I DON'T WANT TO FIGHT!

A GAME LIT NOVEL

CRAFTING A NEW LIFE

AMELIA SIDES

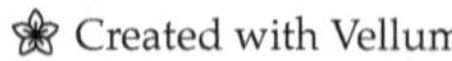 Created with Vellum

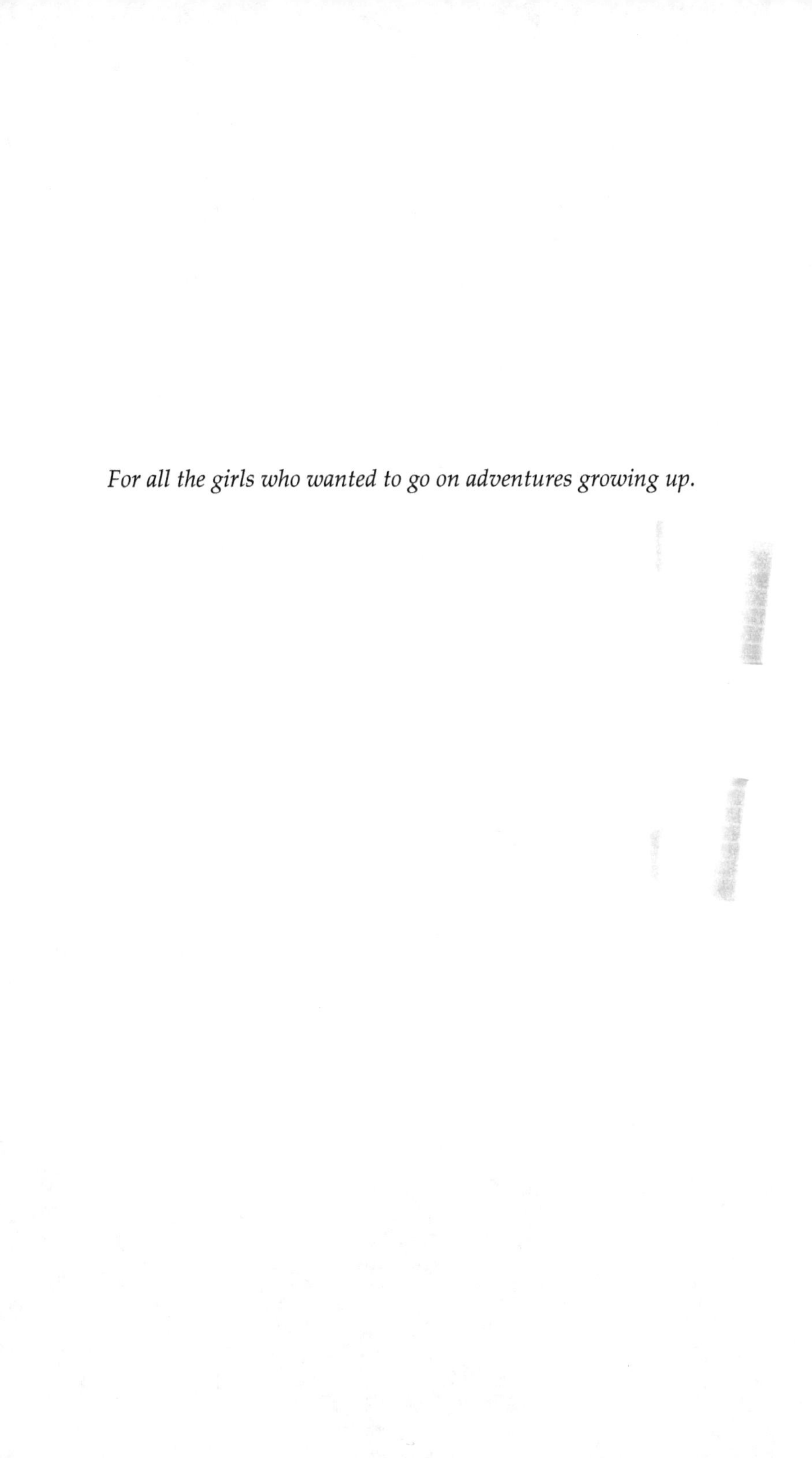

For all the girls who wanted to go on adventures growing up.

CHAPTER
ONE

A VOICE CALLED out as she blinked to awareness, snapping her attention forward. The room about her slowly resolved into focus, shifting to an white blur outside of the man before her. From behind an oak desk, the only spot of color in the room, an older man sat beaming at her like a beloved grandfather. The only color in the room was drawing her forward.

"Welcome, please come and take a seat! We have a lot of things to go over before you can continue," He said pleasantly, waving her forward as she patted down her pajamas with a frown. Was she still asleep?

"Hello," she replied, hesitantly walking to the waiting wooden chair and taking a seat, "Nothing hurts. Why doesn't it hurt?"

"Yes, you had a rather rough time of it, didn't you?" the man said, flipping through a stack of folders before opening one, "Fairly normal if sickly childhood, sicker at eighteen, worked hard through school and college, ignoring your health before collapsing at thirty because of chronic health issues and spending five years fighting against your own body. Arthritis, muscle pain and spasms, nerve pain, exhaustion, migraines. You didn't have it easy."

"I'm sorry. Who are you exactly?" she asked uncertainly, glancing about the room but unable to make anything else out. It was like she hung suspended on a vast plain of nothingness.

"No need to apologize. I am the god, Ume," he said, waving a hand and making a pottery tea set appear.

Weirdly, nothing was frightening. Was this shock?

"Am I dead? The last thing I remember was going to bed," she asked, needing to know. Was she going crazy?

"Yes, I am sad to inform you that you have died in your sleep," Ume announced sadly. He gave a broad smile and settled forward, watching her with an avid expression. Now, you have the honor of being chosen for a new life. You must decide whether to be reincarnated or stay in the afterlife."

She sputtered, fighting for breath, "Reincarnation?"

"Yes, we can't send you back to your world, but there are a multitude of others in need of new souls. We like to refresh the magic and rebalance a world's systems occasionally, and sending a reincarnation allows us to do both simultaneously. You would help an entire world by allowing your reincarnation to move forward. However, you may move on to the next plane if you are truly tired of life. I would recommend reincarnation myself."

"Am I allowed a say in where I go?" she asked. Was there some grand list of new worlds and possibilities the gods kept?

"No, we will send you to a world you are most suited to survive and ultimately thrive in once you adjust. You will choose your strengths and skills in this next body; however,"

"Strengths? What do you mean?" she interrupted sharply. She had never been called strong for anything. What did they even consider a strength?

"What did you want most in your last life? Overpowering strength? Agility?" the god pressed, filling in some form using a golden pen as they spoke. Was she just another number to him, a cog in the cosmic machine?

"That sounds like a game system," she murmured. She'd played a few as a child but rarely had enough time to devote to games, unlike her peers.

"It can be seen as such. I find explaining rebirth as creating a new video game character works best for those from your world," Ume agreed sagely, offering her a page of characteristics and skills to look over.

"So I pick my stats and class?" she asked, looking over the small font.

"Exactly. Would you like to be a warrior, hunter, adventurer, or mage? The options are limitless," he said, gesturing and smiling. The adventure in a rough and tumble life was an attraction for her.

"Wait, a mage? This world has magic?" she asked in shock, giving up trying to scan through the document that seemed to add more items the further down she went.

"Yes, magic and the monsters that go with it. You must be prepared for a more rural life than you may be used to." Ume agreed, sipping from a cup of tea. "We have time if you would like some tea."

"They don't have technology?" she pressed, ignoring the offer. She'd primarily worked in computer systems and call centers, and neither of those skills transferred to a world of swords and magic.

"Not like your world. They have created little of what you have known in Arda. The beings of Arda use magic instead of electronics or technology. You will, however, be sent with a complete knowledge of the language, the ability to read, write, and calculate their currency."

"Will I be near a town? I don't think I'd last long with monsters in the middle of nowhere."

"Yes, you will wake up within walking distance of a city. Once there, go to the temple or guilds to be tested for abilities and receive an identification card." Ume smiled. "Would you like to pick your abilities?"

"I was always so sick and tired in my last life. Can I have the highest health so I'm never sick or tired?"

"This world has its dangers. Wouldn't you rather have skill with a weapon or strength?" he asked, "Perhaps using a sword or a bow?"

"No! I don't want to kill anyone. I don't want to fight!" she snapped. Was this new world that barbaric?

"Very well, the non-fighting classes tend to lean towards healing, crafting, or trading. Do any of these appeal to you?"

"Crafting, I always enjoyed making things with my hands," she insisted, glancing down at her knobby, swollen hands and sighing. That was the most painful thing to give up as her joints got worse. Even lying in bed, she could read, but making things was just too exhausting and painful.

"As you are going completely non-fighting, I'll add a defense skill and up your stats for health and constitution or stamina," he murmured, making several notations and gesturing with one hand, causing the document she was holding to float into his outstretched fingers.

"Will I be able to run?" she asked hopefully, glancing down at her thin legs.

"Anywhere and everywhere your heart desires, with high health and stamina, you should be quite the distance runner." Ume murmured, chuckling, "I believe that covers everything. If you wish to discuss things further, head to a temple. Most religions celebrate many gods, and having a small personal shrine is common in most homes. You can earn blessings and skills as you level, but you will start at level one even with your increased health, so take care."

"Is it really that dangerous?" she asked uncertainly. Was her rebirth going to be even worse than her last life?

"Off the roads and outside of cities, it can be. As your level increases, you will be more able to deal with the challenges, I am certain." Ume reassured her, "As long as you are not searching out dangerous areas, you will be fine."

"If I'm level one, will I be an infant?"

"No, a child around eight years old," he huffed, adding, "Few infants would have a defensive skill, and it is not one activated at birth."

"It is a rebirth. I'll be healthy?" she asked again, needing to be certain.

"Healthy and looking to live a long life with few problems barring accidents." Ume agreed, watching her smiling, offering her the final document for her signature.

"Thank you," she whispered, signing and returning the pen.

"You are most welcome; I hope you enjoy your time on Arda." he said, smiling as her body glowed with an inner light, "I will watch over you if you have any doubts; simply reach out to me in prayer, and I will do what little I can to ease your way."

CHAPTER
TWO

WAKING up in a new world was as easy as waking from a dream. She lay in the soft, dark green grass under a large tree covered in amber leaves, the wind playing with her hair. The sky was a deep blue she'd only ever seen in movies, filled with towering clouds that slowly marched across the horizon. Her lungs were full of the crisp morning air with just a hint of chill that would fade as the sun rose, the scent of trees, grass, and warm earth filling her.

Sitting up, she blinked, dazed by the bright sun and the vivid colors. Everything was sharp and more real than ever in her last life of concrete and computers. A road wound its way past further down the hill, snaking its slow way through the foothills to a walled city set against a distant purple mountain backdrop.

It seemed this world's god was more competent than Earth's had ever been. She was clothed in form-fitting brown pants and leather boots, a blue belted tunic, and a cloth backpack sitting to one side. Waking up healthy, alert, and equipped for a journey was more than she'd been expecting.

"Just a normal traveler looking for a place to stay, nothing to see here," she muttered, grinning, blinking at her unfamiliar voice, chirping like a happy eight-year-old. She wondered what color her eyes were.

Pulling herself into a tailor's seat, she rummaged through the bag. Ume had given her enough basics for a few days. A change of clothes, a coin purse, a few coins jingling inside that she guessed wouldn't last long, a bedroll, what was camping food to eat while traveling, and a slim book.

She never could resist a book, so that was the first thing she grabbed. It listed chapters on the world, its culture, history, and magic system basics. Probably enough not to get her ousted as a reincarnated idiot, but she'd still have to be careful about what she said. She would need to find a library fast and get caught up. Maybe they had a newspaper?

"Do I have to change my name? I wouldn't mind earning a new name, but maybe I can go by the old nickname I used online, Kenko," she said to herself, blinking as a small pop-up appeared on one side, just like in a video game.

Name Selected

"Okay, so it's like a game? Status?" Kenko asked, glancing around when nothing happened. "Right, read the book first."

The language wasn't English, Japanese, or any other language she'd ever seen, but she could read it quickly enough, so that was one worry to set aside. She could read and speak the language here. Everyone here was born with a set class and basic stats that they could slowly improve with time and effort to an unlimited scope. There were a handful of spells that all classes could use. Most children first learned the *Status* command, which opened a screen that only they could see, showing their base stats and level.

It took a few tries to get her status to show. Before attempting to cast the spell, you had to envision your magic flowing throughout your body. Maybe meditation would help later. For now, she was just happy it worked.

. . .

Kenko [Level 1]
 Class: Artificer (Magical) [Level 1]
 Skills: Regeneration, Skin Deep, Marathon
 Additional Skills:
 Cooking (Basic), Crafting (Basic), Spell Craft (Basic), Housekeeping (Basic), Design (Intermediate), Organization (Advanced), Magic (Basic)
 Titles: Blessed of Ume

———

Kenko wiggled her toes in delight, magic! Blinking, she wiggled her toes again. It didn't hurt! Nothing hurt. Stumbling to her feet, she stood gasping and blinking back tears. She couldn't remember a time when nothing hurt. Maybe when she was a child, before she learned, she would never be the fastest or the most graceful. Shoving the book back into her bag, she flexed every joint, wiggling in the tall grass, laughing in delight. She could move!

How long had it been since she could move without overthinking every movement and praying it didn't hurt? Decades of joint pain and temporary relief that left her too drugged to function only for that to stop working, and the struggle to find the next medication that might ease the pain for a few brief hours a day went on. How long had it been since the good days stopped being pain-free?

Kenko flexed her legs and picked up the bag. She might as well try out her legs while she could. Asking for health had been a gamble, but who knew what dangers lurked in this world? She would be safer in the town than sitting around outside in the woods. Walking down the hill, she started to skip, only to stumble and roll the rest of the way down, cursing.

Sitting up, she was standing and dusting herself off before realizing it didn't hurt. Maybe her dexterity was still at level one as well. She'd have to see if there was a way to see all the status screen items instead of just the basic level and skills. More things to add to the to-do list, but there was all the time this life could give her, she thought, smiling.

Reaching the road, she joined the small trickle of others wandering towards the town, towing carts or packages. Maybe there was a market she could walk through to get an idea of the cost of things. One small gold coin, ten large silver, five small silver, and ten copper coins were all the money in her purse. She knew basic trigonometry, but nothing told her how much one copper was worth in goods. Was it like a penny? A yen? Nothing in the book had mentioned how currency worked here. She sent a small mental prayer to the god Ume with a note to update his introduction booklet and thank him for her new life.

Foot traffic and small carts drawn by what looked like massive goats steadily moved closer to the lines of travelers waiting at the gates. She only saw one or two horses on the road, so she assumed this was simply a more rural area without the funds to purchase them. The riders were moving fast, so maybe they were only used by messengers, not the public.

It was still early morning, and the gates had not been open long, according to the surrounding chatter. The walk was peaceful, with only one or two rushing past, grumbling about the traffic. Kenko listened to the idle chatter, storing away small bits of information. It was market day in Arrowview, and most of them were traders arriving early to shop or set up small stands.

A brisk breeze carried the scent of fresh-cut grass and pine to her nose but didn't give her much in the way of guessing the lay of the land around the area. Rolling hills, forests, farmland, and dirt roads seemed standard for the region. Mountains sat in the distance at her back, but in front of her were more hills and forests continuing past the horizon.

"Headed to the Adventurer guild?" One older gentleman asked as she paced her steady way up a hill alongside his cart stacked with cabbages.

"Maybe; I'm not sure what guild I'd like to join yet," Kenko said, frowning; that was another question the book couldn't answer. Where did a crafter fit into the guild system?

"You should visit one or two, even if you aren't sure of a good match. The office workers are skilled at finding jobs that will use just about any class or skill. If you purchase a membership to the guild, they will even reach out if they know you have a useful skill while you are in town."

"Thank you, I will." she agreed, smiling, "Is it rude to ask what class you are in?"

"That should be obvious, Miss," he said with a belly laugh, gesturing to his cart, "I'm a Farmer. I have skills that help me grow my cabbage faster and larger than anyone else in the region."

"That's a wonderful skill!"

"I doubt many would agree with you, but thank you, Miss." he chuckled, "Arrowview is a delightful city, well protected by the local guard and within two day's ride to a bustling river port. Even the monsters avoid this area, so the Adventurers have to head to the woods and caves to hunt. Even then, most requests are for small monsters that don't require much strength. That's why I thought you might be headed there. They specialize in training up young adventurers."

"Oh no, I don't want to fight. I'm a crafter, but I haven't mastered much. Would the guilds take me on to do errands or gathering quests?"

"You could work as a messenger if you like to run. Too much work for me." he huffed, laughing, "Try the Potions guild for gathering quests. The Adventurer's guild mostly takes animal and monster requests. The Healers might take you on, but they pinch a copper tighter than a bone snake. I doubt they would pay you fair value."

"Thank you for explaining so much. It's my first time in a town this big," she said, wincing internally at the small lie. Nothing she'd seen so far suggested the large cities of her past life were an option here.

"You remind me of my granddaughter, Miss; I'd not want her wandering into town lost and fearful. The gate doesn't charge on Market day so that you can enter freely, but the rest of the week, it's a copper to enter without a guild card."

"Really? They charge an entrance tax?"

"It's rather cheap for so large a city; you'd spend a silver at the capital, River-deep. However, the King pays most of the guilds here to train his troops, so they keep the taxes low to keep the townsfolk happy. The guilds also rent rooms to members at a discount if you are looking for lodging in the nicer part of town."

"Think she's a little old for you, Grandfather." One passerby called out, braying with laughter at his joke as Kenko flushed red.

"As if you could pull so comely a lass, Darrick Handover!" The farmer crowed, shaking a fist at the man's back, "You better believe I'll be letting his grandmother know just how stupid a son her daughter's raising when I get back."

"Are you from the same town?" she asked, hopping over a large rut from the last storm that blew through.

"Tiny group of cottages called Bluff's Rise, where loggers and miners live straight back up the road. You probably passed it yesterday, heading in if you camped the night outdoors."

"Am I that obvious?" Kenko asked, laughing, tucking her braid back behind her shoulder. The dark blue hair kept making her twitch when she saw it. The farmer's sandy blond hair was typical among those on the road, but she'd already noted red, pink, and green among the mix of passersby.

"Those with forest blood aren't often comfortable being indoors for long if a forest is nearby. It was a guess." he offered with another grin, nodding to her hair, "Your mother or grandmother? You look human enough otherwise."

"I don't know, sir, I'm an orphan," she said with a small smile, hoping he would not inquire further.

"I'm sorry for bringing it up, Miss," he said, giving her a quick bow from his seat, "but none of that Sir nonsense; I'm Guss Brokenridge."

"It's a pleasure to meet you; I'm Kenko." She returned his quick bow and smiled. "Do you come to town every Market day?"

"If the weather is passable during the winter, there is little enough to sell, but for the next few months, I'll be back and forth every seven days. Find me when you need to get food. I'll steer you to the best stalls."

"Thank you, Guss." Kenko grinned, returning to the road, bouncing as they neared the gates.

"You go ahead—no reason to stay with the old folks. The guild row is off the main square. You can't miss it. Straight on in and on your left."

"Are you sure I can stay and help unload?" she asked, glancing at the long line of carts and the quicker-moving foot traffic.

"Go enjoy your day, child. I have a friend who unloads the boxes when I arrive. He's already setting up the stall by now."

"Thank you, Guss. Hope your cabbages sell," she said, returning to the city and quickly jogging past most of the slow-moving carts.

The crowd grew, and more adventurers and armed citizens filled the road. They wore a mix of leather, cloth, armor, and a dazzling array of colors and patterns. The farmers and laborers dressed conservatively in greens and browns, while the younger adventurers mainly wore brown and neutral tones that could blend in if needed. The older members of the crowd were strangely the most colorful, clad in red cloaks, sky-blue tunics, and emerald scarves.

Many had badges and animal motifs trimmed on the edges, marking them as part of a group. Only a few wore gold jewelry, but copper, silver, and other metals she'd never seen before were used as earrings, hair ornaments, and rings.

Eventually, Kenko would have to learn what all the designs and even the swirling grey tattoos many had meant. The tattoos caught the light and drew her gaze. All the fighters had them on their arms. A scholarly-looking man in an orange and grey over-robe had them wrapping his throat and hands outlined in silver.

The city walls were tall, with guards walking the tops and stationed at the towers in the distance. She blinked as her feet stumbled in a rut. Had she been able to see that far? The guards at the gate waved her through without a word, eyes on the lookout for something only they knew how to spot. Their uniform of white and orange would stand out even in the darkest night.

Kenko did her best to ignore the crowd as she moved past the morning travelers, going both ways. Most houses were two stories and sat close together, with small gardens and trees bordering the front and sides. The shops were open-air fronts with colorful cloth overhangs.

The goods and vegetables passing by were identifiable, but some were just odd colors or scents for which she had no reference. What did blue grapes taste like? The shops were set to sell in bulk ingredients and items waiting to be weighed and measured for packaging. Where were the magic items sold?

A group of large men wearing swords and leather armor passed, heading down a road to the left of the vast square where the traffic spilled out like water from a hose. To the right was the market, with small flags and banners hung across the stalls to attract customers. Her stomach rumbled at the scent of cooking bread and other things, but she forced herself to head towards the left fork and the guilds.

The guildhalls lined the road with long walls and stone walkways but not much else. The traffic had changed to rugged-looking fighters and harried staff or customers rushing back and forth. Large gates allowed carts of supplies, burlap-wrapped dead animals or monsters, and other boxes to access the back of the guildhalls.

She was glad to escape from one adventurer carting the head of something with razor-sharp horns wrapped in stained fabric over one shoulder. Dust, sweat, and the copper scent of blood permeated the area around the adventurers' guild hall. The grey-stoned adventurer's guild sat across from the ivy-flocked potioner's guild hall in almost a mockery to the death being dealt out, a prison of stone next to a college or library with expansive windows. Across the street, the potioner's guild was quiet, but adventurers wandered the entire lane chatting and complaining about quests or broken gear.

The doors to the Adventurers' Hall sat open, filling the air with the chatter of their booming voices. It sounded more like a tavern than a guild. Further down, the white marble-like stone welcomed everyone to the Healers' Hall, a short line of patients and callers waiting to be seen filling one side of the sidewalk's benches.

Kenko decided to start with the quieter potioner's hall. None of the people entering seemed to be in the boisterous mood the adventurers' hall exuded, like it was secretly a bar or tavern in disguise. The adventurers unnerved her with their strength and confidence in the way they moved.

Inside the potioner's hall, the feel was more like a library as the door eased shut behind her. The smell of herbs and other green things filled the air, potted plants dotted the floor, and a massive shelved area to one side was full of bottles, bags of ingredients, and what she assumed were potions. The room was dim, with tiny crystals set high on the walls and desks to give the workers enough light to write by.

"Is there something you need?" A woman called from the counter, a small smile as Kenko approached.

"Good morning. I'm interested in joining a guild, but I'm not sure where my class will fit in best," Kenko said, glancing around at the others going about their day in the guild. Most seemed hurried to return downstairs or hunt the shelves for a specific potion.

"I'm afraid this year's training for alchemists and potion crafting is full. You could try another of the larger towns or the capital, but we've seen more students hoping to increase their skills lately."

"I'm an Artificer and was wondering if there were some gathering quests or messages I could run for the guild? I'm still learning and need the practice."

"That is a rare skill!" she said with a wide grin while the other man at the desk looked down at the young woman in shock, "Where are my manners? I'm Marie. Welcome to the Potioner's Guild."

"I'm Kenko."

"You may want to try the markets, dear. Many shops are looking for inventory if you have any new crafts or inventions. They may rent a small spot in their workshop if you can get your foot in the door."

"I need money for supplies right now. I have nothing ready to sell." Kenko said with a grimace. Crafting wasn't an option yet. The book of instructions had been rather vague on how her abilities worked with crafting and designing.

"Well, we are always looking for fresh herbs. If you get out early, gather them before the adventurers trample the evening's growth."

"Do you have any manuals or herbalist books I can study to know what to pick?"

"If you join the guild, you will have access to our library and discounts on the potions we offer. Sadly, unlike the Adventurer's Guild, we don't offer room and board, but we allow students to use the workrooms downstairs after hours if any are open."

Marie laid out several flyers and forms for Kenko to review, explaining what the guild offered, how to request a potion supply and other essential tasks the guild could perform for a price. Although the library offer was tempting, Kenko wanted to see her options before joining a guild.

"Thank you. May I take these? I'd like to look around town before I decide."

"Of course, take your time. If you are new to town, I can recommend a pleasant inn to stay further into town if you are interested?"

"That would be helpful, thank you."

"The Iron Boar is popular with the adventurers and guards in town and fills up fast. If they are booked up, you can try the White Cat. It's a cheaper inn, but the food is good, and the staff won't overcharge you. Both are further down the road to the left if you keep going. If you reach the river district, you've gone too far."

"Thank you again," Kenko said, gathering the paperwork with a smile for the staff. She walked over to a table to one side, putting her papers away as the guild staff chattered behind her, waiting on their next customer.

"She's much too young to become a full member!" The man at the desk chided Marie in a hissed whisper.

"With that hair, she's at least half, if not full, Forest Elf." Marie said, sniffing, "They age slowly. She could be twenty for all we know."

"True; when we issue her guild card, we can scan her abilities. That will list her age, skills, and level. The Guild Master would never let us live it down if we hired a five-year-old for errands about town."

"Ten, at the very least," Marie huffed. "she could be on the short side. Plus, with that Artificer class, she would be a catch for any guild."

"Elf, and what else do you think? Those eyes are unusual."

"Can't be dwarf. She's too thin, even if she is a crafter. But you are right; the eyes look more like a beastkin. She's unusual, polite, at the very least."

Kenko waved goodbye and headed to the door, chuckling. No one else in the room seemed to have noticed the whispered conversation about her. Was her hearing better than human? She never played an elf in any of the games she'd tried in her other life. Usually, she was some animal hybrid or human when she crafted a character.

CHAPTER
THREE

WHEN KENKO ENTERED THE ADVENTURERS' hall, a short line of men and women waited before the front counter. Waiting men and women of every race imaginable packed the room, seated at benches and chairs along the far wall, eating breakfast or chatting with other group members before they headed out on a quest.

The room was full of the smell of sausages and hot bread, making her stomach rumble. She didn't need the reminder that she needed a job to eat. Kenko knew the cost of never having enough money and the stress it could bring. She was pretty confident that was what had led her father to a premature death.

The only ones she couldn't see were elves or anyone else with blue hair like hers, she noted, mildly annoyed, twirling a loose strand of hair. Were elves from a distant land or not common in cities? She'd have to learn more about all the races, especially the beast people, since having a humanoid bunny serving drinks was just too much like a game. At least she wasn't dressed differently than anyone else.

"Next!" the guild staff called, waving her forward briskly. "I'm Goff. How can I help you?"

"Good morning. My name is Kenko. I was hoping to learn about your guild and see if I could run any gathering jobs or errands for the guild."

"I'm afraid we only give quests to guild members," he said, talking quickly as he laid forms on the counter. "Here are the forms you'd have to fill out and a list of our basic services. If you are planning to hunt or take monster quests, you will have to go through testing with the other new members later in the week before you can start work. We hold weekly training sessions for our younger members that you will be required to attend until we deem you competent enough to rise above rank F."

"Oh, no," Kenko huffed, waving her hands, "I just want to gather herbs or craft supplies. I'm an Artificer, and I need money for supplies to raise my crafting levels."

"Well, if you join, we have several rooms upstairs for rent, booking for one seven-day at a time. We also take member requests for information and allow access to our library to those above rank E." The group behind her was getting restless as Goff continued to explain while other lines were served much quicker; a massive tusked fellow growled in annoyance, making Goff talk even faster, "As I said earlier, we hold training sessions if you want to raise your fighting skill levels or practice with new weapons. The harvesting room is in the back of the guild, and you can access it through the back entrance if you have any animals to slaughter or pelts to clean. The cost to join the guild is one silver. If you are interested, bring the money and the forms back here when ready. We will issue your guild card then and explain things further."

"Thank you," Kenko said, accepting the paperwork thrust at her and stumbling out of the way of the tusked man as he shoved his way to the counter.

Making her way back outside, she did her best to ignore the side eyes the other adventurers gave her as she found a small bench to one side and started reading the forms. The Adventurer's Guild offered more services, but most were geared toward hunters or fighters who needed room to stay while healing from a quest gone wrong or waiting on gear to be repaired. Those using a room without an injury or valid reason will be asked to leave if an injured member needs a room for healing.

Both guilds only charged a silver to join so she could manage it, but it would be a chunk of her money gone that she'd struggle to recoup soon. She'd need to buy tools for harvesting herbs and crafting, probably taking most of her gold once she settled. She purchased one meat pie for a copper penny and grimaced at the fatty, flavorless meat inside, but it was something to fill her stomach until she found somewhere to stay.

The Iron Boar Inn was packed when she finally found it after half a day of walking; it was closer to the docks than the markets and guilds. It wasn't even evening; drunk adventurers and working folk filled the front room. No thanks. She'd have to try the Cat. Her stomach growled from the little she'd eaten, but the prices in the market were higher than she'd thought they would be. She would eat from the penny street carts until she made at least a little coin.

She'd hoped to buy some bread or fruit to add to her backpack, but most sold by the bushel, and there was no hope of her eating that many or carting it around with her, and the price went up if you couldn't provide a bag to cart the goods away. The small loaf of bread and two sausages she'd bartered for still cost her smallest silver coin, leaving her eying her rapidly deflating purse with a frown.

10 small copper pennies = 1 large copper
10 large copper = 1 small silver
10 small silver = 1 large silver
10 large silver = 1 small gold
10 small gold = 1 large gold

———

The White Cat was a much smaller inn hidden off the main street near a small park filled with playing children and exhausted-looking mothers putting their feet up for a moment. The servers were all beast-kin, the half-animal hybrids she'd seen about town. Most of the staff and customers were of different races, with only a few humans to be seen. It surprised her to feel herself relaxing in the quiet bustle of the small inn.

"Welcome to the White Cat Inn. Can I help you?" a woman called from the bar, waving Kenko over. The large fluffy white tail and ears marked her as the owner. "If you are looking for a meal, you can have a seat wherever you like."

"Someone recommended the Inn. Are there any rooms available?" Kenko asked, trying to sound older than she appeared even as her stomach grumbled at the fantastic smells filling the tavern area.

"If you don't mind it being small, I have a single-occupancy room available. It is five coppers a night, and breakfast is included. The most we book in advance is ten nights."

"I'll just pay for tonight," Kenko said, handing over the coins. "Is it too early for dinner?"

"We are just about ready to start serving. I'm the owner, Gatha. I hope you have a pleasant stay." Gatha said, handing her the key to her room.

"Thank you. My name is Kenko."

"Welcome to Arrowview. Is this your first time visiting? I don't believe we've had an elf as young as you through in some time." Gatha said, her whiskers twitching in amusement.

"I am an orphan and raised human, so I can't say much about elves," Kenko said, wincing. She could feel this would be a recurring conversation. "Are they not that common?"

"More that they don't travel outside their forest homes very often. The ones we get here are often rangers or messengers on the way to the capital." Someone waved from across the room, catching Gatha's attention. "Pick a table, and we can talk while you eat."

"Evening. For dinner, we have vegetable soup, boar steak, or fish." The server said, dropping a clay mug of water at her place.

"How much is everything?" Kenko asked, trying not to blush, but the tabby cat teenager just recited the prices without batting an eye, ringed ears flicking at someone stomping down the stairs, making the small rings chime faintly, "I'll have the soup."

"I'll have it right out."

"Thank you," she muttered to the woman's retreating back, fiddling with the glass of water they had left her with.

"You truly have been raised human; how strange," Gatha said, taking a seat with a happy sigh. She tucked furry cat paws delicately crossed at the toes under her chair.

"Is it that obvious I'm an elf?"

"Ears, hair, and the eyes to those who have met one." Gatha said, frowning, "Most around here would take you to be a halfling or a random throwback in a bloodline, given the eyes. It happens occasionally in individuals with powerful magics."

"I grew up pretty isolated, and I'm sure I'm saying things wrong." Kenko groaned, face flushed with embarrassment, fighting the urge to hide her face.

"That right there is a giveaway. Most elves that leave the forest are several hundred years old and well past the need to overreact to minor inconveniences. If you don't want to deal with any issues, say you are a throwback with human parents but distant elf relatives you've never met."

"Will it show on the guild card if I join?"

"Are you considering one? The merchants' or clothiers' guilds are normally willing to train someone with even a minor talent."

"I'm looking at the adventurers and potions guilds. I have a crafting ability, but I need tools to work on it."

"Which takes coin," Gatha agreed, frowning. "I mean no disrespect, but you don't strike me as a fighter. Do you have any protective skills?"

"Healing and a defensive skill, but it's all self-healing. I can't heal others that I know of." Kenko offered shrugging.

"I'm more worried about you wondering about the countryside alone doing quests. You may wish to join a small party if you have any skills that might contribute to combat, even against small monsters. There is more safety in numbers."

"I'm just considering guilds right now. The adventurer's guild has more open quests for gathering, but it seems like the potion's guild has a better library."

"Do you have any issues with other races?" Gatha asked, glancing around the slowly filling inn.

"No, I've not talked to many. However, I'm kind of afraid of accidentally insulting someone."

"Trust me, if they are in a city this big, then they have heard it before, and at least in your case, we know it is coming from a place of ignorance, not spite." she said, waving her hand at the crowded room, "My Inn is welcoming to all races, and any discrimination will see you tossed out. The Adventurer's guild may seem rough and tumble, but most are good people at heart, simply using the abilities the gods gave them as best they can."

"Is there much race discrimination here?"

"Not like you would see in the capital. Now, that is a city to watch your tail in," she huffed, her fur fluffing in irritation. There will always be idiots with ideas about who should be above or below them. We all do what we can to ensure they aren't the loudest voices in the room."

"Here is your order," the tabby called out with a wink, dropping off a large bowl of soup, bread, and a cup of milk.

"I'll leave you to eat. I have a few books that may answer your questions. You are welcome to borrow. I'll leave them at the desk for you in the morning."

"Thank you, Gatha."

Kenko glanced around the Inn between slow bites of delicious food. Bodies crowded the room with beast-kin, green-skinned people she assumed were a kind of goblin, heavily bearded dwarves drinking ale at the bar, and a handful of mixed groups with one or two humans relaxing at the tables drinking.

The meal was filling, but something about the meat in the soup put her off. Did elves not eat meat here? Her trail food that Ume supplied was all nuts, honey, and hard bread. Maybe this was her body's way of warning her away. She wasn't sure she could afford enough food if she wasn't eating meat. She'd need extra beans and things for nutrients, right?

She'd try going without tomorrow and see how she felt. Her stomach was churning uncertainly, but she forced herself to finish the broth and milk. She probably could stretch her coin for a while just eating breakfast at the inn with bread for her other meals, but it wouldn't be a long-term solution.

Several others had left tips on the tables when they were done, so she did the same, biting back the grimace as she left two more copper pennies on the table and headed back to her room. Cracking the window open, she laid out the forms on her small bed. No matter how she looked at it, the adventurers' guild was the best place to get her start. Once her skills and level were sorted out, she could start trying to sell in the market or join the merchant's guild in town.

Once she'd filled out the forms to the best of her ability and put them away, she sprawled under the covers, groaning. She couldn't have walked that far today, but her brain felt melted from everything she'd seen and learned. She reincarnated into a fantasy world with dwarves, elves, and cat people and spent the entire day trying not to stare like an utter idiot.

Magic was real. She was a very young elf and a Magical Artificer, even if she was only level one. The first thing she needed to do was to learn more about this world and its problems. There had to be minor annoyances that magic couldn't solve, but inventing or reinventing something from her past life could. She needed to understand what tools she needed to work magic as well. Was it all in her hands, or did she need something special?

With a chuckle, she imagined a drafting board in her mind and started absently doodling possible contraptions she could invent. She'd yet to see a fan or anything electronic, so she'd need to figure out a power source. The lights were all candles, oil lamps, or magical crystals and lines that seemed to glow a soft blue in the top corners of every building and around some doorways. She drifted to sleep, never noticing the minor alert that popped up.

First Design Achieved

Fan: version 1 added to the archive

———

Kenko [Level 1]
   Race: *Elven*
   Age: *8*
   Class: *Artificer (Magical) [Level 1]*
   Skills:
Regeneration, Skin Deep, Marathon, Darkvision, Perception, Meditation
   Additional Skills:
Cooking (Basic), Crafting (Basic), Spell Craft (Basic), Housekeeping (Basic), Design (Intermediate), Organization (Advanced), Magic (Basic)
   Titles: *Blessed of Ume*

CHAPTER
FOUR

KENKO LAID out all her worldly goods on the bed the following day and started a list on the paper and pencil she'd begged from the maid downstairs. She owned two sets of clothes, one pair of boots, a ribbon she used to tie her hair back, a backpack, one book, one light bedroll and its covering tarp, a coin purse, and a small stack of coins.

If she joined the adventurer's guild, she would need to buy several things.

One sturdy jacket or cloak and gloves

Harvesting tools, such as a trowel and hooked knife.

Canteen

One stout knife for carving and defense

A belt and sheaths for the knives

Small burlap bags to sort out what she was gathering

A notebook and pencils

She owned twenty large silvers, twenty large copper, and two small copper pennies to her name roughly. Gatha's sharp eyes had seen the flash of the small gold coin when Kenko paid the night before, and that morning, she asked for help to change the money to something more reasonable. Only nobility carried gold openly, and unless she were willing to spend the entire coin, few would take the money to finance a small purchase since it meant cleaning out their ready coin on hand.

Breakfast was uncomfortable after two servers took her on as a pet, ruffling her hair and cooing over her mane of curly locks from the rain that morning. Kenko hadn't bothered trying to tame it, instead leaving the curls loose and tying the ribbon around her neck so it wouldn't be lost. The handful of regulars watched in amusement as the tiny elf ate her porridge and milk grudgingly before demolishing the apple the fox beast-kin presented her as dessert.

The guilds never really closed, but she headed toward the markets instead with determination. She wanted to have her gear ready when she joined the guild. She was a crafter, and she would be useful, dammit!

It was an hour past noon by the watch tower bells when she finally reached the guild row and dropped to a seat next to a lone tree. Why was shopping still so exhausting when she was finally healthy? She always hated shopping for anything because she'd go fuzzy with exhaustion halfway through and buy things she didn't need or even really wanted just to hurry the shopping along.

She managed to get most of everything she wanted, but she was sure they had overcharged her on nearly every item from the looks of disgust a few passersby gave the merchants. She couldn't afford to touch her large coppers, and two silvers were already promised to the guilds, leaving her with eighteen large silvers to spend on food and gear for the next several months.

The short grey waterproof wool cloak that fell to her knees had been the worst of it, costing nearly two large silvers all by itself, but it was sturdy and would last her years if she was careful. All the tools she'd found needed to be sharpened, but they were sturdy and rust-free. Not a single pair of gloves would fit her tiny hands, so instead, she purchased leather strips she could wrap around her palms while she worked with thorny plants or rocks.

Buying the short sword or long dagger, as the merchant insisted on calling it, was the worst. She'd been laughed out of the first two stalls for asking about daggers and weapons. When asked why she needed it, gathering herbs had been the wrong answer. Eventually, she bought a used blade from the cart that sold her the gathering tools. All of them were worn and the leather thin, but she would invest better once she made some extra coin.

The most disappointing aspect was the lack of books. Most were handed down within a family or kept in a guildhall. Few people outside of the nobility bought books to read because they were expensive to produce. Magical printing presses had yet to be created.

The hints she'd heard so far made magic commonplace and rare. Everyone had simple magics, the ability to cast sparks to light a fire, to cast a weak light, or to sense an element. Only the more rare classes had a magic of their own or incorporated magic into their mechanics. Most warrior and hunter classes had innate skills that acted like magic but used their natural magical core to boost their attacks.

Only the rare mage and healer classes used magic, as Kenko had known it in games. They needed long incantations and decades of practice to master the skills required to cast protection wards and heal, while genuine spell casters varied wildly in ability and the type of spells they had control over.

The handful of books she'd flipped through, cheap mass-produced booklets, gave the bare basics of how to cast each element and leaned heavily on repetition and mental fortitude. She doubtfully added meditation to her list of tasks before bed each night and a handful of pushups and sit-ups but didn't have much hope of ever openly casting magic like in the fantasy movies she remembered.

Standing up, she dusted off her pants and headed to the adventurer's guild hall with a determined stride. No tusked green troll kin would make her back down from joining. She had a right to work the same as any other race.

———

Goff watched the young girl from yesterday march towards his desk, smiling. He'd been afraid she'd run scared after the troll barged past her yesterday morning. It seemed they made her of sterner stuff than he'd imagined.

"Good morning, young miss. How can I assist you?"

"Good morning. I want to join the guild as a gatherer," she said, pushing the papers across the tall countertop.

"Alright, this looks in order. I need your payment, and we can create your guild card." he agreed with a polite smile.

"Already?" she asked, blinking at him in surprise.

"If you want to do more than gathering quests, you would have to wait for the next testing session, but as long as you stick to the nearby forests, you should be good," he said, grinning and carefully pulling out the crystal tray. "Place your hands against either side and imagine pushing your magic into the tray. It will automatically fill your card with your name and base levels."

"Okay," Kenko said uncertainly, imagining magic flowing from her hands and nearly dropping the tray as it started to glow.

"That should be enough," Goff said hastily, taking the tray back and glancing over her card before noting down her stats on a form as part of her membership, the metal card and a copper pendant on a chain handed back with a happy smile, "Welcome to the Adventurer's Guild. You are ranked F right now, so you will look at the last board on the right for jobs. Don't forget to wear the tag to identify yourself to the guards. If you need more information, please let me know how I can be of assistance."

"Is there a map of the area I could use? I don't want to get lost on my first trip out." Kendo asked quickly.

"I will have one ready at the desk when you find a request you want to take on. Bring the flyer here, and we will log it to your guild record. If you cannot complete the quest, a fine will be placed on your membership of one large copper, and the fine goes up with each offense. Should it happen consistently, your membership will drop rank, or we will ask you to return your membership card. Here is a pamphlet with the general rules of the guild and our services."

"Goff, do you have a moment?" a voice called from upstairs as the girl hurried off to check the boards. "Come to my office."

"Guild Master, how can I assist you?" Goff asked as he hurried upstairs and ducked into the open office, sighing, taking a seat before the older gentleman, already knowing what had piqued his interest.

"The young elf that just joined. Who is she?" Guild Master Banner asked, setting his cup to one side, sighing.

"I have her status page and her membership form here." Goff said, handing it over, "Kenko, age eight, full elf, with a class of Magical Artificer."

"Magic levels?"

"My guess would be humans raised her, and she does not know how to use her innate magic. She nearly overloaded the guild card tray on the first try, but her magic skills are missing, and her magic level is only one." Goff said, frowning.

"See what magic users we have in town at the moment or that are soon to return. I want to get her in basic lessons before she burns down half the town during a nightmare."

"Are you afraid she's repressed her training?" Goff asked with concern, should they have allowed her to join so young? He'd only waved it through because it was gathering quests only. Most kids who tried to apply couldn't afford the fee to join.

"Hard to say. I've never seen an elf that open with their emotions before, and she spoke without a hint of the arrogance most elves show humans. It could simply be her parents died while she was too young to remember them or their teachings. However, being raised outside elf forests would be the same thing."

"I'll get you the list by tonight. Is there anything else?" Goff asked, moving to the door.

"What is her stance on learning to fight?"

"She insisted she didn't need the trial when I offered yesterday. She only wants to earn money for her crafting materials by gathering."

"I'd be hesitant to offer her a membership if she did. Without a party or an apprenticeship, she won't survive a level F quest for even something like a boar. She's just too small. Was she carrying any weapons?"

"A used dagger. On her, it's nearly a short sword on one hip; on the other are gathering tools." Goff said, waving to the documents, "What about her skills? I've never heard of a specialized skill called disengagement."

"I'll have to do some research. I have a feeling it's a non-fighter defensive ability. It's probably something like parry or evasion. Get me that list when you have a moment. I want that kid trained. The last thing we need is a rogue magic user causing havoc while also a member of our guild."

"Yes, Guild Master," Goff agreed, returning to his post. There was bound to be a ton of extra work for the next few days if the guild master was sticking his nose into a new member.

———

"Found anything likely?" Goff asked as the young elf jogged back to the front desk.

"Three, can you tell me where these are found? I'm still new to town." Kenko asked, handing over the three requests.

"Sure, let me show you where on the map." he said, unfolding a small map of the area and marking each location with a pencil, "This is Arrowview here. We are in the town center with the west gate behind us and the north gate to our left, straight down the road. Heading that way puts you here on the edge of the forest, and following this path leads to the meadows along the cliffs where most of our herb and plant gathering quests are sent. Mushrooms and ferns will be on the south end of town, closer to the river along the forest edge. Just don't go too deep. There are bears and other beasts there that can be dangerous."

"I understand," Kenko said, nodding, orienting herself mentally on the map and adding the few roads she'd found from the last few days.

New skill acquired: Map Reading

Kenko blinked away the annoying pop-up and added moving the alerts to her mental list of needs. What if she was trying to stay alive and got a new skill while sprinting to safety? She understood gods were divine and above mortal concerns, but that was just a buggy feature. If it was a mental and magical feature, there had to be a way to edit it.

"Are there guides about the plants to keep an eye out for? Like ones that the guilds would always need?"

"I can write you a list, but I'm afraid my drawing skills are limited." Goff grimaced. "If you like, you are welcome to come by the library on an off day to write up any details you might need."

"I can do that tomorrow afternoon. I want to find my way to the path by the end of today so I know where to head in the morning."

"I'd suggest starting with this quest for Penny Queen. Bittersweet is an easy one to start with. The herb is bright purple and keeps to the base of the larger oaks. There isn't a technique to harvest it. Just don't crush the leaves if possible, or your hands will be purple for days."

"And just storing it in a bag is fine? They don't want the roots and all?"

"No, just the stems and leaves. You want to leave the roots so they will regrow in the coming month. It flowers in the second growth after a cutting to reseed the area. Leave any with flowers alone."

"How much do they want?"

"One large bag at most. It loses potency once it's dried, and the guild can only process so much at a time." he said, pointing to the next sheet, "This next one is in the same area, Greater Gallberry. It's late in the season, so there might not be much to find. The spiny red fruits are popular for adding to pies, and the juice has a slight wit-sharpening ability some mages use. You can bring back whatever you find of those. They are always needed."

Kenko nodded eagerly, "Right, I can do that."

"This last one, Lamb's Rum Lace, save for another day. It's a rough walk to the marshes, and with last night's rain, the path will be a mess. Just hunting for the moss in the dunes can take most of a day."

"Thank you, Goff."

"No problem, be safe out there," he said, grinning.

"I will," she said, running to the door and out on her first quest with a bounce in her step.

The first stop on the way was the blacksmith's shop. She needed to sharpen her tools and buy a whetstone with the little coin she'd saved. A nearby pair of dwarves had recommended the Quiet Hammer when she asked as they grabbed breakfast before heading towards a local mine that morning.

The heat of the forge rolled out from the wide doorway, but strangely, the sound was missing. She hovered at the entrance, eying the pulsing line of blue magic scrolling its way around the door and walls of the room beyond. Inside, four people danced around each other, trading off as they worked.

A tall female troll worked at the back of the shop doing detail work on a massive chest plate while two apprentice dwarves worked to keep their master moving by tending to the forge as he hammered and shaped the piece he was crafting. The troll waved Kenko in with an amused look at the frantic apprentices. Inside, the heat and sound were suffocating, the metal banging on metal in a constant rhythm in her chest and head.

"What do you need?" The troll asked, turning back to her work.

"Varath Smeltbow recommended this forge to me. I need to have some tools sharpened, but I have little to spare. I can do the work myself if you can show me how."

"It's not often that a Smeltbow sees fit to give advice. What did you do to gain his attention?"

"I don't know. I was trying to list what I needed before I joined the adventurers' guild, and he recommended buying my tools second-hand and having them reworked."

"Kraddas, come take a look at this lass!" The troll bellowed, silencing the workshop.

"How is it, Esha, that you can interrupt me with the smallest task, yet if I dare question a line of enchantment, I'm the one in the wrong?" Kraddas huffed, setting his tools down and gesturing for his apprentices to return the metal to the fire. "How can the Quiet Hammer assist you, lass?"

"She comes recommended by a Smeltbow, no less. Asking to rework her tools."

"Does she now, and what do you know of Dwarven lines, lass?"

"Nothing, Master Dwarf, only that I also work with my hands and seek to one day make such amazing things as you craft with yours."

"No elf would class as a blacksmith, child." he snorted.

"No, Master Dwarf, I am an artificer." she said, forcing herself to meet the gruff dwarf's eyes and not back down, "I may have no great inventions yet, but I am willing to work hard and dedicate myself to my craft."

"An artificer, that is a rare class, and you are low on coin and need second-hand tools reworked." he huffed, gesturing her over to a table. "Let me see your selections."

She laid out her dull and worn items, wincing. On the pristine wood bench, they looked all the worse for wear. The handful of wood-working tools she'd added were just as severely used. Her hands were already scratched and red from testing the tools on a splintered piece of cast-off wood.

"You need gloves until you learn to hold the blades with enough strength and flexibility," he said, lifting one of the carving tools with a disappointed cluck of his tongue.

"None would fit, sir," Kenko said, blushing.

"I am not royalty, elf; do not call me such." Kraddas snapped, pulling out a pipe and filling the bowl, frowning.

"Sorry," she whispered, hating how uncertain she was about everything.

"You are taking quests for the adventurers' guild?" he asked, nodding to her copper tag sitting just outside her shirt.

"I'm headed to the forest for a gathering quest."

"Take your gathering tools for the day and return here after you finish. I'll have your carving tools ready. We will discuss payment then."

"Thank you, Master Dwarf," Kenko said, quickly gathering the dagger, trowel, and curved harvesting knife.

———

"What are you thinking, Kraddas?" Esha asked, watching as the girl ran off, returning to her work while he continued examining the elf's tools.

"No elf would be out of the home forests so young without a guide. Nor would an artificer be working with such pitiful tools if they were patron'd. Most magical crafters would have been promised to a patron at birth." he stroked his beard and waved at one apprentice, "We need to send word to the rangers at the capital of a lost child found in Arrowview. Meld, go fetch my writing case."

"And her tools?" Esha asked, looking over the lines of hammers and etching tools she used to enchant each piece.

"We will rework them. She's likely to lose a finger to a weak tool like this trash. If she does a few errands along with her quests, we will call the matter of cost closed." Kraddas huffed, "Perhaps if she stays in the city, she'll remember our shop, and we can supply her the metal parts needed for her inventions to come. If not, then we have done right by a lost child of the elves and will have earned a boon either way."

"An elf working as a simple gatherer," Esha huffed. "Do you think she would accept crafting minor items here as work?"

"As a way to level up, possibly, she doesn't seem to have been raised by other elves from how she was acting. Once other elves find her, she may change her ways, but if a Smeltbow sent her, then I doubt it. He wouldn't have sent anyone with even a hint of prejudice."

"Where did Smeltbow meet her?"

"That's what we need to find out. If she's joined the adventurer's guild, she's probably staying at an inn near the guild row. My second letter will send word to the Smeltbow clan, thanking them for sending such a reference for future work. Then we can discuss how our clans will work together to support the young lass."

"You think they will continue to support her?"

"An elf and a magical artificer? Every guild and master worth his salt will try to tempt her away." he laughed. "Guild Master Banner snagged an uncut gem. If he plays his cards right, she will continue supporting his guild and the community even once she reaches mastery."

"Will the other elves accept her?"

"That I cannot say. She is more comfortable here among what most elves consider the lesser beings. It will depend on whether she caves to their pressure to return to the home forest."

———

Kenko *[Level 1]*

    Class: *Artificer (Magical) [Level 1]*

    Skills:

Regeneration, Skin Deep, Marathon, Archive, Darkvision, Perception, Meditation

    Additional Skills:

Cooking (Basic), Crafting (Basic), Spell Craft (Basic), Housekeeping (Basic), Design (Intermediate), Organization (Advanced), Magic (Basic), Map Reading (Basic),

    Titles: *Blessed of Ume*

CHAPTER
FIVE

RUNNING down the paths toward the forest outside of town was amazing. She couldn't remember the last time she'd run so carefree. Her thick-soled boots ate up the distance, but somehow, there was barely any sound when she should have been pounding down the path like a marching band. It seemed like no time before she had to slow down as the forest loomed just off the path. She wasn't even out of breath.

The air was crisp, and it was still early enough in the evening that she didn't have to worry about returning to town for a few hours. The mix of trees wasn't any she could identify by the smell of green living things, and the moist earth surprisingly relaxed her.

Shrugging, she started scanning along the ground, looking for herbs, a handful of already harvested stalks on the edges of the forest, as she'd expected, but that gave her an idea of what she was looking for. Blinking up at what looked like a white-barked oak tree with golden leaves, she smiled; even if she didn't harvest anything today, she could find a pleasant path for tomorrow, and the forest was beautiful either way.

Kenko gathered a few mushrooms and fallen limbs as she walked, taking in the breeze and the rustle of leaves. She'd check with one of the guilds to ensure the mushrooms weren't poisonous. Maybe the White Cat would buy ingredients if she found enough?

She was never outdoorsy beyond the little playing outside she'd done as a child. Even then, she'd been sick most of the time, suffering from severe allergies or fevers at the slightest thing. It took about half an hour of wandering before she found a good patch of Penny Queen Bittersweet, thick and purple underneath its towering crimson-leafed tree.

Even with careful harvesting, her hands were purple by the time she filled up a small bag. She'd also found a few ferns she wanted to press and dry so she could identify them later, as well as a small bag of various nuts. Most of her pack was full of branches she planned to carve at night to increase her crafting skills; even if she made silly whistles or toys, she was still learning how to use her carving tools.

New skill acquired: Gathering

There was definitely something different about being an elf in the forest. She instinctively knew which direction led back to the road, that this game trail was safe to follow, and that one was to be avoided. It was confusing, but she let her gut guide her feet since she had little experience otherwise.

The sun was starting to set when she left the woods and started back to town. The guard nodded at her guild medallion and waved her past with a smothered yawn. Her stomach complained about the lack of lunch, and she bought a day-old apple and bread from the market with a few pennies to munch as she walked.

The adventurers guild was much busier, but Goff waved her over to the edge of the counter by the wall when she entered. "One of the girls upstairs put together a list of herbs and things. She's waiting off the library to review your harvest; ask for Tiss."

"Thanks, Goff," she said happily, trotting off to the grumbles of the others waiting in line.

"Elves getting preferred treatment now, Goff?" One of the adventurers scoffed, making Goff scowl.

"Would you want a kid wandering around here at night with half the crowd drunk? Guild master's orders. You don't like it, take it up with Master Barrow." Goff snapped, and the adventures grumbled, but let it be, considering the nights could be rather bawdy when everyone got into their cups.

———

Upstairs was a long open hallway and a series of doors, most of which were closed. The library was at the end of the hall, tucked behind the guild offices and taking the rest of the space available. Shelves reached the ceiling with more books than most homes would ever boast. It wouldn't have put a scratch on the big city libraries that had several floors, but it was enough to make Kenko's eyes tear up just from the scent of paper and dust that only came from old books.

Several desks sat to one side, but the closest was manned by a fiery-haired fox beast-kin who glanced up from her task and smiled, "Hello, can I help you?"

"Hello, I'm Kenko." Kenko said, slowly blinking in shock at the kimono-wearing beast-kin, "I spoke with Goff this morning, and he recommended I study some herbal manuals and said there would be a list of plants and things to gather that are always in need at the guilds. I was told to ask for Tiss?"

"Oh, you're Kenko. I'm afraid Tiss is out running an errand." The fox said, grinning, "My name is Sadao. I work for the guild, and my clan are information gatherers. Our rates are very reasonable if you ever have a specific need, and we buy information that benefits the guilds."

"Nice to meet you." Kenko grinned back. The fox girl was all but bouncing in place as she gestured about the room.

"I have the list and a stack of illustrated manuals for you at the desk by the windows. If you need anything else, don't hesitate to ask, but try to remain quiet. We do have others who use the library during the day to research quests."

"Of course, will it be all right if I sketch the plants and take notes?"

"You have paper?"

"Right here," Kenko agreed, pulling out the notebook and pencils she'd purchased to note her quests and the items she gathered.

"Perfect, I'll be at the desk should you need anything until we close."

"Thank you, Sadao," Kenko said with a quick bobbed bow; it never hurt to be polite.

Kenko approached the desk and started laying out the books and things she would need. It was quiet, with only the fox and a snake beast-kin researching in one corner to break the faint murmurs from the guild hall downstairs. She'd never had the patience to draw in her last life or hands that didn't scream holding a pencil, but there was nothing but time to learn now. If she was going to market her inventions, she'd need to be able to draw her designs, and it was something she'd have to adapt to.

She still wasn't used to having a body that did what she asked, waking up pain-free and only having the expected level of exhaustion coming from a long day of physical labor to lull her to sleep. She was often up late making notes in her journal or designing projects in her head, her brain too full and spinning too fast to let sleep come quickly.

Waking up refreshed and full of energy after a life of exhaustion was so foreign. She doubted other elves skipped and bounced on one leg down the paths in the forest just because they could, but she revealed the simple ability to move without pain.

The way everyone talked about elves made them out to be very vain, aloof, and arrogant in their views. There was no way she wanted to act any different from in her past life. She wasn't better or worse than anyone else, regardless of race, and she had no intention of snubbing anyone.

"Um, Sadao?" Kenko asked when she'd copied everything from the gathering lists and sketched each plant she'd be expected to gather.

"Finished already?" The fox girl asked, accepting back the small stack of books from Kenko.

"Yes, but I wondered if the guild has any history books. I don't know much about the area and would like to learn."

"Much of what we carry is geared towards battle tactics and fighting manuals. Let me take a look and get back to you. Were there any other topics you wanted information on?"

"General information on the other races and the elves." Kenko said, blushing, "I'm afraid I will say something embarrassing or biased since I was so isolated growing up. I don't know much about the world and want to learn."

"You might do better speaking to your friends, but I'll see if I can find a few general histories and things that might help broaden your education."

"That would be great. Thank you, Sadao." Kenko said, relieved; she hated feeling like she was in the dark about everything.

The Quiet Anvil was just as busy when she returned that afternoon. Only the objects they were crafting had changed in the hours she'd been gone. A line of completed work sat to one side, filling the long tables.

"Ah, the young elf," Kraddas said, waving her over to one corner, "I have your tools and an offer for you, lass."

"What kind of offer exactly?" she asked, only to gasp when he unrolled a leather kit with her carving tools filling each slot, gleaming and sharp as razors, "That is much too much; I can't afford something like that."

"This is a gift. The offer is to pay for sharpening whenever you wish, and I would like you to train under Esha and learn how to engrave. It is a handy skill to learn along with carving, and most start with wood to learn the feel of the tools."

"Why would you want me? You have your apprentices already."

"Meld and Brin are my apprentices and are still learning to work the forge and to shape metal. I can't see an elf prospering with such a task, but learning to engrave for one with magic is a handy skill."

"Even if I can't use my magic yet?" Kenko pressed, needing to be sure; even Gatha had been surprised that she couldn't use heating runes or cast the simple locking spells used on the Inn's doors.

"You won't be carving magical runes anytime soon, lass." Esha chuckled, "I simply wished to offer lessons should you wish to learn. No elf could learn troll magic, but I know enough runes to cast basic enchantments on our armor, so you can start to see how it is done.

Should you wish to learn proper magic, you must find a mage to apprentice to."

"I wish to pay for my tools. Even if I help around the shop, I need to pay something," Kenko insisted firmly, turning back and refusing to look away as the older dwarf cleaned his tools.

"If you are willing to run errands for the forge and take lessons from Esha, we can settle on one small silver." he said gruffly, "You are too young to be swinging a hammer or spending hours in the heat of a forge. Do your gathering quests, but stop by each morning for the tasks we can give you and after your gathering for a lesson with Esha. Will that suffice? We will be busy the next few days pushing through a new order of shields and swords for the army."

"Come collect your tools tomorrow morning. Esha can show you the basic shapes each tool is used to make. Leave your harvesting tools so they can be sharpened tonight."

"That is too much," she protested, only for him to shush her.

"It gives the boys something to fuss over. Trust me, they will do you right."

"If you insist," she said uncertainly, setting down her pack and pulling out her tools frowning.

"I do; no adventurer or apprentice should learn with substandard tools. I will return these to you in the morning; never fear."

"I am taking advantage of you."

"By making my apprentices prove their craft to their master? Gods forbid." Kraddas snorted, "Esha, take her upstairs and show her your workroom. You will be working there instead of dying of heat in the forge, and you are already wilting."

"No, I'm fine," Kenko said quickly, hurrying to follow the tall troll inside.

"You may not mind the heat, but I am much more comfortable working outside the furnace," Esha laughed. I sometimes work in wood myself to relax. Carving can be wonderful after a long day in the forge."

The workshop upstairs was just a simple room with shelves and tables filling most of the space, and the difference was how Esha relaxed as she entered. Tension dropped from her shoulders as she pulled down her wood carving tools and laid them out for Kenko's perusal. The scent of cedar and wood filled the room from a basket full of shavings and a stack of different blocks filling one corner.

"Before you begin any project, you take care of your tools; before you end a project, you do the same. A sharp tool makes for quick work, and a clean workshop makes for a clean finish." she said with a satisfied smile, "First, I will teach you how each tool is used, and then your project for the next few days is to carve several simple shapes and bring one to me each morning. Even with a simple knife, most shapes can be made; it takes more time. The tools allow you to more quickly complete complex cuts, nothing more."

"Tomorrow, we will begin training; for now, think of what you wish to make. In the coming weeks, you will be given more complex tasks until you can start working on your own projects. Then I will advise you on improving your work and set tasks to learn a specific skill with your tools."

"Thank you, Esha."

"Do not look so overwhelmed, little elf. We were all where you are starting at one time. It is the mark of a master of their craft to pass on their knowledge, and it does no good dying with its crafter."

Kenko *[Level 2]*

   Class: *Artificer (Magical) [Level 1]*

   Skills:

Regeneration, Skin Deep, Marathon, Archive, Darkvision, Perception, Meditation

   Additional Skills:

Cooking (Basic), Crafting (Basic), Spell Craft (Basic), Housekeeping (Basic), Design (Intermediate), Organization (Advanced), Magic (Basic), Map Reading (Basic), Woodworking (Basic), Wood Carving (Basic), Drawing (Basic), Calculation (Basic), Gathering (Basic), Pathfinding (Basic)

   Titles: *Blessed of Ume*

CHAPTER
SIX

"WELL?" Guild Master Banner asked, pouring a drink for the hunter and himself as he sat at the darkened bar.

"She didn't seem to spot me, but she also avoids every path that goes anywhere near a monster den I know about." The stout man said, heaving himself onto a bar stool and sighing, "The kid has enough energy for three; I've been running around town all day."

"Where else did she go?" Banner asked, starting to wipe down the bar as he finished closing the Guild Hall for the night. Sometimes, it pays to keep your rooms at the guild.

"The Quiet Anvil and is lodged at The White Cat for now. She is being careful with her money, so she probably will have enough to continue staying there, but if it runs out, that could change. The owner is charging her half price already for a single room."

"Don't bother the dwarves," Banner huffed, "I'll ask for an appointment with the clan chief for that shop."

"You couldn't find enough gold to make me step into that viper nest; there was too much political drama." The man snorted, sipping at his beer.

"Elves aren't much better. We will have our hands full once word gets back to the home forest." Banner said, stretching out his back and shoulders as he moved to cover the light crystals for the evening.

"How long will it take?"

"To get an elf here? It depends on what clan they suspect she is from. I'd wager a month or more. Six weeks or fewer if she's a nobility with a watcher on guard until they arrive."

"No one can spot an elf if they don't want to be found, and for a kid, she's a fast runner. I nearly lost her several times outside town. Thankfully, she's still a kid and spent ten minutes skipping along one path." The hunter laughed.

"For now, just keep an ear out for issues she's having or monsters in her quest area. The last thing we need is an international war with the elves because some idiot decided to bait the wrong kid." Banner pointedly said, "I just want to watch for trouble. Relations aren't great with elves, and the kid is too innocent to realize the political undercurrents she's wading through."

"So far, the locals are leaving her alone. She's staying around the beast-kin and dwarves, mostly." Mayor Dixon said, "Is anyone specific giving her issues about her race? The elves generally keep to themselves, but with the Empire's beliefs spreading, I can't rule out that she will face aggression from those in town who follow Mendite."

"Staying among the beast-kin should keep her mostly safe, but there are enough humans in the guilds and around town to make trouble if they decide they don't want an elf staying here, no matter her age."

"She may start working part-time at the Anvil if the dwarves can talk her into it. Do you think that will cause problems?"

"Not as long as they do it the dwarven way; contracts and rules are their forte, after all."

"And if they lock her into a contract at her disadvantage?"

"I doubt that will happen. They are working for a long-term advantage. Once she levels up her crafting, she could start enchanting their weapons and armor at a tenth of the cost the Mages would be charging."

"No one would kidnap an elf, but sabotaging their trade agreements is fair game. Once she starts building and selling items, we can worry. Until then, make sure no one in the underground is too stupid to live."

"That would be half the idiots in the capital." The hunter snorted, "I'll keep my eye on the girl. Don't worry about that. The only other thing that's strange is that she eats meat."

"Seriously?" Banner asked, setting down his glass, frowning.

"Yeah, keeps buying the super cheap pies from the street vendors. Maybe she can't afford anything else, but I've never seen an elf touch anything with meat. I thought they all were strict vegetarians?"

"So did I; I'll have to check with the local healers. I have no idea if it's bad for their health or not." Banner mused.

"Is it our fault if she's poisoning herself?"

"She's an eight-year-old and a member of my guild. If she's had zero interaction with elves and was raised by stupid humans, it is completely possible she's been eating meat since she was an infant." Banner grunted, digging out a small notebook and pencil, "Mind running a message to the healers for me?"

"Only if you are paying me for it." The hunter huffed, snatching the note and hopping off his chair, "I'll come by at the end of the week unless something comes up."

"You know where to find me." Banner huffed, returning to his office; he had a stack of jobs and quests that were weeks overdue, thanks to the rise of raids along the border. Too many of his members were headed to the army, and many guard positions were available to watch over caravans or take night shifts at border guard.

———

Gatha looked over the assembled group with an amused chuckle. Who could have guessed that a tiny elf could cause so much chaos in a single town by just walking in? Most of the guild masters were milling about: Potions Master Anthea, Adventurers Guild Master Banner, Healers Hall Master Kot, Mayor Dixon, his advisors, and the head of the guard.

"Thank you for coming, everyone. If you can have a seat, we will get started." The mayor called out, waving the last few stragglers to a chair, "I asked everyone here to discuss the issue of the young orphaned elf girl that arrived in town recently. Most of you have inter-acted with the child; she is staying at The White Cat."

"What is there to discuss? She works the same as any adult and is not in debt yet." Guard Bensen asked, snorting, rubbing at his wide, flat nose. It wasn't hard to see how he kept the peace in the city; given his broad chest and deadly-looking horns, one didn't mess with an adult Minotaur.

"Has anyone heard back from the elves yet?" Kot asked, hands stroking the holy grimoire they carried everywhere, goat ears flicking in annoyance.

"Several of us have sent letters to the elven enclave at the capital and the elven territory." Mayor Dixon said, trying to keep the discussion civil, "However, it is much too soon for a reply unless someone is willing to use a mage sending for such a trivial matter?"

"By the Gods, having an elf child in town is not an emergency! She is a child, not some rogue running around bent on destruction. We must ensure she is fed, clothed, and safe until the elves come to collect her." Anthea huffed; Arachne generally didn't keep their children very long and wasn't precisely the mothering kind.

"If she is willing to go with them." Gatha said, "Elves didn't raise her, and she didn't seem to remember much of her childhood before living alone. She is polite and would make a wonderful addition to the city if she chose to stay."

"You don't think they wouldn't force her? She is only a child." Bensen asked, waving off her rebuttal, "Do we know who raised her?"

"And elves treat their children like adults. They are responsible for their actions no matter what their age is. If she wishes to stay, it would be allowed as long as she is not causing herself or others harm." Gatha insisted, "We have no say in what happens to her or where she goes."

"She is staying with you, Gatha. Is she doing alright? Does she require anything?" The mayor asked.

"Her largest concern is the lack of funds at the moment. She spends her mornings running errands and doing quests for the guilds, but she only gets breakfast with her rooms, and I don't think she is eating very well the rest of the day."

"Has anyone else heard of an elf that eats meat?" Banner asked, glancing over the others, "I'm concerned she's making herself sick."

"She eats meat?" Kot sputtered, "You must be joking! Did wolves raise her?"

"Nope, buys those nasty meat pies the street vendors sell to the poor for lunch and dinner, as far as I can tell."

"That would make an elf ill; they can't sustain themselves from meat. It might fill her stomach, but it does little else." Kot murmured, looking a bit green.

"Several guild members have already expressed resentment over what they see as me giving her special treatment. I've brushed it off as making adjustments for her age, but I won't be able to do much more for her in the adventurers' hall. Maybe if we could get her into lessons, I could have a meal provided during that time, but I can't just suddenly start shoving sweets at the kid."

"Sweets won't help the issue. She needs vegetables and fruit." Kot huffed, disliking the idea, "Cheese or milk if you can get her to eat it. I know young elves do eat that from time to time."

"I am serving her salad and milk with every meal, but it is already obvious that she's not getting the same meals as the other customers." Gatha sighed, "No one has complained since it is helping a child, but eventually, there could be backlash. Perhaps we could start offering small take-a-way meals for lunches at the Inn. If I can keep the price low enough, it would cover the cost and give her an option without seeming like charity."

"Please draw up an itemized list of services you've provided her outside your normal duties and send it to my office. I am gathering a report to give the elven representative whenever they arrive." Mayor Dixon said firmly, "I will try to see everyone compensated."

"I do not need to be compensated. I don't wish to see the child taken advantage of." Gatha glared at the merchants further down the table, "She is still leveling her craft, and I know no child of yours would ever be forced to sign a contract of servitude, so put those papers away."

"No one is suggesting a contract of servitude, just a general contract to allow her to work in the merchants guild and sell her wares in the market." One of the merchants scoffed.

"She doesn't have wares to sell!" Gatha snarled, making the human merchant back off, hands raised in defense.

"Then when she does," one of the beast-kin merchants added, trying to mediate only for most of the table to sneer openly.

"Gentle beings, please! Can we keep the tone civil?" Mayor Dixon said, "We are here to look into what we can do to help the child until her guardians arrive, nothing more. There will be no discussion of contracts or sales until she has a guardian present."

"What else is there to discuss? She has access to housing, is earning money, and is working to increase her craft." Athena snapped, ready to get back to her research.

"What about her magic?" Banner asked. "I have letters to several members trying to find a tutor for her, but I haven't received any replies yet."

"Is that something to be concerned about? Elves generally have a natural grasp of their magic." Mayor Dixon asked, glancing at the others, "Who could teach an elf? Their magic is unique to their race, isn't it?"

"We can't assume anything; the last thing we need is her burning out." Healer Kot insisted, leaning forward, "Who have you contacted? I may be able to reach out to a few peers who have also worked with elves in the past."

"Anais and Othall."

"The Blue Mage?! How could you ask her?"

"She has taken apprentices before from the guild." Banner said, waving away their concerns, "I haven't heard back yet either way."

"Well, those of us who have connections should reach out. It wouldn't hurt to have a few mentor options," Kot insisted, accepting the cup of tea he had been passed. Is there anything else to discuss on the matter?"

"Do we know if the dwarves have her in a contract with the Smeltbow Clan or Kaddras Hammersmith?" Another merchant asked tentatively.

"No, she hasn't signed with the dwarves; however, Hammersmith is open to allowing her to learn basic engraving and simple tasks at his shop," Gatha said, glaring at the merchants.

"Is anyone watching her when she's outside the city? What if she is injured while running quests?"

"She has several self-healing and defensive skills, and I've assigned one of my adventurers to keep an eye on her when she leaves the city walls. She's as safe as the guild can make without assigning her to follow another guild member around."

"Is that an option?"

"Not unless someone takes her on as a student or apprentice." Banner huffed, "She has no interest in learning weapons or self-defense, and I can't make her do so."

"What if we started a small weekly class for the more junior members of our local guilds? A way for healers, potioners, and everyone to learn basic skills?"

"Who would teach it? Thanks to the border skirmishes and the tensions with the Empire of Human Nations, I've sent most of my best guild members to the West."

"Is there anyone in the capital we could tempt to come and teach her?" Mayor Dixon asked, fiddling with his pen.

"Not without paying a substantial stipend to do so." Banner grunted, "Most mages are out on the war front or working as healers. Kot, do you have anyone who could teach her the basics?"

"Not anyone I would trust with the duty. She could follow along with my apprentice, but I don't have time to take on another, myself, and we don't even know if she can heal yet. She needs to be tested."

"What if we sent for someone from the capital simply to test her? Once we know her abilities, we can decide what help to offer." Athena offered, hoping to wrap up the meeting.

"That I can approve," the mayor said, sighing in relief, "I will request a mage to test the youths showing magical promise in town. If we make it into an open session for any child who wishes to be tested, we may find more talent in our population."

"Has anyone asked her what she wants to do?" Gatha asked, raising an eyebrow at Banner and the mayor.

"She needs training, and who's to say she doesn't want to learn magic? She seems more than willing to learn what she can from those at the guild." Banner pointed out.

"It is still her decision. If she wants to spend all her time running around as a gatherer, she can do so. We have no say in what she does and are not her guardians."

"We are the closest things to it until the elves arrive, Miss Gatha." Mayor Dixon pointed out, "She seems to respect you and the guilds, which is why I've included you in this meeting. Would you leave an orphan to deal with life in our town with zero support?"

"What of the other orphans? She isn't the only child without parents in our town, Mayor. If you offer her support, the others should be offered the same."

"They are welcome to join the guilds the same way she has. The local church provides meals, housing, and education for those without in town. Kenko is welcome to use the same resources, and all the orphans will be offered testing when the agent arrives from the capital. Perhaps we can make it a yearly event for those in town, a day to approach the orphans and underage with offers of support and information on the guilds."

"Will you be paying for their memberships as well? Most don't have a copper to their names. With no way to earn a silver for the membership, few can join the guilds without support at such a young age."

"I will see if it is possible to supply funding to the orphanage for those who wish to join a guild. However, our budget isn't bottomless, and they will have to earn their own way in life once they have their start. That is all we are trying to offer the elf: a safe start in our city until her guardians arrive."

"Then perhaps a small yearly event can be arranged," one shopkeeper offered. I know many of us are without apprentices from our children. What if we provided a yearly day for our city's children to meet with willing merchants and crafters who need apprentices or workers in their shops?"

"That is an idea worth pursuing, thank you." The mayor grunted, making swift notes, "Are there any other issues?"

"Then let us adjourn the meeting for now. I will contact those who need it once I have more information on the testing and where it will occur. Thank you, everyone, for coming."

———

Kenko *[Level 2]*

   Class: *Artificer (Magical) [Level 1]*

   Skills:

Regeneration, Skin Deep, Marathon, Archive, Darkvision, Perception, Meditation

   Additional Skills:

Cooking (Basic), Crafting (Basic), Spell Craft (Basic), Housekeeping (Basic), Design (Intermediate), Organization (Advanced), Magic (Basic), Map Reading (Basic), Woodworking (Basic), Wood Carving (Basic), Drawing (Basic), Calculation (Basic), Gathering (Basic), Pathfinding (Basic)

   Titles: *Blessed of Ume*

CHAPTER
SEVEN

WHITTLING WAS BOTH MORE complex and more straightforward than she'd imagined. Her hands automatically knew how to follow the wood grain and how much each sliver could bend and give without breaking, but that didn't apply to using the knives or chisels to shape the branch. Her scrapes and bruised fingers healed overnight, but her first attempt at a simple shape was stained with blood and sap as she fought with the green wood.

Each night, she designed the tools and machines she hoped to build one day. This became part of her routine, as she meditated on her magic and reviewed her day as she exercised.

She was stumped on accessing her magic or casting a light spell safely. She'd watched several young children crafting fairy lights and chasing them about a park yesterday. She could feel a pulsing vibration at her core if she concentrated, but nothing she did seemed to change it. No amount of wishing called that light to her hands.

For now, she left it alone as she continued her slow progress. She'd nearly jumped out of her skin when she got her first level-up notification. She was progressing, even if it seemed at a snail's pace.

If she was going to collect herbs and wood for her crafts, she needed a separate bag. Some of the berries she had picked the day before were mushy after being under the sticks all day. The more fragile things needed a basket she could pull out and carry as she harvested them from the forest.

Spending the morning harvesting reeds and long, sturdy grass felt like a waste. It took hours of braiding blades of grass and weaving reeds until she crafted something decent enough that she wouldn't be laughed out of the guild hall the following day.

New skill acquired: Weaving

New skill acquired: Basket Craft

"That is an unusual bag," Goff said with a strained smile, which she greeted with a glare. The guild hall was packed this morning, and two others were working the counter with him, accepting quest items.

"I can't afford another bag. It will work for now." Kenko huffed, shoving her bag of mushrooms across the counter, "Tomorrow, I'm going to get the Lamb's Rum in the marshes. Is there anything else I should be keeping an eye out for?"

"If you are going to the marshes, watch out for snakes. It's spring, so they shouldn't be too bad yet; mostly, it's the bugs." Goff said grimacing, "The flies are bad in the marsh unless it's winter. If you find anything unusual, go ahead and bring it back. You can work with the girls upstairs to sort out if it's a herb the guilds need or not if it's not on your list."

"For today," she huffed at him, annoyed, "I don't want to make them do extra work."

"Can I return your basket tomorrow? I need a runner to take these to the potions hall later."

"If you want, I can do that now. Should I tell them it is from the guild?"

"Yes, and to mark the exchange on our register," Goff said with relief, waving forward the next in line even as he returned her basket.

The potions guild was just as busy when she entered, with several other gatherers and apothecary staff waiting for the next box of potions to be brought up. Coins and boxes of vials steadily changed hands across the counter. A second counter to the side dealt with the freshly harvested herbs and ingredients being brought in.

"Who is next, please? What do you have?" The man barked, waving her forward.

"The adventurers guild said to add this to their register," she said politely, handing over the bag.

"More mangled, worthless ingredients," the guild staff huffed, laying out a few of the mushrooms and some sprigs of herbs, "Tell the guild not to bother with another batch of these. They aren't good for anything but making stew. It's not worth our price to clean and store them. We wouldn't make five copper pennies on the lot."

"Really? I was told they are in season."

"Yes," he scoffed, "and they are so abundant anyone can walk up and gather a handful. Not worth the time, like I said. Next!" he snapped, shoving the basket back across the counter and waving the next gatherer forward.

Kenko hefted her basket and headed towards the inn with heavy steps. Had the guild been lying about needing the herbs? Were they humoring her?

The church bells rang the evening bells, calling the orphans who stayed there to dinner. Several older than her ran past, hurrying to reach their last meal of the day. Her stomach grumbled, but she saved her coins for more scrap wood from the market.

The next day, it was due to rain, and she planned to spend the day at the forge working on her carving. Already, an icy breeze blew through the streets, bringing the heavy feel of rain and building clouds to the west. If her gathering were a wasted effort, she would focus on crafting instead, even if it meant missing a few meals. When she arrived, she took the herbs and mushrooms to Gatha but refused to let the woman pay for them, insisting that it was just extra she'd picked that day.

"Then we will have mushroom omelets in the morning." The beast-kin said firmly, refusing to comment further as she took the basket to the kitchen.

Taking a small block of wood, she started carving, sitting on the back steps of the inn so she didn't make a mess. Today's task from Esha was a chain of wooden links. She'd already turned in to her mentor squares, balls, and pyramids of wood. She was still struggling with fine details, so for now, she was working with larger designs.

She needed a way to find out if the adventurer's guild was

humoring her with the quests they gave her. She doubted Goff or even the guild master would admit to it. Was she overlooking the obvious? Gatha and the dwarves were also helping her, but was it out of kindness or a fear of the elves?

Was it just because she was an elf, and they didn't want to offend that powerful a race? What did it matter if she was alone? She'd never had contact with elves, so it wasn't like she was writing back to them asking for guidance or support.

None of the other orphans in town were being offered discounts and trades the way she was; however, they also didn't seem to be trying to work like she was. It was enough to give her a headache. Was she being humored, or were they hoping to take advantage of her once she leveled up? Was it both?

Putting her knife away, she stalked back to her room in a strop. What was she missing about this world? There had to be some subtext that she wasn't seeing.

———

She wasn't sure why her instincts were fussing about being in the woods today. None of the paths felt safe, and the annoying feeling of being followed that had been haunting her the last few days was still there. Grumpy at the constant mental ping of there, there, there, the follower was giving her, she stomped down the first path she came to.

Whoever was following her had at least stopped following her around town. This had made her paranoid, so she took extra streets and got lost a few times as she wound her way through town, trying to lose them.

Reaching a clearing ahead of her, she slowed, listening as the forest fell silent around her. Her instincts screamed at her to backtrack, but she kept creeping forward. Parting the brush with one hand, she struggled not to gasp as a massive bear came into view just a few feet away.

Kenko froze as the bear turned and reared up with a roar. Slowly back peddling, she watched the animal gather for a charge. Growling, it plowed forward. Run! She twisted, throwing herself backward into a tumble that somehow she came out of already running, body low to the ground, running for everything she had.

Disengagement activated: one minute cool down active

New skill acquired: Flight

Her brain shut off. Dodging and scrambling, she ignored the path, bulldozing through the underbrush. The sound of a fight broke out behind her. The bear roared in anger, and meaty thumps echoed through the trees.

She slowed, glancing back as the animal went quiet. Had the bear found someone else to hunt? Running away wasn't an option; she was going back and checking. What if they were hurt? Steeling her nerves, she started walking back, taking care to be extra quiet as she paced forward. Keeping her body low, she eased through the underbrush in a crouch.

The clearing was a wreck, with broken branches and blood covering the ground. A man stood to one side, frowning, looking over the fallen bear. He raised a dagger as she approached before turning back to the bear.

"If I'd known you could be that silent, I would have left you be." he huffed, starting to skin the bear and gathering his weapons to be cleaned.

"You're the one who's been following me?" she snapped, angry that she ignored her instincts.

"Yes, I hunt these woods often, but few children go this deep into the forest, so I watched while hunting."

"No, you followed me around town too." she snapped, knowing this was the same person that had driven her mad with her instincts constantly on alert.

"I wasn't sure if you'd noticed." he huffed, continuing with his work on the bear, "The guild master was concerned about a child wandering around alone. He asked me to watch over you until we were sure no one in town meant you harm."

"Who are you?"

"My name is Brun. I'm just a hunter who keeps out of the guild politics. The guild master sometimes calls on me to track individuals he has concerns about."

"And do you still have concerns?"

"Yes," he said flatly, not looking up from his work. I want to teach you tracking. It would have helped you avoid the path you chose today."

"I only took that path because I was annoyed at being followed." she snapped, "In a way, this entire situation is your fault."

"Be that as it may, you must learn more skills to continue to frequent these woods on quests."

Kenko considered the man; in a way, he wasn't wrong, but it irritated that the guild master hadn't bothered to inform her of his concerns. Everyone considered her a helpless child, which was starting to annoy her. Confronting him would confirm that she couldn't care for herself; she would need to find a way to prove it to the surrounding adults.

"When would you teach me?"

"When are you coming back to the forest?"

"In two days, I'm at the forge tomorrow and in the library the next."

"What are you doing in the library?" he asked, straightening up and eying her with a look she couldn't read.

"Reading about the history of Arda," she huffed, hating how simple that sounded when she was struggling to understand why so many wars seemed to have been over a tiny insult one race gave to another. For a country so concerned with dealing with monsters and keeping the cities safe, they seemed to go to war a concerning amount.

"Ask for a book on tracking and animal tracks. It wouldn't hurt to add crafting animal traps even if you don't eat meat or hunt yourself. It can be a useful skill to know."

"Right, and you will want me to learn a weapon as well," she huffed, imagining how much time she would lose carving and gathering.

"I won't force you, but what if someone weaker than you was attacked? What would you do? If you were out in the woods and no one else was around to help? Would you run away like today? Think about it."

"Are you going to keep following me?"

"Only in the forest until I'm convinced you don't need me. This area is mostly low-level beasts and monsters like boar and the occasional goblin."

"I haven't seen any goblins."

"You won't as long as you stay out of caves and aren't out at night. The ones around here are nocturnal. If you went further south, you'd find roving bands of fighters in the grasslands, which are much tougher to fight."

"I'm heading back to town."

"Do what you like; I'm going to be smoking this meat before it goes bad," he grunted, continuing his butchery.

Kenko took the first path she found that led toward town. Why was this world so different? Yes, it was more rural, even for a mid-sized city, but she wasn't used to dealing with many dangers. Everyone in the town was dangerous, and the animals attacked openly outside it. The farmers had to be tough to survive and keep their crops safe.

She'd already seen brawls in the taverns and thieves in the market. An argument could escalate quickly in a world where everyone carries a weapon. Usually, the guards would be stationed in the market and around town. Still, thanks to a war on the border, most were too busy covering the walls with limited labor to do more than patrol the busiest streets and taverns, leaving the less frequented areas to violence and theft.

The market was at least vaguely safe if you ignored the refugees wandering through begging for scraps or trying to trade their few valuables for coin to continue their journey. She ducked through one of the smaller gates and headed to the main square at a jog. Lingering around was just asking for someone to harass the elf lately. The town was tense with the flow of wounded and displaced wandering from the border.

Men and women who had served in the army or guard returned with missing limbs and eyes. The healing hall was flooded with patients, and there were not enough healers to help them. Guild Row was a shifting mess of refugees and returning soldiers hunting for healing or work. How the town had changed in just a few short weeks since she arrived was unbelievable.

———

Kenko [Level 3]

 Class: Artificer (Magical) [Level 1]

 Skills:

Regeneration, Skin Deep, Marathon, Archive, Disengagement, Flight, Darkvision, Perception, Meditation.

 Additional Skills:

Cooking (Basic), Crafting (Basic), Spell Craft (Basic), Housekeeping (Basic), Design (Intermediate), Organization (Advanced), Magic (Basic), Map Reading (Basic), Woodworking (Basic),

 Wood Carving (Basic), Drawing (Basic), Calculation (Basic), Gathering (Basic), Pathfinding (Basic), Weaving (Basic), Basket Craft (Basic)

 Titles: Blessed of Ume

CHAPTER
EIGHT

KENKO WAS all but skipping as she made her way toward the potion's guild hall a few days after the bear attack. Brun gave her a few basic lessons on tracking, and she'd humored him by asking the dwarves about basic weapons she could learn.

She decided to take out the middleman for a few weeks and deal directly with the potioners. The forest had finally produced something decent to turn in, and she looked forward to eating as many apples and fruit as she could stomach. She would eat well tonight.

A sudden shove from the side sent her basket flying even as she hit the cobbles hard. Laughter rang out from several kids in the square as she blinked in shock at her broken basket and scraped hands. No one moved to help as she pushed to her knees, the one who'd shoved her watching sneering.

"Hey, elf brat!" A kid crowed, shoving past her and scattering her fallen herbs across the cobbles with muddy boots.

"Don't!" Kenko snapped, lunging for the broken basket; they would ruin the plants.

"You too good for the orphanage? Too classy for the likes of us?" The boy sneered, stepping forward to grind a mushroom into a paste.

"What?" Kenko asked, flinching as another stomp splattered her with crushed plant matter and mud.

"The little princess is too busy for the likes of us." A girl singsonged from across the street, watching with anger in her eyes.

"I'm not a princess," Kenko stuttered. She'd been bullied most of her past life, and this was too much like the taunts she'd received throughout her school days.

"You aren't a gutter rat, too high and mighty." Another snapped, "Where did you get the coin to stay in an inn if you're an orphan? Did the elves kick you out?"

"I bet she stole it, " another jeered. "We should take it, finders, keepers."

"Thief! Gutter rat! Princess!" Rang out around her as tears came to her eyes.

"Aw, we made the brat cry." The girl mocked, "Are you going to run and tell your parents? Oh, that's right. You don't have any."

'What do you want?" Kenko snapped, shoving herself to her feet. She refused to run from another child.

"For you to leave, we don't need some random elf getting special treatment while we barely get meals from the orphanage."

"I work, I don't get special treatment," Kenko said, trying not to let herself cry.

"Do you think you're the first kid to try to work at the guilds? Without a parent's approval, they won't hire anyone until they're fifteen, and the orphanage won't approve. How are you working as a guild member? What are you five? Who allowed you to join?"

"No one, I just joined." Kenko huffed, hating that the kids were right. She was getting special privileges, but she had no choice but to accept what she was offered unless she wanted to be starving on the street.

"Because you're an elf," the dog beast-kin boy sneered, "orphanage probably wouldn't even take her."

"Hey, what are you kids doing?" Someone called out, and Kenko glanced behind her to find the hunter, Brun, walking towards them.

The kids scattered, and Kenko launched herself into a run, ignoring the scattered herbs and her basket. Brun shouted behind her, but she kept going. She raced past the streets she knew and kept going until she was outside the city walls.

She slowed to a walk and forced herself to consider the situation unemotionally. The guild had allowed her to join at eight when they don't take members until they are at least fifteen without a guardian's sign-off. She had no guardian to do so; they had never asked for one.

There were no elves in the area. They only came through traveling to the capital or patrolling the forests outside their territory. She was a lone elf child with no knowledge of the world wandering around their town, and they were breaking the rules left and right to accommodate and protect her. It must be because they feared the elves would do something if she were injured or starving. Were the elves that protective of their kind, or was it just her?

Why had Ume made her an elf when they weren't seen outside their country? Was it intentional or some random roll of the dice?

And what about the other gods? Ume was the major god of this region, but each race seemed to have its gods, and some were specific to a profession as well. She'd prayed nightly to Ume, detailing her life and how things were going, but was that necessary? Did the gods follow along with the reincarnated's lives, or were they just left to fend for themselves?

All the stories she'd heard so far had the gods much more involved and invested in this world than in her last life. Her miracles were uncommon, but receiving a special blessing or skill from a god wasn't rare; it did happen. She had a blessing from Ume, but it seemed to be something all reincarnations were given; no one spoke of such random blessings that didn't have an effect.

She wasn't a sage or hero reincarnated to save the world or stop a war. She was just Kenko. She'd been rolling along with her new life like a vacation since she arrived, just enjoying living her life the best she could.

This was her new life now, and everything just seemed to fall into place so quickly. She was a guild member, mentored by a local crafter, working as a gatherer, and learning about the world around her. What had she missed?

She was an artificer, but what had she crafted outside the random carvings she made? Her designs for dozens of devices filled a notebook, but there was no way to power them without learning magic and runes. She was forced to keep her inventions on paper until she knew enough magic to implement them.

Was it all useless, or was she missing some more significant part of the picture? Ume had hinted that this life was to make up for the misery of her last one, and in most ways, it did. However, she still wasn't a productive member of society. She leaned on everyone around her. Kids were allowed to do that, but was she a child? She had the mind of an adult. If she'd lived, she could have been turning thirty-eight this year. No one had expected her to live that long, much less her parents or herself.

This was her chance to do things over again. How was that supposed to work when she was stuck in the body of a child? How was she supposed to wait years to be acknowledged when she'd died ignored and viewed as broken no matter how she struggled? She couldn't stop; she just couldn't.

———

"Kenko, wait a minute." Goff called, waving her back to the side of the counter the next afternoon, "The guild master wants to speak with you upstairs."

"Now?" Kenko asked, surprised, shouldering her pack. Was this about Brun and the bear? He hadn't bothered her beyond showing up once every few days to teach her a few things for an hour or two before fading back into the forest, as he'd never been there.

"Upstairs and to the right," Goff said, waving her off before returning to the stack of quests he was sorting to add to the boards.

"Ah, Kenko, please come in." Guild master Banner called, waving her through the normally closed door.

"You needed to see me, Guild Master?" she asked, glancing at the surly teenager waiting to one side leaning against the wall.

"Yes, we are looking at fostering more partnership and group work amongst our newest guild members, and I'd like to discuss you joining a small group of other members on your trips to the forest."

"And if I refuse?" she asked, fighting the urge to fidget.

"While you have that right, I would like you to consider shadowing the group for a week at least. They could teach you basic skills they use in the field and on quests."

"You expect us to take a child with us hunting?" The teenager scoffed, "Not only will she slow us down, Guild master, but she has zero combat training. We would spend half the fight working to protect her, splitting our defensive power."

"I don't expect to be defended. I can defend myself." Kenko snapped, "I don't have any weapons ability, but I know how to hide and get away from danger."

"You expect to follow us into a combat quest and run away and hide as soon as danger appears? If you are part of the group, you have to pitch in. Otherwise, you're just dead weight." The boy snarled.

"I don't want to complete combat quests at all," Kenko huffed, "however if the guild master insists on this, that would happen. I don't see working with your group helping either of us."

"I agree. Since she refuses to join our group, I'll see myself out. Thank you for the opportunity, Guild Master." The teenager said sarcastically, bowing to Banner and walking out.

"Was there anything else, Guild Master?" Kenko asked, fuming, why he was pressing this issue.

"If you are going to continue your harvesting lessons this fall, I must insist you learn at least one long-range weapon. I don't care if it's a sling, bow, or crossbow, but you need something on you in case wolves become an issue again this year. Most of the town guards are being sent to the border to assist refugees who are traveling along our roads. No one outside the town will assist you if you get into a dangerous situation."

"So I just need to find someone to teach me?"

"Yes, I suggest looking into the lessons we hold in the evenings for new guild members who want to raise their ranks."

"I will look into it, Guild Master," she said with her own bow to the man.

"I will have to ban you from taking quests outside of town if you can't show proficiency in at least one weapon by this fall, Kenko. The wolves and monsters get worse in the winter, and I can't have an adventurer wandering around without the ability to defend themselves."

"Noted," she said, turning and leaving without another word.

What was the point of having a guild master if they isolated themselves from the guild? She'd never seen the guild master at any of the collection tables or in the bar when she was at the guild hall. He was supposed to live in the building but never left his office or inter-acted with the guild members.

He wasn't wrong about the refugees. However, the roads were full of slow-moving carts and people traveling away from the border. Few bothered to stop in town, but the prices in the market and inns had increased as supplies began to run short with the increase in mouths to feed.

She didn't particularly want to learn to use a bow. It was just so OP for an elf to carry about a bow. A sling would be light enough to pack in her pocket or carry while she gathered supplies or herbs. Throwing daggers would be too expensive in the long-term, as would arrow at her current budget.

It looked like she was going to be signing up for sling lessons. Could her days get any busier? If Ume had sent her here to reclaim her childhood, there was no way that was happening.

CHAPTER
NINE

"WHY DID you bother to contact me, Banner? You know I don't take apprentices." Anais huffed, brushing a lock of white hair from her eyes; she was exhausted and needed to head back to the capital for her next assignment. Something was happening with the nobility there; she wanted to route it out before it became a full-fledged insurrection.

"Just meet with the kid," the guild master snapped. "If after you meet her, you can say that she'd be better off with a different master, then you are welcome to head out in the morning."

"I don't work with elves on a good day," she muttered, fiddling with her silver belt, "You've seen how the elves in the capital treat humans."

"She isn't an elf. Humans raised her."

"And they haven't called her back to the home forest yet?" she pressed; the rangers were more social, at least, and she'd heard they sometimes were sent for lost elflings or half-breeds that turned up.

"We are still waiting for word from the envoys. She doesn't know what clan her parents were, doesn't remember them at all." Banner huffed. "She's an orphan who fetched up at my guild hall. I have to do what I can to help her, or the elven clans could sanction the entire town, and you know it." He snarled, scrubbing his hair and fighting the urge to rip it out. It would not improve his headache.

"That doesn't have to involve me!"

"We have a tester arriving from the capital tomorrow. I need her apprenticed to someone before the capital mages get their hooks in her."

"What training has she completed? Is she a complete novice, or does she have special skills?"

"She's an artificer who refuses to fight," he snapped, "she has zero training beyond basic tracking and woodcraft. She is working with a local forge to learn carving and enchantments once her magic is under control."

"How does an elf not have access to her magic?" she asked, blinking in surprise. All elves were magical; it was in their blood and bones.

"For all we know, she was raised by humans or wolves. She has zero common sense when it comes to living here so close to the wilds. She probably would be safer in the capital with a patron, but this is where she lives." Banner muttered, slugging back his drink and moving to pour a new one, "She has never shown even the smallest spark of magic, and the dwarves say that she has been seen attempting to cast as other children do without any results."

"Are you even certain she has magic?"

"Elves wither and die without it. She'd be sickly if she lacked a magical core. She has magic; she has no idea how to access it." Banner huffed, "I don't have an ounce myself, or I'd be offering the kid lessons. You know most of the guild tends not to use magic."

"I can't help but think that your guild tends to be idiots too impressed with their strength and weapons to understand the fine art of magic."

"Anais, you can consider this a favor I will owe you."

"You barely have the staff to run your guild right now, and all your adventurers are below level C. Don't make me laugh; you have nothing to offer me." she snorted, sipping at her whiskey.

"You know all the level C and above adventurers were summoned to the border last fall. There isn't anything I can do about that." he pointed out, "I need your help, Anais."

"You stayed behind."

"Someone had to stay and train these idiots before they got themselves killed in a milk run, and you know it."

"It didn't have to be you."

"There wasn't anyone else; everyone is either dead or fighting on the border thanks to the constant raids, and now they are attacking trade routes, so the entire country is low on goods."

"What makes this kid special? Why her? Why not any of the dozen other orphans running the streets of Arrowview?"

"I don't know; meet her, and you tell me." Banner huffed, "What eight-year-old calmly chooses a job to advance their levels and crafting? What kid shows up with a palm full of gold and has no idea how money works the first week and then is out bargaining the merchants by the next? She's strange, and being an elf with no idea how to act like one is only part of it."

"She's a child."

"Go talk to her and tell me that again." Banner snapped, "She may be physically eight, but she's mentally older. Something hammered that girl into shape at a very young age, and I can't figure out what since she doesn't have the trauma most would show at being forced to care for themselves so young."

"She's healthy?" Anais asked, looking concerned.

"No scars or injuries that I can see, and beyond needing a few more meals than she is getting right now, is healthy."

"So you aren't pushing her off on me, hoping for someone to heal her." she agreed, sighing.

"Gods, no, she's healthy, just utterly untrained. It took me until last month when the refugees started pouring in to get her even to take up a weapon at all."

"What happened?" she pressed; something must have triggered it if she'd been that adamant about not using weapons.

"She was attacked by a bear, probably a higher-ranked one since it took Brun a minute to take down."

"I take it she ran?" she asked, amused.

"Like a deer, Brun said it was the most graceful panic scramble he'd ever seen." Banner said, "She has several self-healing abilities and a disengagement skill that must have kicked in and got her away. She did go back, however, to check on Brun."

"That is something at least." Anais agreed dryly, "What weapon is she learning?"

"Basic blocks with a dagger and sling practice."

"She chose a sling over a bow?" she asked, frowning; most elves favored a bow.

"Cost may have been an issue, but she is very aware of her situation and has refused a loan from several people."

"So she's a charity case?" Anais asked; the guild generally frowned on taking on costs for a member.

"At least until the elves come to claim guardianship." Banner huffed.

"And that could be weeks or months away if they've already got a watcher in place," Anais added, holding out her glass for a refill.

"If they have, no one has spotted it yet, but given how some of their rangers hide, it isn't out of the question."

"Gear?" she asked, taking a long drink of the alcohol and savoring the burn as it lit her throat and stomach alight.

"Basic but sturdy, she is learning to sew and craft baskets but can't afford replacements."

"Baskets?"

"She's a crafter; grass and reed baskets are quick to make, and they let her carry more herbs or things she's gathered." Banner huffed, sounding like he'd already answered that question several times.

"Resourceful then," she hummed, "Fine, I'll meet her after the testing. I'll take her on if she wishes to learn, but I won't stay in town long. If she wants to continue her training, she'll leave once the elves arrive."

"Thanks for giving it that long."

"Even I know you don't mess with an elven child," she snorted, "I'd rather not be banned from their borders or blocked from their traders in the nation. It's hard enough to find magical herbs and crystals outside of their markets."

"She does have an eye for those, at least." Banner said, settling back in his chair, "She keeps finding rare plants or magical variants of even common herbs in her gathering. We haven't been making a big deal out of it, but she has some natural skill driving her to pick the best of everything she gathers."

"Probably an elf thing," Anais grunted, "where is she staying?"

"The White Cat, Gatha has taken her under her paw."

"I'll book a room then. You can't beat the meals either way," she agreed, gathering her bags.

"Thank you, Anais, you won't regret it," Banner said with a relieved smile.

"I haven't taken her on yet, Banner. Don't count on it happening before the contract is signed."

"You'll understand once you meet her," he said, watching her leave with a rueful chuckle. Anais was one of the few from his guild who made something of herself. Hopefully, she'd repay the favor and train his wayward elf.

———

"What exactly does being tested accomplish? Does it just show you have magic, or does it give you a list of skills like the guild cards?" Kenko asked, glancing over the assembled children as tables hosting the different guilds. Gatha insisted she go to the testing since anyone was allowed to take the testing, but children under 15 were tested for free.

"Yes and no. The test shows the current level of your skill and then the highest level you can attain. Unique skills are shown as part of the test, and the tester will ask the child to perform any magics they already have mastered."

"And those who show promise are offered positions to train?" Kenko asked doubtfully.

"Yes, as an artificer, you will have a few choices of whom to train with. You could even go to train at River-deep if you were able to secure a patron."

"But a patron expects to be repaid at a later date."

"Well, it is more that you will be willing to do a set number of projects for them every year they offer you patronage. They are paying for you to learn in exchange for future inventions."

"They would own the rights to those inventions?" Kenko asked, alarmed. The last thing she needed was to lose her rights to her work.

"It depends on the contract you make with that patron. Most are very fair and only expect you to work in their business for a set number of years before allowing you to go on your way."

"And I need a magic instructor to learn how to use runes," Kenko added, fingering the stone she'd picked up in the forest. She had no idea what attracted her to the smooth, dark pebble, but rolling it across her palm calmed her.

"Or to be apprenticed to a magical crafter, but we have none here in Arrowview." Gatha agreed readily, making Kenko sigh. Nothing ever seemed to ruffle the beast-kin innkeeper.

Kenko watched the line of children, recognizing a few as the bullies from the orphanage who delighted in pelting her with rotten fruit or pieces of bark whenever she was in the market. The slur of bark-eater had started to follow her about town, and even a few adults had sneered it as she passed on her way to the guilds.

The merchants had turned the event into a tiny festival with carts offering fried dough, roast meat buns, or sugared plums. The heavy scent of grease filled the square, making her stomach turn.

The mage conducting the testing watched over the strange hovering crystal orb each child was instructed to touch. He looked bored out of his mind as he handed off the parchment sheets listing the child's power levels and magical skills to their guardians. Few, if any, seemed to know more than one or two of the most basic spells. Most looked ecstatic to have any ability, no matter how small, but a few were angry at not being an all-powerful mage.

Kenko stepped forward as the line grew shorter, trying to swallow her sighs. So far, only the forge and Gatha seemed to be helping her out of simple compassion, and everyone else was either hoping to use her abilities once she gained a few levels or were looking for ways to profit from her stay in town. One of the shopkeepers had gossiped behind her back, not knowing of an elf's excellent hearing about the meeting they'd attended and how the elven nation would reimburse them for any loss of profits from her business.

"Please step forward to be tested," the mage said, looking like he couldn't care less. At least he looked like a proper mage, wearing long dark blue robes and carrying a long crystal-topped staff that he'd left standing by itself to one side of the stage, drawing all the children's needy gazes, if only they had enough power to use a staff like that.

"Name or identification?" he asked, pulling out the next sheet of paper and marking a line in his ledger for the testing.

"Kenko," she stepped forward and handed over her guild identification card, waiting for his order to touch the floating stone. The entire table and stage glowed with soft blue and gold designs, especially around the stone. Even the papers he used to capture the children's stats were covered in minuscule scrolling runes and lines of glowing gold magic that drew her gaze.

"Known spell work?" he asked, pen ready to jot the answer down.

"Nothing," Kenko said quietly, ignoring his surprised look.

"Please touch the stone and press a small amount of mana into the orb if possible."

She stepped forward without a comment and pressed her fingertips to the stone. It was shockingly cold, and it took a moment of concentration before she could summon her magic to her hand and ease it into the device. A sharp pulse of light made the mage gasp even as Kenko released the orb and stepped back. The mage nearly dropped the paper as he hurriedly drew the page across the orb, gathering the information and turning it so he could read it.

"Is something wrong?" Gatha asked after he stood frozen for a long moment, not recording Kenko's statistics in his ledger as he had for the previous children.

"Ah, no," he said, blushing, jotting a long line of text in his ledger, "your child has several unusual skills we rarely see during their first testing. She will be very powerful when she reaches her full potential."

He waved the next child forward more eagerly while Kenko accepted her results and moved away.

"Don't read it here," Gatha cautioned, "let's return to the Inn."

"Okay," Kenko agreed, sighing. Nothing she did was typical in this life. Most children had received a small list of abilities and statistics on their magical core and skills. Her page was covered nearly front and back with thin black text.

Several guild tables and merchants looked disappointed as she walked away without a glance. Kenko had no intention of apprenticing to anyone, much less signing a contract with a small-time merchant hoping to use her to support his failing business.

The White Cat was crowded, so Kenko headed to her room, Gatha murmuring about discussing her options once the dinner rush calmed down later that night. She glanced over her tiny room with another sigh and flopped onto the small bed, curling into a ball. It seemed that life in any world was complicated.

Unrolling the scroll, she noted the number of options that weren't on her status menu. Her status seemed only to show skills activated at least once, while the test showed all her possible magical skills and statuses. It even broke things down into racial abilities versus unique skills.

Racial Passive Skills:
- Darkvision
- Meditation
- Perception
- Pathfinding
- Stealth
- Longevity

Racial Magical Skills:
- Forest sense
- Spirit sense
- Taming

Passive Magical Skills:
- Regeneration
- Skin deep
- Marathon

Unique Magical Skills:
- Archive
- Rune carver
- Inscription
- Shield

- Light
- Thorn Whip
- Environmental Entanglement
- Elemental Control

Upgrades possible for Meditation, Stealth, Forest sense, Spirit sense, Taming, Rune Carver, Inscription, Shield, Thorn Whip, Environmental Entanglement

Current Magic Level: 1/1000

———

Kenko [Level 3]

    Class: *Artificer (Magical) [Level 1]*

    Skills:

Regeneration, Skin Deep, Marathon, Disengagement, Flight, Darkvision, Perception, Meditation

    Magical Skills:

Archive, Rune carver, Inscription, Shield, Light, Thorn Whip, Environmental Entanglement, Elemental Control

    Additional Skills:

Cooking (Basic), Crafting (Basic), Spell Craft (Basic), Housekeeping (Intermediate), Design (Intermediate), Organization (Advanced), Magic (Basic), Map Reading (Basic), Woodworking (Basic),

Wood Carving (Basic), Drawing (Basic), Calculation (Basic), Gathering (Basic), Pathfinding (Intermediate, Racial Boost), Weaving (Basic), Basket Craft (Basic)

    Titles: *Blessed of Ume*

CHAPTER
TEN

KENKO REFUSED to call it brooding, but she wasn't in the best of moods. Gatha was pushing for her to receive training in her magics, and Esha had refused to teach her further, citing that their magics were too different to be of help. Her carving was coming along, and she'd started etching small designs onto flat boards, curling vines, and one lopsided pinecone adorned the chunk she was working on now. She wanted to toss the entire thing into the fire and start over, but Esha refused to let her destroy even her practice pieces. Each was kept on a shelf the orc had cleared in her workshop to show her progress.

Tucking her tools away, she headed to the enormous fireplace inside. As summer drew nearer to its end, the wind howled outside, making her cold no matter how many layers she was trying to wear. Her clothes weren't enough to block the wind, given how threadbare they were becoming. She would have to spend the last of her coin on winter clothes soon if she wanted to stay here much longer. None of the other races seemed bothered by the cold as much as she was, so maybe it was an elvish thing.

She had just settled down on the wood floor near the fire with her notebook when someone else came over to warm their hands by the fire. The woman wore thick silver cuffs and a long leather belt covered in large blue stones that caught the firelight. The scars wrapping her forearms caught Kenko's attention; heavy, discolored scars marbled her tan skin with white. To survive such an injury, even with a healer, was chancy. She either had a backbone of steel, or her family paid her body weight in gold to the healer's guild to let her keep her hands.

"You have the entire town in a flutter over your testing." The woman said, a tired smile breaking over her face as she pulled a stool over and sat, "Half the guilds in the capital would probably take you on merit alone from that once the tester reports his findings to the main guilds at River-deep."

"What do you want?" Kenko asked tiredly, setting her notebook to the side so the woman could stop trying to figure out what it was.

"I wanted to ask what you plan on doing. You have many options with that strong a magical reaction to the testing orb. Most townsfolk here would catch the first carriage or horse to River-deep and the mage college there."

"I don't want to go to a college. I want to work with my hands and learn to craft while learning magic at the same time. Classes won't let me do that." Kenko pointed out, tucking her tools away into her shoulder bag.

"No, I doubt the college would let you be out in the forests gathering herbs either." The woman agreed, picking up a glass of wine to sip.

"What, have you been around asking about me?" Kenko snapped, annoyed; why was everyone so interested in her?

"No, the adventurers guild master is a friend of mine. He told me I needed to meet the elf working in his guild hall. That she was unlike anyone he'd ever met."

"Do you agree? Am I unlike anyone you've ever met?" Kenko huffed. Come to Arrowview and meet the weird elf. Great, she is a sideshow act now.

"You certainly aren't like any elf I've met before, but of course, no human would be allowed in contact with an elfling until they were over fifty."

"You know elves?" Kenko asked perking up.

"Of them, yes," she nodded, returning to the fire, "I've even visited the home forest several times on business for guilds and quests. I can even call one a friend, though it has been a few years since I've done more than exchange letters with her."

"I've never met one," Kenko admitted, fiddling with her stone. Would they think she was too strange?

"You probably will get the chance in a few weeks, if not sooner; word has certainly already reached the elven territory of a lone elfling working here."

"Why would they bother coming to find me? I don't know any elves," Kenko asked, refusing to say too much. She knew the merchants expected the elven nation to pay them back, but why would they care about a single elf child?

"All elflings are protected by the clan they are born to, as they don't know your clan; they will send a representative to meet with you and bring you back to the home forest to allow you to grow to adulthood safely."

"And if I refuse to go?" Kenko pressed; she didn't want to be isolated and alone in the woods for years.

"If you cannot prove to them that you can provide for yourself and have a guardian or master to rely on," The woman looked her up and down before continuing, "they will force you."

"Let me guess, you want to be my master so I don't get sent home?" Kenko huffed, yet another adult trying to use her.

"I'm only one option. You could always find someone else. If anything, I'm the harder sell anyway since I won't be staying in Arrowview very long. I travel the country taking quests and assignments among the guilds and from each territory's royal families and nobility. If you were apprenticed to me, you wouldn't stay in any place for more than two weeks at a time. I stay on the road year round no matter the weather, dealing with monsters and magical mistakes. It would be dangerous, and you would have to learn fast to survive." The mage said flatly, "I don't have time for someone who doesn't want to be there or is unwilling to work."

"What is your name?"

"I'm Anais, the Blue," she said with a small self-deprecating smile. "Once you become a mage of the realm, you give up all ties to the land of your birth and travel the world helping where you can."

"So you serve Arda, not just this kingdom." Kenko pressed, frowning.

"This part of it, at least." Anais chuckled, "We aren't exactly paid well, but we are hosted in every town we travel through, and whenever we return to the capital, we are given rooms in the palace. You would see the finest of luxuries and the poorest of slums with never a single day the same."

"What would you teach me?"

"First, we need to get you ready to travel and have you fully outfitted. It would be best to learn to ride or at least stay in the saddle, along with basic defensive magics to add to your current skills. Mostly, I would teach you to survive. Magic is simply a tool. Most mages learn a tiny portion of their abilities and then use one skill for the rest of their lives. If you travel with me, you will learn all of your abilities and how to twist them to any situation you may find yourself in."

"Runes?"

"Runes," Anais agreed, "cantrips, elemental casting, how to use the environment around you as a weapon against your attacker, how to camp outdoors in any weather and travel without getting injured, forest craft, trap making, fishing and foraging, casting defensive barriers, warding homes and objects, enchantments that would work with your artificer class. Anything and everything, if you can think of something and I don't know it, I would find someone to teach us both."

"Would we have a contract?"

"Yes, I would want to wait until the elves arrive or head to their territory if you want a magical binding."

"When do I need to decide?"

"You have until the end of the week. By then, I will have finished my business in town and be ready to ride out."

"I'll let you know in two days," Kenko said firmly, a plan starting to form in her mind.

"Very well, it was nice to meet you, Kenko. I will see you again in two days."

"Thank you, Anais," Kenko said with a distracted nod. She headed upstairs to start figuring out what steps she needed to confirm the woman's story and find someone neutral to review the contract. Perhaps Kraddas would be willing to review the contract once it was drafted. Dwarves were supposed to be the best at bargaining for trade since it was part of every aspect of their culture.

———

Two days later, Kenko was as ready as she was going to be. Kaddras, Gatha, and Esha had agreed that traveling with Anais would be her best bet for becoming an apprentice without going to the capital. She would learn more from the blue mage; not even an elf could challenge the apprenticeship. Her belly rumbled, and she did her best to ignore it. She was down to a handful of copper coins due to the lack of gathering lately.

"Good evening," Anais said, teasingly smiling as she sat at the table with Kenko, "would you care to join me for dinner?"

"I don't have the coins to spare," Kenko said, flushing even as her stomach rumbled sharply at the scent of the stew being served.

"Consider it my treat." Anais said, waving for the maid and ordering stew for herself and a slew of vegetables for the table, "Anything you prefer?"

"Steamed boto?" she asked the waiting beast-kin server. Hopefully, she'd come to love the strange purple vegetable that was somehow more like a fruit than a potato but was still cooked and used like one.

"One bowl of steamed boto, coming right up!" The server chirped, grinning and trotting off to place the order with the kitchen staff.

"I heard a rumor you've been eating meat," Anais said, sipping at the tea the server left behind, "are you aware that it isn't healthy for elves? It might fill your stomach, but you don't get anything from it."

"It was cheap." Kenko huffed, "My gathering slowed because I was doing extra training at the guild every evening."

"Yes, sling and dagger work. I spoke with Banner to see what you needed to learn, and it will be a rough few weeks before we hit the road, I'm afraid." Anais said, "If you accept, that is."

"I would like to accept your offer, and I'm willing to do what I must as your apprentice," Kenko said carefully.

"Even if that means killing?" she asked, watching Kenko flinch, "I can't guarantee your safety, Kenko. I walk a dangerous road most days, and we will be faced with monsters and men looking to kill us both. I won't always be able to let you flee from a fight."

"I don't want to kill; I don't want to fight at all, but I know I have to know how to defend myself here," Kenko said, wincing at the slip of the tongue. The last thing she needed was for her new master to realize she was reincarnated.

"I'll teach you everything I know, but I can't say that you won't need to kill at some point. Hopefully, that will be years from now, but only the gods can see the future."

"I want to be your apprentice, Anais, but will you want me to call you master all the time?"

"Gods, no." Anais laughed, "All it means is that you move into my room at the inn, you'll have your own bed, and we'll start training you for a life of travel tomorrow morning. I've arranged with a friend outside of town to teach you horseback riding and to find you a pony. We can get you outfitted in the evening with more clothes and a few necessities."

"What will being your apprentice cost? I don't have much money." Kenko pressed, needing to know all the details.

"As your master, it is my duty to see you outfitted to the best of my ability. Considering I am a Mage of the Empire, I have more funds than most. Leave the cost to the penny pinchers at the capital." she said, grinning, "You need gear to travel with me, and you are going to learn to use everything I give you. My price is your sweat and blood during your years of training."

"You don't wear armor," Kenko pointed out.

"I have; it depends on what I'm hunting. This trip was more relaxed, so I only packed the essentials. I tend to travel light, but in most hunts, I wear leather armor or chain-mail layered under a tunic. You'll be outfitted for leather armor, just the basics, helmet, greaves, and chest and shoulders."

Kenko stared in shock when their food arrived, as it barely fit the table. Over a dozen plates of vegetables, sides, and extra bread and stew filled the table. Anais had tea with her stew, while Kenko was served a large mug of milk and her boto.

"Eat what you want; you'll need the energy for riding tomorrow. You will be hellishly sore this week, but your muscles should adapt quickly, and I'd rather get you comfortable in the saddle before we hit the road."

"What weapons do you want me to learn?" Kenko asked, grabbing a fork and muttering a quick prayer of thanks to Ume.

"Right now, you can continue with the sling and dagger. As we travel, I'll teach you the bow, crossbow, and staff, along with using magic to attack and defend. Since you're elvish, you will have an affinity for elemental, plant, and animal-based magics. We can use that to your advantage in a fight."

"I don't want to make an animal fight for me." Kenko huffed, nibbling at the hot apple salad mixed with nuts, carrots, and some sweet sauce.

"That's not what I meant; one thing that always affects a fight is footing. If you take steady footing away from your enemy, you give yourself the advantage, even if it's only more time to run away. Tripping them or making them fall is even better."

"Eat up," Anais said, waving at the surrounding plates as she started her stew, "I expect you to eat three meals a day unless unusual circumstances prevent it. You are still a growing elf and need the energy."

Kenko started to eat, doing her best not to stuff the vegetables down. It was the best meal she could remember since she came to this world. They even had stewed apples as a dessert with tea while the conversation shifted to Anais' adventures over the years.

"Go get some sleep, Kenko. Gatha said your room is yours as long as you are in town. We are starting bright and early tomorrow with your riding lessons."

"Alright," Kenko agreed. It had been a long week, and the enormous meal had her yawning.

In her small bedroom, she pulled on the oversized tunic she wore as a sleep shirt and laid out her clothes for the following day before making sure everything else was packed. She wanted a tidy room in case they had to leave quickly, and she had a feeling Anais went where she was sent without much notice.

———

She'd left working at the forge after explaining to Esha and Kaddras, who were understanding. They at least revealed they had been mostly helping teach her to keep her from burning out her magical core on accident. A low-level mage could destroy a small village if they fractured their core accidentally. Considering most elves were highly magical, it would have been an epic disaster if hers were damaged with unsafe magic.

The training was more challenging than she thought it would be. Kenko practiced horseback riding for four solid hours before walking around town to stretch her muscles out, with Anais talking about magic and the history of Arda. They spent hours debating war tactics, exploring the inner workings of magic and runes, and talking about herbs and monsters she might see in their travels.

"One of the things townspeople never realize is that monsters evolve and form stronger and stronger mobs if they aren't culled within a certain cycle." Anais said softly, waving Kenko to a seat by the deserted courtyard they were passing, "It varies by the monster, but with every evolution, as the monsters gain strength, that cycle gets shorter and shorter. Eventually, they gain followers among their kind and start forming hunting parties and mobs."

"Does that happen often?"

"It hasn't always. It can take fifty years for a goblin to become a goblin king, but once it does, no one below rank B can take it on, not even an army of lower-ranked adventurers and hunters."

"So the adventurers hunt the monsters to keep everyone safe?"

"Yes, but all the high-level adventurers were summoned to the border. With the war dragging on and most of the city and town guards out on the border being soldiers, there isn't anyone left but low-ranking adventurers to handle the monsters around town. All it takes is a big enough mob and a single high-ranked monster to destroy a village or a town." Anais said, frowning, offering Kenko a few seeds from a pouch.

"So you are hunting them instead?" Kenko pressed, cracking the chestnut-like seeds and nibbling on the meat as Anais slowly cracked a handful for herself.

"The ones I can get to, yes. Sometimes, even if I'm not strong enough, we have to send word to River-deep to send reinforcements. Generally, by then, it is too late."

"But the larger towns are holding out?"

"Honestly, it depends on the town. Thanks to the river and the forests the elves control, the nearby monsters are kept in check."

"The only ones I've seen are at the guild harvesting tables."

"Be thankful for that," Anais said thoughtfully, "you have a good guild master who makes sure the local monsters are hunted and knows to keep them away from the town. Some guild masters let a few monsters roam so that there are sightings at the nearby farms or by the guards. It lets them raise the prices they charge the city for their annual cull."

"But doesn't that," Kenko trailed off as Anais gave her a grim smile.

"Yes, eventually, those random monsters get strong enough to damage the town, and the hunters aren't strong enough to handle them. Not understanding how monsters reproduce or strengthen themselves leads to most of the attacks we see. And most often, that lack of understanding comes from greed more than ignorance. Someone who was raised in a large city with few monster attacks thinks the large fees the guilds charge for the seasonal hunts are unnecessary, and they cut funding to services they didn't understand were keeping their people safe."

"How do you stop that?"

"Make the hunts and the monsters killed each season visible. You haven't been here for a full hunt to see the monster corpses laid out in the square while the Mayor tallies up the kills."

Like deer hunting, Kenko thought frowning. Without wolves to hunt the deer, their population exploded, leaving the herds to destroy farmland and crops when they ran out of natural forage. The adventurers guild and hunters acted like the wolves of this world. They kept the monsters in check.

"Where will you go next?" Kenko asked, changing the subject, "Will we be hunting monsters?"

"Once the elves arrive and we can travel, I have a social visit to make." Anais said with a grimace, "Mages of the realm are required to take quests from the local nobility in the areas we travel through if there are no more pressing quests. Baron Armland rules the next territory and requests my presence whenever I travel through his lands."

"What is his quest?"

"The man is a monster collector and keeps them caged in his walled garden around the estate. Generally, he wishes to know of any new species I've seen or heard about and to show off his collection. However, it will be an excellent opportunity to show you rare and dangerous monsters in a safe setting..."

"You don't like his collection," Kenko said with certainty. She wasn't sure if Anais liked the man, but she kept that to herself.

"No, I would not submit any animal to the cruelty of being caged and watched from afar with little food and no room to move about or run. They often die in agony, and the Baron simply calls for his hunters to find another."

"That is horrible," Kenko whispered. She knew rich people who collected rare animals, but at least in her previous life, such practices were generally monitored for animal cruelty.

"We weigh the nation's safety over the safety of the monsters." Anais said, glancing at the girl beside her for a long moment, "The animals are just that, animals, but monsters crave violence. If you cage a monster and move it to an area without humans, it will find its way to the closest human settlement to start harassing them all over again."

"Do they breed like animals? Could culling the females help?"

"No, it has been tried, and some seem to appear spontaneously in remote locations as if they are some strange accident of wild magic. Some areas produce more than others, but no common factor seems to cause it every time that anyone has found, and it has been studied for centuries by the elves and other long-lived races."

"Not even the elves know?" Kenko asked; the elves seemed the best at collecting knowledge from everything she'd read.

"If they do, they aren't saying." Anais laughed, "I admit I like you, Kenko, but most elves are rather stuffy bores by the time they are allowed out into the human territories. The rangers are among humans more, but those who rarely leave the home forest come off as arrogant and appear to believe all humans are barbarians."

"That is ridiculous. I've met so many lovely people here." Kenko scoffed in annoyance.

"I'm not saying it is all of them, but I've been insulted by many in River-deep for wasting my talents as a mage, gallivanting around the country hunting like a savage instead of assisting my people in some useful manner."

"That sounds like a quote." Kenko pointed out, grinning.

"It is," Anais snorted, shaking her head, "the one elf I deal with the most is a magical advisor to the crown, Nevarth Olamys. He is a masterful mage, but his personality seems to have decayed in the last five hundred years."

"Five hundred?!" Kenko sputtered, letting Anais haul her to her feet.

"Yes, elves live a very long time," she said, giving Kenko a weighted glance. Once you've mastered the basics, you have centuries to hone your craft. Let's get lunch, and then we can work on your sling accuracy."

They continued their walk while Kenko contemplated living to be five hundred. Do you stop aging at some point and just exist? People's personalities tended to stay unchanged unless they consciously tried to change their mentality and actions. Would they be stuck in a medieval point of view? Would they speak like Shakespeare or use old jargon and terms no one else knew about?

It seemed like an infinite amount of time considering her last life. Would she eventually come to dislike the changing world around her? Would she stop caring about those around her after surviving all her friends and family?

The entire concept made her depressed. She had all the time in the world to learn whatever she wanted. For now, she would deal with surviving her apprenticeship, and whatever the elvish kingdom would throw her way, she could deal with the following centuries as they appeared.

The one thing she knew for certain was that change was constant. For now, she would have to try to flow with whatever was thrown her way until she understood this world and its underlying secrets.

CHAPTER
ELEVEN

THE DAY the elves finally arrived, Kenko worked with Anais to cast wards around a small clearing outside town. A guild runner came to retrieve them, but Kenko had already noticed the watcher following them before they left town and mentioned it to Anais. She had been apprenticed for almost a month and was learning many practical survival skills for this world.

She still wasn't sure how she felt about fighting. Even if she didn't want to fight, it never hurt to be prepared to fight. Anais stressed that she was learning to fight only enough to get herself and any innocents to safety. If that meant killing something to make an opening, she needed to know how to survive the attack and ensure her safety.

"You think it's a ranger?" Kenko asked as they worked together to tear down the wards she'd crafted and gather up the handful of rune-etched stones she'd made earlier that morning.

"I'd be able to mark anyone else; the only ones who've evaded my tracking before are elves," she offered, smirking, glancing at the nearby forest. "It is good, however, that you can sense them, even with it being an elven ranger. They are the best of the best when it comes to hunting and stealth. You can't hide from an elf in the forest or anywhere in nature. Only by isolating yourself in a large city would you even have a chance, but if they are gifted enough even, then it is still possible."

"How is that possible if they use nature to enhance their skills?"

"No one is ever completely outside of nature if you think about it. Most houses have flowers and plants in most rooms, windows let the breeze through, and if the room is wood or stone, a powerful nature mage could sense every person inside a building just by touching or walking on a natural material."

"But that isn't super common, right?" Kenko asked; if it were, there would be no absolute privacy, even in the city.

"Let me know if you get one of the elves to answer that question." Anais snorted, "Elves dislike lies or even mild falsehoods; they are known for honoring their promises and bargains even centuries after the deaths of the original parties. They will, however, skirt around the truth and convince you in a debate that the grass is red and the sky orange."

"Shouldn't the ranger have come out to say hello at the very least?" Kenko asked. Wasn't announcing your presence the polite thing to do?

"No, he is acting as your guard, not a friend." Anais insisted, "I've played the same role at times. The only time you see a good guard is when there is danger. If you can't mark him, neither can the ones hunting you, and it gives his attacks more power."

"I see," she agreed, frowning as she joined the mage in walking back to the city, "so I don't need to worry about them out in the cold or not having dinner then; they already have taken that into consideration?"

"Exactly," Anais grinned, "it does show your kind heart that you are worried about such things."

"I hate seeing people go without," Kenko mumbled, not seeing how she could explain how poor she'd been in her past life with every bit of her money she made going to her rent and medical bills.

"What do you want for lunch? The White Cat had fish today, so they will be packed with beastkin. Care to go somewhere different?"

"As long as I don't have to eat that stew again," Kenko shivered, thinking about the grey stew she'd been served at one shop they stopped in. It had been the only supposed vegetarian dish they offered, and she'd been sick the rest of the night from what turned out to be monster meat.

"Monster meat is cheap for the poor, and some are considered delicacies by the nobility, but I'd rather not eat it myself. I'm guessing it was some form of dark magic or decay-casting beast. Most elves are susceptible to the more unnatural magics that twist natural laws and cause disease." Anais said, glancing over at the girl. It was several days ago, but it wasn't good for an elf to eat meat either way.

Kenko yelped as a tall figure in grey and green stepped out of the woods ahead of them. He held his arms up to show he wasn't carrying any weapons, but a bow and sword were ready by his side.

"Apologies for the scare. Is the child in need of healing? " the elf said, looking over Kenko with concern. His voice was somehow more resonant than Kenko was used to.

"I had her checked by the town's main healer, but you are welcome to check yourself if you wish." Anais offered, clasping Kenko's shoulder to keep her in place, "No one here in town is very used to treating elves and could have missed something, but she claims to be recovered."

"I will inform the envoy when he arrives. They are traveling with an elvish healer who will see to her either way," he said, giving a firm nod. I merely wished to check that she was seen to myself."

"Can I ask your name, Ranger?" Kenko asked carefully, looking up at the elf. He was tall and lean but with broad shoulders and muscular arms from wielding a bow for what must have been decades, if not longer. Tan skin, blue eyes, and ash blonde hair marked him as what townsfolk would call a sun-blessed elf, and the moon-blessed were dark-haired and light-skinned like Kenko.

"I am called Orrian," he said, giving a curt bow that made Anais raise an eyebrow, "The envoy will be most astonished when he does meet you. Try not to take offense; our kind does not do well when we are surprised."

"Have I done something wrong?" Kenko asked uncertainly if she had managed to breach some unknown elven taboo in the few short months she'd been on Arda.

"No, nothing beyond your birth, and that is to blame on your parents. You have done no wrong to the elves; if anything, we will be currying your favor for centuries to come."

"I doubt that," Kenko snorted with a wry grin, "you haven't seen my bow work yet."

"Sadly, I have." He agreed, looking mildly amused. "I will merely point out that everything takes time, and with practice and diligence, you will be a much better archer in a few years."

"True of most skills." Kenko agreed, sighing, "Are you coming with us to the city?"

"No, I only wished to see that a healer had treated you. As you are clearly in decent health, I will bid you both good afternoon."

"Have a good afternoon, Orrian," Kenko called, watching as he faded into the woods with barely any sound.

"So, what do you think of the first elf you've ever met?" Anais asked in a teasing tone as they continued on their way.

"He knows how to use his weapons, and I've never seen anyone move that fast and quiet," Kenko said softly, watching the trees as they passed but not spotting the presence she could almost feel moving ahead to check that the road was clear.

"Rangers are like that; they train for most of their lives running about hunting monsters and patrolling their territory." Anais huffed, eyes watchful as they made their way into town.

Kenko had been spared most of the chaos her arrival caused, but lately, more and more were becoming vocal in their anti-elven statements. The refugees they passed gave holy hand gestures and the fingertips to the forehead, mouth, throat, and heart gestures of the Mendite followers from the Empire of Humanity.

The Empire espoused complete segregation from all races that weren't human and declared humanity the proper race and power meant to own all land on earth. It had made traveling as a nonhuman close to the border dangerous even before the raids started, and now it was next to impossible.

"Go back to your trees, Bark-Eater! You have no place here! " one man shouted, his arm missing below the elbow. His wife started a mumbled prayer to Mendite to cleanse her soul of impurities.

"Will Orrian be okay?" Kenko asked as they hurried past.

"No ranger would allow themselves to be caught by a human; to do so would be a major blemish on their pride." Anais said softly, guiding her into the guild hall and up the stairs to the library, "He will be fine. You find a table while I get us some lunch."

"Tis won't like us eating up here," Kenko muttered even as she waved to the spider woman scaling the shelves in the back, the first time meeting her had been an experience. Even here, the surrounding humans shuddered to see the Arachne in a joint racial phobia that not even a new planet had eased. Giant spiders were the stuff of nightmares to most.

"Let that be my issue; find something to read for now."

"Alright," Kenko huffed, "You can just say you need to be somewhere else, right? I can entertain myself."

"Pardon me for forgetting your competence, apprentice. Find a map of the route from here to the elven forest and write out any obstacles or towns we might encounter."

"Yes, Master," she said with a smirking lisp.

"One day, you will explain why that is so amusing." Anais huffed.

"As you command, my master." Kenko agreed, limping away and dragging one leg. Now, they just had to wait for the envoy to arrive. It should only be a day or two since they had received a magical message from Anais that one was on the way that morning.

———

Kenko was at her riding lesson when the elvish envoy's party finally arrived in Arrowview. She had graduated from a horse so dead it was one step up from a stuffed animal to a pony so ornery it kicked and tried to scrap her off on trees if she wasn't paying attention. Anais promised her a decent mount when they left for their next destination, but she was now rotating through the worst the local stable could throw her way. She could only hope the elven deer mounts were more sensible than the horses she'd ridden so far if she ever got to ride one.

Covered in mud and sweat, she blinked at the frantic runner from the mayor shouting for her to stop. The stable master hurried over to criticize the man even as Kenko forced her tubby mount away from the tempting bushes and closer to the gate where the two men were arguing. Butters was a bare step up from a pony, but his barrel-like gut made her knees scream every ride.

"You are needed at the mayor's house, Miss." he called as she came over, "You need to get cleaned up and find your master. Both of you are to see the mayor as soon as possible."

"Anais is out on an errand. She won't be back until late." Kenko said, wincing, stumbling as she dismounted with aching thighs, "I'll go start getting ready, and if she's not back in an hour, I'll come myself."

"Very well," the young man agreed, twisting his hands. The entire house is in an uproar. Some big noble envoy arrived and stormed in without even letting us open the doors first. It is a right mess, Miss. You need to hurry."

"I'll hurry." she agreed; the elven envoy must have arrived finally. Handing off the reins to the stable master, she stuttered an apology that he waved off.

"Next time you leave a mount hot, I will have you cleaning the stalls for a month, but today, you get a pass. Get moving, Miss."

"Thank you, sir." she agreed with a quick nod before darting off down the lane, not bothering to dodge the puddles or patches of mud. She was already covered in sweat and smelled like a horse, and it couldn't get much worse.

Kenko considered her options as she ran, but none of her clothes had been purchased to make her look good. They were meant for utility and protection. The best she could manage was the blue coat that showed her status as an apprentice and a velvet vest she'd purchased to have something to wear to the baron's manor when they arrived.

The only nice thing in Anais' rooms at the White Cat was the tub that filled with hot water after a quick application of magic. It was expensive to enchant, but they were becoming more popular at the good inns around the country as people were willing to pay more to bathe in peace instead of at the local bath house. Kenko filled it part way and scrubbed herself down quickly, rinsing with a pitcher full of warm water, which she refilled from the tap.

Her braid was still damp when she bolted back down the stairs and out the door, cloak flaring behind her, but she was as made up as she could be at the moment. A dark blue wool coat set against a royal blue velvet vest that nearly matched her hair, and a white shirt and grey slacks rounded out the outfit. Her plain brown boots would have to do. Her foot was too small to buy expensive boots, and she would outgrow them before they wore out. She refused to purchase custom-fitted or wear ill-fitting boots. Her grey cloak covered it all and, more importantly, hid her elven features from the newcomers wandering the streets.

She thought she caught someone dodging through the shadows a block behind her, but she ignored it. It was either her ranger or someone from the town tailing her to keep her safe until she went on her way. So far, no one has offered her violence, but the lack of work and the rainy summer weather leading into fall was making everyone cranky. Someone shouted behind her as she reached the mayor's home, "Go home, Bark-Eater!" tugging her cloak's hood lower over her hair.

A small crowd gathered across the street, jeering and catcalling the staff as they worked. Kenko pulled up her cloak hood and ducked into the side lane to enter the rear entrance, going out front was asking to be yelled at.

"Kenko to see the mayor," she told the butler, handing over her cloak as she caught her breath, tucking a few stray bits of hair behind her ears.

"Right this way. Is your master on her way?"

"I left her a message at the inn, but she is outside of the city at the moment." Kenko offered shrugging.

"I see; I will tell the master when I see you inside. The elven envoy and his staff are in the main parlor with the mayor."

"Thank you," she said, pausing outside the door to straighten her vest. The butler waited on her nod of readiness before swinging open the door.

"The elf, Kenko, apprentice to the Blue Mage." The butler announced, waving her through and easing after her to whisper in his master's ear.

She gave the room a low bow, glancing at the elves from under her lashes. The envoy was dressed in silken robes of pale rose and grey, highlighting his glowing white skin and pastel green hair. He was notably older than the other elves, which meant he was well into several centuries old, possibly, while the others were dressed as guards similar to the ranger except for one wearing robes of gold and white. They were all men, and she really hoped elves weren't misogynistic as well as arrogant.

"I take it punctuality is not something you have been tasked with learning yet. I will have it noted to add to your lessons." The envoy sniffed, waving away the cup of tea a trembling maid offered.

"I'm afraid you weren't expected to arrive so promptly," Kenko said with a bright smile as she straightened; if he was going to be an asshole, she would show him the exact amount of respect he gave her, "Thank you for the invitation, Mayor Dixon. I am afraid I haven't been introduced to your guests."

"Thank you for coming. I apologize for interrupting your lessons this morning. How are your horsemanship skills coming along?" Mayor Dixon asked, waving the maid to prepare her a cup of tea.

"Slow and steady." she said, smiling as he followed her lead of snubbing their guests, "I believe I'll show more progress once I have my own mount."

"That is wonderful to hear. Let me introduce you to my guests." he said, turning to the fuming envoy and the white-robed elf next to him, "Almon Morlar, envoy to the elvish nation, and Merrill Leosatra, an elvish healer for the noble house of Morlar."

"Pleasure to meet you both," Kenko said, bowing and frowning slightly when the healer gasped and stared at her openly. "Is that not a greeting elves use?"

"Apologies, Lady Kenko, I was simply surprised to see your eye color. It was not noted in any of the reports we received." Healer Merrill said quickly as the mayor gestured her to a seat and poured a cup of tea with a dollop of jam like she'd become accustomed to at the White Cat.

"The traditional greeting between elves is 'merry met.'" Envoy Morlar huffed, frowning as she sipped the tea after adding a slice of lemon, "It is also considered rude to eat during discussions."

"Surely drinks would be permitted to allow one to speak easily?" Kenko asked, taking a larger sip before setting her cup down, "May I be blunt and ask what the elven nation expects of me? I have lived in Arrowview for almost a season now and had no issues, and I am learning to protect myself and to survive in the wilds."

"Such an education is expected of all elves, but you are missing many subjects we teach our children from birth. You are years behind your peers in terms of elvish education. We also have a report of you eating meat, something a full-blooded elf would never consider."

"You do what you must when you are poor and without other means," Kenko said, simply settling back in her chair. Sometimes, you just had to wait for the supposed Boss to get over his power trip, something she'd seen far too often in business meetings.

"Your manners are wanting." he snapped, nostrils flaring.

"Apologies, I was raised by humans." she returned mildly with a polite smile, still waiting for the man to get to the point.

"Then you have no memories of your birth parents?" he huffed finally when she showed no intention of continuing.

"I only remember my human parents," she said, glancing at the mayor as he fiddled with his cup before deciding. If she had kept things polite, they would have been here until next week, with the man still insulting her. Mayor Dixon, might I speak with the envoy alone for a moment?"

"Of course, the room is yours for however long you need." He quickly agreed, bowing to the envoy and waving at his staff to leave.

"You wish to speak of something private? I will not be sending any of my attendants away." Envoy Morlar huffed.

"Frankly, I doubt you could survive without them." Kenko snapped, snatching up her cup and draining it, "I have no memories of this world before six months ago. I woke up under a tree about ten miles from Arrowview and made my way straight here."

"Were you injured?" The healer asked, shifting in his chair.

"No, I was perfectly healthy when I awoke." Kenko said carefully, glancing between the two men, "What do you know of reincarnation?"

"So, you are one of the Reborn." Envoy Morlar scoffed, leaning back in his chair in disgust while the others shifted silently, "It has been several centuries since the elves have seen one and even longer since one was an elf themselves."

"You don't sound happy about that fact," Kenko noted, trying to keep her tone firm but unemotional; she would be perceived as a child with little knowledge no matter what she did.

"Those that are reincarnated introduce massive changes in our world, both for the good and the bad. They seem to bring bad luck to those around them simply by existing, and the gods delight in meddling with their lives. Do you have your memories from a previous life?"

"Yes," she said flatly, watching the envoy with sharp eyes; his view of her seemed to be getting worse instead of better.

"I suggest you forget them entirely; introducing ideas and items from your last world will only bring tragedy."

"You can't be serious." Kenko blurted in shock; surely it couldn't be that bad.

"Sadly, I am. The reincarnated seem to attract the unwanted attention and chaos that our race finds abhorrent. However, as you are one of our race, you will be expected to uphold at least some of our traditions and knowledge and will have a tutor assigned to teach you our ways. Your education can begin in earnest once you return to the home forest."

"And if I refuse? I have no intention of leaving Arrowview at the moment, nor do I want to isolate myself from the world." Kenko asked, arching an eyebrow. She might dislike conflict and negotiations, but she was used to dealing with powerful old men who pouted like angry toddlers if they didn't get their way.

"The reincarnated are known for their stubbornness. However, you are still a child and require guardianship as an elf, which falls to the clans. Those who have been reincarnated are given to the royal clan." He said, giving her a long look. Should you refuse, I am authorized to use whatever methods I have at my disposal to force the issue."

"I am apprenticed to the Blue Mage, Anais. I already have a guardian. You can ask your ranger. I've been well taken care of in the days he's been following us around." she snapped, ignoring the minor signs of amusement the other guards showed at that statement.

"You would do well to watch your tongue around elven nobility, child." The healer huffed, offering a hand, "Are you willing to let me check on your health?"

"I have never been a child, Healer Merrill," Kenko said softly, allowing the healer to pull her to a standing position.

"Few reincarnated have been allowed that luxury, it seems. Most of our records show that those who were reincarnated are given the chance because of a painful previous life, with few chances for change or improvement. At least in reincarnation, they are given new bodies without the previous scars and injuries."

Healer Merrill took her hand between his and cast a spell that glowed gold, soft radiance and warmth seeping into her body a wash of magic. The spell seemed to settle into her bones and hum against her muscles as if seeking potential flaws. After about a minute, it withdrew back to the healer.

"You are healthy as any eight-year-old can be. You still have much growing to do, and the brush with monster meat did no harm that I can see," he said calmly, both of them ignoring the muttered insults from the envoy at the mention of eating meat.

"I was given a dish that was supposed to be free of meat." Kenko huffed, "It wasn't like I was trying to eat it."

"I will give your master a list of recommendations for your diet and health."

"Then I will be allowed to stay with the Blue Mage?" she asked, carefully glancing at the envoy.

"That is your decision," Healer Merrill said, only to be immediately overridden by Envoy Morlar.

"It's Impossible. She must return to the elven forest and continue her education. Not doing so would be irresponsible and childish for one of our kind." He sneered, but Kenko ignored him and faced the healer.

"You mentioned my looks were startling. Why is that?" she asked Healer Merrill, hoping he would ignore his companion and answer honestly.

"That is of no consequence! You will be returning to the elven nation." The envoy declared, waving the healer off.

"Be that as it may," the healer said smiling, "I commented on your looks because your eye color is unusual for our race. Only one clan has the golden eyes you share."

"Enough, Merrill!"

"You would deny her knowledge of her heritage?" The healer asked mildly, turning to his counterpart, "The head of her clan will be most unimpressed with your behavior this day, Envoy Morlar."

"She will be presented to her proper clan when she arrives at the palace. To announce it before would be placing unnecessary danger on her."

"She is the only one here who would know," the healer said flatly, turning to Kenko, "do you wish to know where your clan rests in our hierarchy, or do you wish to know simply the clan name?"

"I wish to know everything about my elvish heritage. I am unable to leave for the elvish nation without taking leave of my master, which I have no intention of doing." Kenko said honestly, "Is there a way for me to learn what I need while I travel with my master?"

"That would be the decision of your Clan leader. Would your master agree to bring you to visit the palace at Ernsari, perhaps?"

"I am sure she would, as she has visited the elven forests previously. However, she has other duties that must be seen to first."

"I will write the King tonight to inform him of this encounter." Healer Merrill said firmly, giving the envoy a sharp glance, "We will speak to your master when she arrives, but it must be done soon."

"Soon by human standards or elvish?" Kenko asked, pouring herself a fresh cup of tea now that negotiations were finally moving on.

"Before the winter solstice," the envoy snapped, "as for continuing your education, you will at the least be provided with a guard and someone to train you in the skills the clan deems necessary."

"Are you always this unpleasant, or is it merely reserved for children?" Kenko asked, mildly sipping her tea and considering the tray of sliced fruit to one side. Would anyone else care for fruit?"

"You are a barbarian." he hissed.

"And your poor opinion has no impact on my life or my choices." she pointed out tiredly, selecting a piece of blue apple that she hadn't had before, "I wish to see the elven territory and the palace, but it will be at my master's discretion, if she decides you are too hostile to be dealt with I will continue as I have been without the knowledge you are offering. If I am part of a prominent clan, arrangements will be made; if not, I will still have a long and healthy life with many years to correct any inaccuracies I may have in my knowledge and spell craft."

"You would," he sputtered, forcing himself to take a breath, "you are saying you would abandon your heritage?"

"As you have pointed out, I am reincarnated, and technically, my heritage is human, even if it is from another world. If most of the elves are as rude as you have been today, I would be better off living among those you consider barbarians." she snapped, setting the fruit aside uneaten, "I am returning to the inn when we are staying. When my master arrives, we will return to continue this discussion, as you are unable to continue at this time without insulting me."

"Insulting you!" he screeched, "I have never been treated so in my entire life."

"Then you have been truly sheltered." she huffed, giving the healer and guards a bow before she left the room.

Outside, the Mayor was waiting wide-eyed in the hall, "I would give him a few moments to collect himself before attempting further conversation." Kenko said, giving a sympathetic smile, "I've rarely met someone so willing to insult a child."

"I am shocked, and I apologize that you were forced to deal with such a man without your master present."

"They have placed you in an uncomfortable situation, Mayor Dixon." Kenko grimaced. "I'm returning to the White Cat to wait on my master. Please let me know if you need me before that."

"Of course, my butler will show you out," he said, waving her out as shouting rang out behind the closed door.

CHAPTER
TWELVE

KENKO INSISTED they continue their training like usual, refusing to wait for the envoy to call for them. They had offered to meet once already and had been ignored. They headed to the practice yard with their weapons, trailing several elven guards and rangers to Kenko's amusement.

"Why exactly is this situation so humorous?" Anais grumped, annoyed at all the attention they were drawing.

"They get to see exactly how bad an elf can be with a bow." Kenko snickered, pulling out the first arrow.

"That is not something to be proud of," Anais scoffed, but she agreed that the looks of shock as every arrow missed the mark were hilarious. While Kenko was decent with her sling and daggers, she was genuinely dreadful with a bow.

They were finishing a light lunch at the White Cat when the runner finally came requesting their presence. Kenko dressed for war in her traveling leathers and blue apprenticeship coat, so Anais did the same, both wearing daggers and other small weapons. Their small squad of guards marched around them as they walked, drawing far too much attention and forcing the group to go through the protestors that the mayor was hesitant to disperse by force. Shouts of 'Bark-Eater' and

'Forest Trash' followed them into the guild hall where the meeting was held.

Anais looked over the meeting room at the guild the following day with a polite smile. The elvish envoy was clearly annoyed that Kenko wasn't showing him the level of respect an elvish elder generally received and was working himself up to a massive tantrum. The fact that Kenko has zero hopes of showing him respect while he continues insulting her existence is being ignored completely.

Healer Merrill was polite and helpful, however. He supplied several lists of foods, recommended magical exercises for Kenko to learn, and recommended areas of study she should consider introducing. The subtext made it clear that they needed to get to the elven home forest and the palace as soon as possible.

She would write to the King as soon as this meeting ended and pay for a mage messenger spell at the healers' guild hall to see it arrived promptly. Educating Kenko might become her next assignment in between magical disasters. She was at least an elven noble, given how the guards were deferring to her during the day. She had never seen a ranger defer to anyone, even those above their station. Rangers were a class unto themselves in elvish society and answered only to the King and his staff.

"Healer Merrill, may I ask a potentially rude question?" Anais asked as everyone was getting seated. The envoy was apparently late for his own meeting.

"With the understanding that I may refuse to answer given the subject, yes." The healer said with a polite smile that didn't touch his eyes, glancing over to Kenko, who was animatedly speaking with Orrian about how rangers were trained.

"Having two rangers and four guards escorting a missing orphan is a bit excessive. I was expecting one guard or perhaps a ranger. It may be my imagination, but she is treated much more like a missing noble than a random elf that was orphaned."

"There are a few clans among the nobility that have specific traits passed down to every generation, and she shares one such trait. She could be an unacknowledged child or the child of a missing brother or cousin in the clan. It will take some time to determine where she is concerning her actual station, so we are erring on the side of caution."

"That is understandable," Anais agreed with a frown, "will there be issues if she does not wish to stay among the elves?"

"That will entirely depend on the clan's decision when her status is determined, I am afraid. There is a good chance she will be allowed to continue as she is your apprentice with required visits once a year or so."

"Will she require a guard to travel with us or a tutor?"

"That will be up to the head of the clan; given that you are often headed to dangerous areas, a guard is possible with them acting as a weapons instructor for the child during the downtime."

The elven envoy stormed in, sternly glaring at the healer and guards for arriving before him. Anais waved Kenko to a chair in the middle of the table and sat beside her as everyone settled and tea was served.

"We are here to discuss the guardianship of the elvish orphan, Kenko. You are her master, Anais Gens, the blue mage?" Envoy Morlar asked, glancing at the guild master and mayor seated to one side with annoyance, "Must there be so many present for this discussion?"

"She is a member of the Adventurers Guild, and as such, it is my duty to make sure she isn't placed in an uncomfortable situation while under my care." Guild Master Banner said gruffly, fighting a frown.

"She has a guardian, and we are already bending the rules of propriety by allowing Mayor Dixon's presence." The envoy snapped.

"If I am no longer needed, I will continue with my day," the mayor said firmly, standing and nodding to the room. I hope the discussions are fruitful."

That was not what the envoy meant, and he fumed as the man left. Kenko watched this in fascination; where was the vaulted composure the elves were known for? Was this man so used to everything going his way he no longer knew how to deal with any disagreement?

"May I ask a rude question, Envoy Morlar?" Kenko asked, giving Anais a quick smile when she raised an eyebrow at her.

"You have been nothing but rude in our encounters, and I have no doubt you will continue to be even with the addition of your guild master and the blue mage," he snapped, waving the guard away who was pouring his tea. Was he using his guards as servants?

"Why exactly am I being treated like a bratty child when I've already explained that I have no knowledge of Elven culture or their social structure?"

"You are an elf! It is beneath us to behave in such a sloven fashion."

"Sloven?" Kenko blinked, glancing at Anais and continuing carefully, "I am uncertain of your meaning in this situation."

"You greet everyone, no matter their station, as having the same rank as you. You treat rangers with the same respect that you give beast-kin. You are possibly one of the highest clans in our society, and you treat those around you as equals."

"I see," she said, glancing at the table, but Anais clasped her shoulder, silencing anything she might have said as she stood.

"I understand now why Kenko was uncomfortable fully explaining what transpired yesterday in your meeting with her. You may inform the royal family and any noble clans you need to that I will bring Kenko to the palace to be evaluated; however, it will not be with such an uncouth man as you." Anais sneered, "I have worked with elven rangers, guards, and even members of the royal court. Never have I felt so insulted and belittled in an official meeting, and I won't have you spewing such degrading rhetoric in my apprentice's ears. I will be lodging a formal complaint to both the King of Arda and the Royal Elven King and Queen over your actions as envoy."

"You can't be serious! The child needs training, protection, guards!" he sputtered, waving one hand about in annoyed grand gestures.

"You may assign a ranger and one guard if necessary. Either way, we will leave in the morning for my next assignment; I have already wasted too much time here." Anais said firmly.

"You can't simply take her," the envoy said, ignoring the looks the rest of the room gave him.

"Why ever not? She is my apprentice, and I am her official guardian and master. Until you can produce official documents stating that you have the power to override those titles, I will remain so." Anais snapped, "Kenko, we will be retiring."

"Yes, Master," she agreed, standing and offering the room a bow, "It was a pleasure to meet you, Healer Merrill, Ranger Orrian."

Anais fumed as she stalked out of the guild hall. The nerve of such a man being sent to recover a lost child! Did the elves have no compassion? They nearly returned to the Inn before she stopped and calmed down.

"Are you alright, Kenko?"

"Yes, he was rude, but I wasn't raised with the same beliefs as the other noble elves. I'm starting to think that might have been a good thing," she murmured sadly, eying the small scattering of leaves in the gutter; fall was already on its way.

"Not all of them are like that, Kenko. I'll do my best to prepare you for meeting with the Elven King and his court before we leave for the Elven forest. Theirs is a powerful nation, and few are willing to openly attack when the very ground you walk can be controlled and used against you."

"Ranger Orrian, have you been assigned to us?" Kenko asked, glancing into the shadows to one side.

"I volunteered; however, that will be decided later tonight. For now, I will guard your backs," he said, stepping into the light.

"You can't be on guard all day; every day, you need at least one other. Not even an elf can evade sleep forever." Anais pointed out.

"A point I have already made," he said, chuckling, glancing at Kenko, "you have a question, young one?"

"Why exactly is the envoy so annoyed? I know I don't have the elvish manners or greetings learned yet, but I have done very little to have offended someone I have only met twice."

"Sadly, I believe it is a matter of being poorly informed. Originally, the guard was alerted to an elvish orphan living in Arrowview, and it was set aside to be reassessed once a more formal report could be made. However, the prince heard word of the report and insisted it be investigated. His twin brother was lost to goblins as a child, and he has always believed that he survived and wandered lost. He insisted that the incident be fully investigated as he does every report we receive of a lost child." Orrian smiled sadly, "He knows his brother is lost to him in his heart, but he wishes for no other elves to suffer that pain if it can be remedied."

"That is kind of him." Anais hummed, "I take it the Envoy has suffered many false reports?"

"More along the lines of having found many elvish commoner's children and half-elves that were abandoned instead. He believes bringing such bloodlines back to the forest damages the nation."

"So he believed I was a half-blood; however, given that I have the features of a noble clan, he assumes I'm a bastard." Kenko said, glancing at Anais, "Is he hoping to use me to gain power among the nobility? Would returning with a bastard child of a noble elf bring down someone in power?"

"What clan does she share features with?" Anais asked Orrian, noting his barely there wince at the probing question.

"I have been ordered not to share that information," he said, giving them a slight bow of apology as they started to walk again.

"What color are the prince's eyes?" Kenko asked, glancing at Orrian with that thoughtful face that made her seem decades older. She rarely acted like a child, but occasionally, she appeared decades older than she looked.

"You are far too perceptive, elfling." he huffed, shaking his head in amusement, "The Prince of the elven kingdom has gold eyes, like all those within his clan. I will say no more on the matter. Have a good evening, Ladies."

"You as well, Orrian," Kenko replied, blinking in shock.

"You suspected as much, didn't you?" Anais huffed, leading them towards the inn; they might both get a drink tonight, no matter the kid's age. Finding out you were a royal bastard at best wasn't the typical ending to a day, no matter who you were.

"I hoped I was wrong," Kenko muttered, "is it wrong not to want to be royalty?"

"No, I doubt any royal wants to be given that amount of responsibility," Anais said, tugging the young girl against her for a quick hug before urging her on; they couldn't talk about such things in the middle of town.

"We will have dinner in our rooms tonight. Can you also have a pitcher of mead sent up?" she asked Gatha when they reached the White Cat, sending Kenko on up to get cleaned up first.

"Is she alright?" The cat beast-kin asked in concern. "She was looking rather pale."

"The elven envoy arrived yesterday, and we heard their demands today. The meeting did not go well. I'm afraid we may leave tomorrow after things have been finalized."

"I am sad to hear that, but she should travel with her master." Gatha agreed, glancing outside and frowning. "Will the guard be staying?"

"Probably until we leave. I'm sorry for causing so many issues for the Inn."

"I understand it isn't your choice, and I know you don't like even the attention your role as blue mage brings." Gatha said, "I will arrange everything tonight. Just leave it to me. Would a pot of tea help?"

"Sadly, this isn't a conversation for tea. Perhaps you could bring some juice for Kenko. She loves the fruit juice you have."

"I'll arrange dessert as well. You both could use something sweet."

"Thank you, Gatha."

———

Kenko watched her master fussing about the room with a frown. Was Anais worrying over offending the elves or something else? Did she not want Kenko as her apprentice if it came with so much drama?

"Anais?" she asked uncertainly, "Are you okay?"

"I should be asking you that, Kenko. I know this has been a lot in the last few weeks; we've just started getting to know each other. Are you alright with me denying the elves their request?"

"Of course, the envoy was being impossible. I wouldn't have wanted to travel with him, anyway." Kenko quickly reassured her, "I know being elvish nobility will make things harder, and they will expect more of me, but I have years to catch up with the elves; I want to learn what I can from you first."

"All right, I just wanted to check." Anais said, dropping into a chair, heaving a heavy sigh, "I suspect that we will take at least one ranger with us to Baron Armland's estate before we make our way to the elven nation. I'll send a letter in the morning to my superiors to explain the change in my route. I've already alerted them that I was taking on an apprentice and might need to make adjustments to further your education."

"Will the elves cause you problems?"

"No, they might have placed trade sanctions on the town if you'd been mistreated, but I've little they could mess with personally. It's you that I'm worried about; if you do turn out to be related to the royal family, they may try to force you to stay in the elven forest, or even if we are allowed to continue traveling, they may have us travel with additional guards. It all depends on what the elven test reveals."

"What if I refused the tests?" Kenko asked, needing to know every possibility.

"I fear they might force the issue if you refuse to allow them to test you. As an elf, you fall under the elven nation's rule; they could order you to be forced back to the palace in chains if they wanted. Meeting them halfway by allowing the testing to be completed is our best bet of getting you into a position of strength and allowing the nobility to discuss the matter civilly."

A knock at the door interrupted them, and Anais went to open it, letting a maid in with their meals. Kenko was too nervous to eat earlier before today's meeting, so she was starving. The covered dishes huffed steam and the scent of spices into the room as each was opened and laid out on the table.

"Come get some food, Kenko," Anais said, pouring each a small glass of mead and a larger mug of juice for the elf. Tonight isn't a day to discuss things without a drink. I'll allow you a small glass, but we will purchase supplies and a few last things for the coming months tomorrow. It will be a busy day, and neither of us needs to be sporting a sore head."

"What else do we need to discuss?"

"Options," Anais huffed, filling her plate from the dishes with rice, a thick curry, and vegetables that had been sent up. The separate plate of chicken and sausage meant Kenko could have some of everything else on the table.

"What options do we have? I have to report to the elven forest, eventually," Kenko said, slowly taking a seat and taking a slice of the thick rye bread and a spoonful of fruit.

"You haven't had to deal with arguments between different nations before." Anais snorted, "Just the negotiations over whom to send as an envoy can take weeks. Given that I plan to send a mage message to the elven kingdom and my contact in the palace, we might be sent to River-deep instead. It all depends on how the royals of both nations wish to appear to the other. Currently, the elves have misstepped and managed to insult an apprentice to a Mage of the Realm. That means my supervisors will press the royal family to respond in my favor while the elves try to save face. If the King demands you go to the palace and the elves come to him, we will do that. However, if the King wishes to curry favor with the elves for upcoming trade agreements or other proposals in the next few years, he may send us an escort to take us to the elven nation. Either way, I fully intend to visit Armland's estate as it is on the road we will be taking."

"Is this showing me how horrible humans can be with their caged monsters?"

"Ignoring his hobbies, the man is a devoted magistrate and serves those under him justly. While he isn't someone I would run to in a fight, he is still a fair man to those in his care. You can't expect much more from the landed nobility in Arda; some are better, and some are worse than you would see in any race or position in society."

"And we are staying at his estate just to discuss monsters?"

"The forests around his territory are dangerous at night; I'd rather push through and stay in a walled keep than force both us and our guard to deal with potential ambushes while both the elven and human guards around us have reason to dislike the other."

"They won't be fighting each other." Kenko huffed, nibbling at apple and pear slices even as she served herself a small bowl of curry and rice.

"No, they will just be trying to outdo each other if we encounter any monsters and get in each other's way. It makes the situation more dangerous than it would normally be. The more people you add to a fight, the higher the chances of someone doing something stupid."

"Would it help to ask for female guards?" Kenko asked, taking a bite of curry and humming happily. The inn really had fantastic food.

"There aren't many female royal knights, and the few I know are all posted either as guards for the queen or on the border dealing with night raids at the moment," Anais said, shrugging, refilling her mug and setting the pitcher of ale out of reach of them both.

"You think they are going to send a knight?"

"The elves sent rangers. The Arda Kingdom has to answer in kind, or they appear weak. As I'm already a Mage of the Realm, they can't send a higher-ranked mage, so they must send someone better than a guard troop." Anais said, "It is a show of strength."

"Is that all politics is here? Trying to outdo your neighbors and earn favors whenever the chance arises?"

"People are always trying to better their situation; it is a standard policy for all life." Anais chuckled.

"Even monsters?" Kenko asked, looking amused.

"I'm sure the packs have a social hierarchy, and most animals are driven to breed and hunt for better territory and mates. Monsters may have the same instincts, but their drive to kill anything weaker than themselves overrides any attempt to tame them."

"What about bindings? I read that some demons can be bound and used to hunt?"

"Those are very weak demons, and more mages die from attempting a binding than manage one successfully. Something about a monster's magic and energy is corrupt, allowing them to break magical chains and wear down bindings over time. Even Baron Armland has to refresh the spell work on his cages constantly. The only reason his cages work long-term is that his family has created a unique method of binding that is part of their bloodline. You will have to ask him on the details, and I've yet to make sense of it myself."

"So certain bloodlines have uncommon abilities?"

"For humans, certainly, you will have to ask the rangers if it is the same for elves. My family is known for crystal-based magics or using stones to hold our wards; a friend uses wind-based magics, while another works in glass. Most mages can work in any material, but some will always come easier, and those abilities tend to run in families."

"How does that work for the elves?

"You would have to ask the head of your clan once you are tested. I've never heard of elven clans having bloodline abilities, but it isn't impossible. They will want to test your elvish magical abilities at the same time, I would think. We will have to work with the rangers on your pathfinding, nature sense, and elemental abilities."

"We can do that on the road?"

"More likely in the evenings after we camp. Magic on horseback is never a good idea unless you have a horse used to your gifts."

"What will I be studying while we wait on the knights? More weapons?"

"Shield work. Your footwork with the dagger is still too hesitant," Anais said, ignoring the elf's grimace. I know you don't want to fight or hurt others, but sometimes there is no choice. You must commit to the movements as if your life depended on them now."

"I understand the need in my head, but my body still freezes or flinches with every blow."

"I generally don't push bringing emotion into a fight, but you need something to push you forward. You need to meet each blow, step into the fight, not away from it."

"How can I when everyone is so much bigger and stronger than I am?"

"I'll arrange a demonstration with the rangers tomorrow. You don't have to be the strongest to win a fight," Anais said, grinning. Tomorrow would be interesting.

CHAPTER
THIRTEEN

THE NEXT DAY, the war started. Kenko could no longer step away from a fight or leave the ring if she got scared. The two elven rangers and Anais brought Kenko to the training grounds behind the adventurers' guild hall, not saying what they planned to work on that day. She generally avoided the fighting rings, focusing on her archery and sling on the targets slung along the back wall. Today, Anais towed her over without comment, stuffing her into the training padding and shoving her small shield and long dagger into her hands next to one of the deserted practice rings.

"I thought I was going to watch a fight," Kenko said uncertainly, fiddling with her dagger and shield. She was still new to the shield, and the weight stretched at muscles unused to such strain.

"First, the rangers want to see your footwork in a fight, then you can watch how they approach the same kind of attacker," Anais said, waving forward the guard she'd hired for the day, a hulking man with broad shoulders and a permanent scowl thanks to a scar bisecting his right cheek and lips.

"What are the rules?" Kenko asked, stepping into the ring and readying her shield; she felt she would need it this morning.

"No, rules. Just don't kill each other or take off any limbs; too much paperwork." Anais called, smirking, "Begin!"

"What?" Kenko bleated, twisting away as the man's club missed her by a hair's breadth, sinking into the dirt of the ring with a solid thump she felt in her heels.

"Start fighting, Kenko. I'd hate to lose an apprentice this quickly."

Kenko knew Anais was joking, but it didn't stop the sheer terror coursing through her body as blow after blow was barely deflected by her shield or dodged in a flurry of sand and limbs as she rolled out of the way. The guard stayed completely silent, only the occasional grunt showing the effort he was putting into the bout, seeming to barely shift with each strike. Kenko gasped for air, her frantic scramble to keep a distance between her head and the club soaking her in sweat and grime.

"Enough, Kenko, come out and let Orrian show you what you are doing wrong." Anais called, waving her out and shoving a cup of water at her, "Sip that and calm down."

"I don't appreciate your training methods, Master Mage." Kenko huffed, taking a long swallow of water and setting it aside.

"Complain to me again when you've been in a proper fight." Anais huffed, "How much of that was your disengagement skill?"

"None of it; I would have been thrown out of the ring and running if I'd used that."

"So that was what? Evasion?"

"Some of it, yes," Kenko agreed, watching as the guard stretched and turned to face the waiting ranger.

"Watch Orrian and how he handles his opponent. You would agree that the guard is bigger than him, correct? Both in height and weight?"

"Yes, he's a lot more muscular." Kenko agreed, eying the hulking form frowning.

Kenko watched dumbfounded as Orrian surged under the first blow, blocking the second with his staff before riding the guard to the ground and delivering a finishing blow. He held the last position for a long beat before relaxing and helping the guard to his feet like they were old friends.

"Why was he so close? Isn't it dangerous?" she squeaked. There was no way she could have done the same.

"It's a matter of strength and balance. It won't always work on an opponent, especially one used to fighting one-on-one. If you crowd a sword fighter, you take away their reach. The blade becomes a blunt weapon they are forced to club with, forcing them into a grappling position. Most fighters start punching to gain distance; some will reach for a dagger or short blade. Trip them up and take them to the ground, and you gain the upper hand, but that doesn't stop the fight. The battle isn't over until someone yields or dies."

"And waiting before letting him up?" Kenko asked, hating that she probably should have known the answer; she hated fighting.

"You never assume your enemy is down and out of the fight until they are dead. You can't take a fighter down and turn your back only to have them get up and stab you while you are distracted with the next enemy on a battlefield."

"We won't be fighting on a battlefield."

"If we get attacked by ten or more bandits, it counts just the same. Anytime you are outnumbered, it becomes a battlefield." Anais said, watching her apprentice with a careful gaze.

"What did Orrian do to make him fall? He used his legs?"

"Your entire body is your weapon, not just your shield and sword or dagger. You can kick, punch, bite, whatever it takes to win." Anais said, watching Kenko worry at the end of her braid, "I'm not teaching you to look pretty in a duel, Kenko. I'm teaching you to survive. Go back in and show me your disengagement skills. I want to be aware of what it does before you use it in the middle of a fight."

"Right," Kenko agreed, huffing a breath and pulling her shield back onto her arm. It has a cool-down effect as well. I can't use it for a few minutes afterward."

"Good to know, show me," she said, watching intently as the guard and Kenko faced off.

Kenko felt like time slowed as she let the club descend towards her. Disengagement activated, and she flew backward, twisting to land outside the ring, flight blurring the ground under her as she ran from the danger. Suddenly, she was across the square and several blocks from the guild hall, watching as Orrian jogged over to her.

"That, elfling, was impressive," he said, grinning, clasping her shoulder as they started the walk back, "Did you mean to scale the wall?"

"I didn't; I went out through the gate," Kenko said, frowning, glancing at the tall elf.

"No, you ran up it like your feet were made of tar." he grinned. "Your ability chose the path, ignoring the one you planned in favor of the shortest distance to safety."

"That could be a problem," Anais agreed as they approached her outside the hall. "We will have to test the limits of your ability, Kenko. We must know it won't throw you onto unstable ground or off a cliff."

"How exactly do we test that?" Kenko asked warily, glancing at the elf, who gave her a wide grin.

"Very carefully," he offered, getting a snort from Anais, "do not fret so, elfling. We are testing to ensure you are safe when danger is present."

The rest of the day turned into a trial by fire as they forced her to use disengagement in every scenario they could come up with. Enemies on all sides, hands bound, weaponless, holding a spear, hemmed in against a wall, every possible way they could think of was tested without placing her on a cliff and asking her to throw herself off of it. She was covered in bruises and exhausted by dinner, limping from a sudden tumble off the top of a wall when her skill landed her on a loose stone.

"Now, do you understand why we want you trained in weapons even if you aren't going to fight?" Anais asked a bit rhetorically as she hauled the exhausted girl to her feet.

"I understand, but I still don't like it," Kenko grumbled, rubbing at a bruised hip.

"I don't care if you like fighting or not as long as you can survive any encounters you get dragged into. I don't fight because I enjoy it. I fight because if I didn't, I would be dead or have the blood of innocents on my hands from doing nothing." Anais snapped, "Very few people actually like fighting, Kenko. You have to do it to survive in this world."

"I dislike the idea of hurting others, but if it stops them from hurting me or others, then I understand." Kenko sighed, "With all the monsters about, why are people still attacking each other? Shouldn't they be more worried about the monsters?"

"People are a weaker target than most monsters. Some simply like preying on the weak. That doesn't seem to change no matter where I travel."

Kenko didn't comment and went to bed early that evening. Curling under her quilt, she compared her previous life to the current one in Arda. Was her safety in one really that different from her danger now? On earth, she'd been physically safe but constantly belittled and viewed as weak, struggling to find common ground with anyone else around her thanks to her illness. Now, she was seen as weak for not knowing how to or wanting to fight. In both worlds, strength was seen as power, and intelligence could only get you so far unless you had a way to back it up with social connections or money.

In her past life, she had few friends beyond the handful she made online. She never truly felt like she had a connection to anyone. Everyone drifted in and out of her life without doing much beyond making her feel more useless. Were you genuinely living if no one needed you?

Most of the people she saw daily were more of a hindrance than a help when it came to getting by. People liked to think they were helping even if they did more harm than good. People donated to charity but wouldn't stop to help a person struggling across a traffic crossing. It was easier to ignore someone's struggles than to step up and offer a helping hand. Everyone was too busy with their own lives to look up, anyway.

Her parents in her first life had been crushed by medical bills even long after she left and tried to work and live on her own. They had refused the money she wanted to give them, but she felt guilty for most of her life for taking so many options away from them. Her mother had given up on so many dreams to take care of her as a sick child; her father worked himself nearly to death trying to pay back the companies they owed money to and help her get through college. Debt constantly hung over her head when she finally moved out. No matter how much she scrimped and saved, no one considered her a safe bet for a long-term job, so she floated from place to place, job to job.

In her last life, you worked to get paid, not to enjoy life or your job. She didn't feel like she'd taken a deep breath or relaxed for the last two decades of her life. That was the last thing she wanted now. She was finally breathing, and she refused to go back to that hopeless grind.

She had people here who genuinely wanted to spend time with her, talk about her day, and share time together over meals. In her last life, she had always felt like the affection her parents and other family gave was forced. They were her parents, and they had no choice but to do their best for her no matter how much they came to hate it. Ultimately, they would have been relieved that she was no longer burdening them.

Here, she had a chance to choose her path all over again without the pain and exhaustion that had limited everything she did. She finally had a chance, and nothing was going to take that away from her, not the elves, not monsters, nothing.

She wanted to commit to something in this new life. Even if forced to fight, she would do her best, no matter how much she disliked it. She would not be a burden to those around her this time.

———

"I understand that many issues with the elves are a matter of politics, but beyond my eye color, you have no reason to think I'm a noble. For all you know, I would be a throwback to a distant cousin from a side branch of the clan." Kenko pointed out, sighting down the archery lane and releasing with a soft puff of breath.

"It doesn't matter if you are or not. We will treat you the same because the potential is there." Orrian said, giving her the next arrow, "You are dropping your shoulder."

"So because you can't rule it out, you will treat me like an unknown royal." Kenko huffed, taking a breath and loosing the arrow at the swinging target, "That is somehow worse, what if the test shows I'm a commoner?"

"Then you will have a chance to meet and spend time with several rangers, guards, and nobility that few commoners ever meet."

"It just seems like a waste."

"You are thinking like a human," the other ranger, Gaelin, huffed, glancing up from the arrow she was fletching, "Elves live a very long time compared to humans and have few children. Every child is precious to us."

"You could both be on patrol and traveling the countryside hunting monsters or keeping an eye out for others in danger. Instead, you are stuck playing babysitter to me. How is that fair?"

"How is it not? Others are assigned to the forests and borders while we are here." Orrian said, offering the next arrow, "You are not old enough yet to realize that we have centuries before we will be seen as old. We have walked the forests for over a century already. You are but a blink of an eye to us, elfling. We can only hope we come to know you as closely as those we have worked with for decades or longer."

"I don't know how to judge time that way." Kenko huffed, fighting the urge to sway in time with the target. "I just take things one day at a time. Nothing much matters past that if you can't see yourself surviving or making the next meal."

"I thought elves were born with a bow in their hands. It's nice to be proven wrong occasionally." Guild master Banner said, smirking, wandering over with someone new at his elbow, watching the elves interact.

"She has a good eye even for one so new to the bow." The other man noted with polite interest as he glanced over the trio, short and thin for an adventurer with a head of shockingly white hair worn in a thin braid down his back and hidden mainly by a pageboy cap.

"Do you need the lanes, Guild Master?" Gaelin asked, starting to pack up her gear.

"I wanted to see if Kenko was up for a different kind of lesson," he said, clapping his companion on the shoulder.

"What kind of lesson exactly?" Kenko asked, glancing at the man sharply when her senses urged her to ignore him.

"Good, my skills don't work on you very easily. You have already passed the first test." The man said, tucking his cap under an arm and offering her his hand, "I'm called Owen."

"It is hard to hide from an elf, even with skills such as yours, thief." Orrian snapped, taking the bow and quiver from Kenko, "I would speak with Anais before training with this one, Kenko."

"What skills are you using? Misdirection, presence extinguish?" Kenko frowned as she eyed him, and her gut told her he was both harmless and extremely dangerous. "Are you using a skill to seem less harmful?"

"I see why you thought she could do with the lessons." Owen huffed, "It generally is considered rude to point out a person's skills in mixed company, but you caught the gist of most of them. I started life as a pickpocket living on the streets, and most of my skills support that kind of life; however, my class is that of a healer."

"You defied your class?" Orrian asked, sounding impressed, "That is a hard path to walk."

"Healing made me no coin, and I had no patron to finance an apprenticeship with the healers. My country wasn't as blessed as this one; the poor starved no matter their potential or went to the army to die in the mud. Through rote repetition, I defied my blessing and learned skills outside of my class."

"How long did it take you to gain the first skill?"

"After months of constant practice, you must throw a rock one thousand times to gain the throwing skill. To level it up, you must multiply that by ten for every level," he said, giving her a bitter smile. It is not a path I recommend to most, but you look like one fighting her class. What is your level in archery?"

"I don't have any weapons skills." Kenko said with a bitter smile, "I am a magical artificer with defensive skills only."

"If you must have a weapon, then you need to practice at least an hour daily. You can get a level on a single skill in six months if you have the hours. It would take you a year or more to get to level three. Most don't bother reaching above that."

"Do you use all your abilities? Did you use your healing in battle?" Kenko asked, eyeing the scars littering his arms.

"I was a battlefield medic and healer for years; now I teach those who wish to learn outside their skills. Natural born thieves who hate to steal are sent to me to learn how to turn those skills into abilities they can use outside of their set class."

"But I can learn to fight, eventually?"

"Yes, but you will never be a natural at it. Not like these two," he said, gesturing at the elves by her side, "They were born archers, skills set to turn a bow into an extension of their body without thought. Once you are confirmed into your clan, you may gain some small abilities that make such things easier, but that depends on the clan."

"What do you know of elvish clans?" Gaelin asked sharply, hand falling to her sword.

"Little enough," he said, "I was asked to meet the child because she is fighting her Class. I have worked with a handful of elves in similar situations, but not while I have lived in this country."

"You know of the mountain clans?" Orrian asked, stiffening.

"Yes, I visited their valleys for several years when a young pair of elf twins were born without the normal fighting skills, and their tutors were at a loss."

"You trained the royal heirs," Orrian said, watching Owen with something close to respect.

"For a time, yes, I did." he agreed, glancing at Kenko before asking the group, "Would you care to talk inside? Sadly, my old bones are no longer up to so much travel."

"Can you tell me of the Mountain elves? I haven't heard much about them from the book here beyond that many are known to be healers and often bond with animals."

"All elves have the ability to bond with animals," Gaelin huffed, opening the guild hall back door and waving everyone through, "Most simply do not because we no longer live such rural lives. Many rangers who devote themselves to patrol bond with an animal that lives in the part of the forest they frequent. The mountain elves travel less and have more set routes to patrol than in the open forests as we do."

"It would be cruel to force a wild animal to travel with you constantly, I guess," Kenko said with a hum, not noticing when the sound made the others blink.

"Do you sing, Kenko?" Orrian asked, watching the way her face shuttered at the question with a frown.

"No, never," she said, blushing hotly. She'd been ridiculed in her past life for her accent and how often she lost her voice whenever she got sick.

"You should. You probably have a delightful voice." Orrian said before turning back to Owen, "What exactly are you hoping to teach Kenko if repetition is what she needs?"

"I am here mostly to provide the training schedule I use with my students as a guide. I won't be able to travel with her and her master, but I wanted to offer my services should they be needed at a later point." he said, turning to Kenko as she helped gather the tea set and plates, "Your master is welcome to write to me should you need assistance as well."

"I'm sure she would appreciate that, sir," Kenko said, bringing the tray to the table before the other servants could help.

"You are rather independent, aren't you?" Owen said musingly as she poured the tea and settled in her seat with a fruit dish at her elbow.

"You say that like it is a bad thing." Kenko huffed, picking up a fork to stab a small chunk of the mango-like fruit in season.

"It can be your plan to focus on raising your fighting skills, but that means you will have little time for anything else. What else are you studying?"

"Anais has declared my writing and maths proficient in common. I don't know calligraphy yet, but she saves most of my etiquette lessons for the human kingdoms this winter when we will be in the capital. I am focusing on elven culture, etiquette, and lessons in strategy and history."

"Along with archery, horseback, sword, dagger, and shield work." Owen huffed, "You need to narrow down your weapons focus. Archery can be done while traveling with the rangers or in the forests, but I would focus on your sword and shield work every morning. You can gain the horsemanship skill just from how much riding you will get traveling with your master."

"He does have a point," Banner agreed, "we have been trying to introduce you to several skills to see what weapons and actions you favor, but it will be hard to drill every day once you are traveling. You are still studying herbal manuals but don't have the time to gather anything; you could be spending that time on sword work or something else."

"I want to learn more about the world; I want to know how to care for myself in the woods and outside of a town. I need to understand the plants, animals, and monsters I might encounter for that to happen."

"You have decades to learn all that, elfling," Orrian said gently.

"What if I don't?" Kenko asked, needing them to understand. "You keep saying I have all the time in the world, but Arda is at war with her neighbors. It might not spread this far, but it could. Anais is already concerned about the rise in monsters because there aren't enough hunters to cull them before they evolve. I won't stay in the elven nation forever; I won't isolate myself to stay perfectly safe."

"We aren't saying you need to isolate yourself," Banner said, trying to calm her down.

"But you are, you want me safe, but you also say I'm learning too much, taking on too much. I understand I don't need to know everything if I travel with Anais or a party, but what if I get separated? I need to know enough to get by on my own." she insisted, pushing out of her chair, "I don't want to know how to use a sword, but I need to in case I'm attacked. Learning about monsters and herbs is the same as learning the sword. I need to know how to survive independently if I have to. If you don't understand that, there is no point in this."

She darted out of the room without another word, ignoring the startled denials. She needed to be able to support herself. If she couldn't do that, then what was the point of learning how to fight? If she could never defend herself well enough to be trusted to travel alone, then why was she being pushed so hard?

Was she misunderstanding the limits of this world? Was it because she was a child? An elf? What underlying reason was she missing?

———

"You have half the guild and most of the elves downstairs worrying over you." Anais said, coming inside and closing the door on the elven ranger behind her with a glare, "Do I need to be concerned or start finding a back entrance to sneak you out of?"

"I have a question for you, and I want you to answer it as if it's any other mage's apprentice. Not me, not someone my age, not an elf. Can you do that?"

"I'll try my best," Anais agreed, taking off her boots and coat and dropping into the chair across from where Kenko was curled up.

"What would you expect a human mage apprenticed to you to know? Would you be teaching them everything I'm learning?"

"Most apprentices coming to me would be fifteen or older." Anais said slowly, "They'd likely be closer to thirty. They would already know the basics of local history, magic, economy, horseback riding, and some form of weapon at a basic level. Most of my training would push them to get out of bad habits and learn new skills."

"Banner and Owen think I need to narrow the focus of my training. I disagree; I feel like I am horribly behind because I didn't have the same childhood everyone else seems to have had. I don't understand this world, and until I do, I feel like I will be a burden to anyone I am traveling or fighting with."

"Frankly, if I had my way, you wouldn't be fighting for at least another two years." Anais said, "Given how much time I spend on the road, I can't guarantee you won't see your first kill in the next month. I've been pushing your training because I want you at a decent enough baseline that I don't have to focus on only protecting you the moment we leave the safety of the road."

"So I won't always be learning everything like we are now?"

"Gods, no, I'm hoping by the end of next month you will be decent enough with a sword to take a few blows and run away if necessary. I want you strong enough to survive a fight if I am too busy dealing with bandits or monsters to protect you, Kenko. No one expects you to master the sword in a few weeks suddenly, and it takes even people with the class of weapon's master years of training."

"I'm horrible with the bow." Kenko pointed out flatly, sighing.

"You don't have the archer class, Kenko. I don't expect you to pick up every weapon instantaneously, even if you are an elf. As long as you are consistent in your practice every morning and most evenings, I don't care how your progress is going. You have plenty of time, so stop stressing about learning about every monster and poisonous plant. Even I don't know everything, I will teach you what I do know for as long as you will allow it."

"You aren't going to kick me out if I never learn the bow?" Kenko pressed.

"No, frankly, I'd rather you learn something useful. You have your sling; stick with that and maybe work on the small crossbows. The rest can wait until the winter when we are stuck in River-deep."

"Owen wants to give you some schedules for training he used on his other apprentices who were working on gaining skills that weren't part of their class."

"I will speak with him tomorrow," she huffed, gathering her boots and hanging her coat correctly. Was there anything else we need to discuss? Have you had dinner?"

"No, I needed to think."

"Be a good apprentice and draw your master a hot bath while I arrange for some food. It was a long ride today testing out your horse."

"Did you buy one?"

"Yes, you get to meet him tomorrow. It's even an old elven mount, so it is used to a light hand and leg, but it's not so tall that you'll have to worry about outgrowing him anytime soon."

"I was kind of afraid I'd get a pony."

"Ponies are well enough, but you need something with a bit of leg when we need speed."

"Okay," Kenko agreed, heading into the small bathroom to start the water.

"You can stop worrying. She isn't thinking about running." Anais said, ducking out the door and giving the elf outside an amused glance.

"She is still young, and the young overreact at times." Orrian huffed.

"True enough, but she's an old soul in that body. Whatever happened during her childhood aged her mind faster than her body. She reminds me of the touch-starved orphans I've met in the River-deep slums. They lash out at everyone around them even when offered kindness because those with honeyed words tended to cut the deepest in the end."

"I would not call her broken,"

"I never said she was," Anais sighed, glancing at the elf, "that child has a spine of steel and determination to do better for herself no matter the odds against her. No child I know would have lasted this long on her schedule without at least a few tears."

"Elves aren't ones for tears unless the pain is life-ending."

"Then she hasn't reached that point yet," Anais huffed, heading downstairs, "I think she will have a few more surprises in store before we reach the elven forests. I hope you rangers are ready for a hard ride."

"Might I ask a favor?"

"Ask away," she said, pausing a few steps down.

"Have you heard her sing?" Orrian asked, crossing his arms and leaning back against the wall.

"No, but her voice is well enough. She probably sounds lovely. Why?" Anais asked, slightly suspicious.

"She hummed in the guild hall, and the sound resonated in my chest. Even the frame of the surrounding building thrummed in response. I've never seen a child with such control ignore the sound completely and deny having made it when questioned."

"Did she say why?"

"She claimed that she never sings." he offered grimacing.

"Perhaps we can get a few sea shanties and ballads going on the road. Song is a good way to learn languages, and she needs to learn elvish, eventually." Anais mused, sighing.

"Fair enough," he huffed, returning his post beside the door.

"As long as you two don't expect much from me, I have the voice of a crow," Anais added with a snort, heading downstairs to place their order for dinner.

THE FOLLOWING DAY, they slept in, and Kenko was surprised to be told she had the day off to do as she wished. Before heading out, she stole an apple and a slice of cheese from the waiting tray for breakfast. It was still unusual to have so many people care that she ate properly and had all the things normal children needed: food, shelter, and even affection in a limited fashion from the people in her life.

She wasn't sure if Anais enjoyed teaching or saw her as a long-term investment. Anais seemed to have few expectations on how much she expected Kenko to learn or master while under her care. Instead, the lessons were more off the cuff: stories of monsters she fought in the last few years, the history of the area they were heading to next, and weapons and magic practice wherever it could be fitted into the day around all her other lessons.

Magic flickered around her fingers as she walked, trying to decide what to do with the day. Anais pushed the habit of using magic whenever possible, crafting tiny runes or fireflies of colored light to flitter about her hair to get used to casting and slowly increase her reserves. It unnerved the locals, but it did mean that the children who were bullying her only did so from a distance now.

Anais had said they would be leaving today, but perhaps they would wait on the knights instead. It probably depended on the elves, Kenko thought, sighing, coming to a stop and waiting to see if her shadow would come out or not. Orrian dropped from the roof's edge with a smile, keeping pace with her when she started walking again.

When they reached the marsh road and headed down the path that curved along the town wall, she asked, "Has the envoy decided who will be traveling with us?"

"Gaelin and I will continue to guard you. The knights will arrive in the next few weeks. However, Anais would like to start tomorrow morning," he informed her gravely.

"We aren't waiting on them?"

"You would have to ask your master about that. I was merely told to be ready to leave at dawn," he said, glancing over her clothes, "When we reach Ernsari, you will understand the elves more easily; we will have to find clothes more fitting to your station before your presentation."

"I don't have a station, Orrian. I'm an orphan and an elf, nothing more."

"And if the test reveals you to be more than that?"

"Then it will be up to the royal family to convince me I must stay in Ernsari. I don't plan to end my apprenticeship anytime soon, Orrian. I have too much to learn before I can do that."

"You could be apprenticed to an elven mage," he offered, holding up a hand to stop her outraged defense of her master. "I am speaking of options, not saying your master isn't suited to her role. She is very suited to you; it is rare to have a human mage so comfortable with all races, and she is even noted as a friend of the smaller trade villages she has visited on her travels."

"You think I'll be pressured to stay after the testing, even if I don't fall under the royal clan, don't you?"

"You are a powerful mage and crafter, Kenko. Many people will want to sway you to their side, and our society thinks in terms of centuries of profit and improvement for our nation. Investments in our children are rarely a terrible choice as they will be the ones who continue our struggle when we return to the forest's heart."

"Envoy Morlar wants to use me to improve his station." Kenko sighed, "Why was he so angry that I might be part of the royal clan? What does that change?"

"As a poor commoner, he would have been your only access to those in the nobility. He would have introduced you to patrons and helped you adjust to our society. You have a foothold in the royal clan, so he has very little to offer you, which robbed him of his normal approach."

"I don't have any power over him or his actions," Kenko pointed out, biting back a sigh. Everything was so complicated when it came to politics.

"You will be speaking to the royal family; all it takes is one word in the wrong ear, and he will be delegated to a remote posting. He knows he has offended you and your master, so he seeks to distance himself from the entire affair."

"He is angry at himself, then?"

"Yes, he was unable to control his actions. That is almost a crime amongst elves, and we are raised always to consider our actions and tune our thoughts to the world around us. He misunderstood the situation and refused to bow to someone he saw as his inferior. He has caused his own injury, and he knows it now."

"Tune your thoughts to the world," she repeated, glancing out over the surrounding fields, "do the elves have a religion they follow?"

"Not as humans believe in religion," he said, gesturing her to a lone tree to one side and stroking a hand down the rough bark. Come have a seat and tell me what you feel."

"From the tree?" she asked, sitting and touching the bark.

"What do you feel from the tree, the air, the ground under you, everything?" he asked, leaning back, closing his eyes, and resting against the enormous trunk.

Letting the tiny sparks of her ever-present spell fade, she leaned back, sighing. The weather was warming up as summer peaked, welcoming the light breeze. The mosquitos and gnats she remembered from her last life seemed to leave elves alone, so she sat unbothered, resting in the flickering shade.

She looked inward, meditating on her magic, settling her mind before reaching outward with that inner sense she couldn't define. The surrounding energy pulsed with its own heartbeat, the tree's much slower than hers. The grass hummed along with the breeze, rising and falling as the sun shifted over its length.

"Why is the tree so slow?" she asked, blinking as she opened her eyes.

"We call them the dreamers. They see the world through seasons more than moment to moment," Orrian said, smiling, leaning back, and closing his eyes; Kenko copied him a moment later.

"And the rest?"

"Most flowers live only for a season before they go dormant in winter or die until the next spring when their seeds will be reborn. The grass and the bushes are much the same."

"Do all elves mediate like this?"

"All are taught as children to feel the surrounding forest, the life around them. We are charged with protecting that song from those who can no longer hear it."

"Why does it feel like magic? It's the same as when I reach for my magic to cast a spell."

"All beings have some magic; even the most non-magical rabbit has a tiny spark at its core."

"Can you sense them as well?"

"Yes, that is what forest sense is at its core—learning to feel the world around you and its power even while your eyes are open. Practice while you meditate, reach out with your senses, and feel the flow of the songs around you. In time, you will even be able to tell what magic is being cast or active."

"Is that why the wards and enchantments glow?" Kenko asked, sitting up and twisting to look at Orrian, "The others in town don't see the lines of power on their doors and walls, do they?"

"No, not even all elves have mage sight."

"It isn't forest sight?"

"No, I can feel the play of spells and wards while I meditate or if I step across one, but I cannot see the lines of power after they are cast."

"So it isn't a common skill for elves," she sighed, yet another thing to mark her as different. "Anais was wrong then, but she did say she wasn't aware of many skills that an elf might have that could be different from humans."

"I take it she can't see the lines of power either?"

"No, nor does she know of anyone who can. I guess I can ask the Clan whenever I get tested." Kenko said, standing and brushing off her leggings, "I probably should go to the market, but it has been so crowded with all the refugees coming through."

"I am surprised they aren't camping around the city yet." Orrian agreed, glancing toward the long line of travelers making their slow way past along the main road, headed towards the river ferries.

"I will see what horse Master purchased; she said I would like him."

"Is it being kept where you ride? We can walk there next," he agreed, standing and offering her a hand that she ignored to jump down to the road.

"Do elves ever keep pets? Like cats or dogs?"

"Of course, however, few rangers have such companions unless they are a bonded familiar, and no, I don't have one of my own," he said, giving her an amused grin; she was full of questions today.

"Does Gaelin knit?" she asked, fiddling with a leaf.

"Knit?" he repeated, blinking at the abrupt subject change.

"Yes, making mittens or scarves with yarn. Is that not a thing with elves?" she asked, glancing back when he came to a halt at the unfamiliar word.

"The southern forests rarely get cold enough for such things; perhaps the mountain elves have such a skill." he offered, shrugging, "Why do you ask?"

"I wanted to try making a scarf. I carved some knitting needles but can't find the yarn I like in the market."

"This is a skill you have?"

"I used to make hats," Kenko said, grinning as she remembered the hats and socks she'd leave about for the homeless; knitting was something she could do from bed, and it was nice to have a finished product after weeks of nothing going right.

"You didn't keep them?" he asked, frowning, stopping yet again; the child continued to confound him at every turn.

"As you say, we don't need them now. It's too hot for a knit cap or mittens, but they might be nice in the winter. I could get started now, and it is something to keep your hands busy while you wait," she offered. Her mother hated the clutter the yarn made and threw it out several times. It wasn't until she lived on her own that she could finally do as she liked, not that it had lasted very long.

"Having a simple hobby is always useful," Orrian agreed as they started off again. After the stables, we can speak with the innkeeper; she may know someone who does a similar craft and can supply your yarn."

"That is a wonderful idea," she agreed, starting to skip. Today, she had a new horse to meet, a chance to restart her old hobby, and a new magic to learn. It was a good day.

———

Sadly, meeting her new horse wasn't like the books she'd read as a kid. It was just a horse, big-chested and more than willing to wipe green drool down her back. It was a chestnut brown with dark eyes, four white socks already stained with mud and a soft black nose it used to nip at her braid.

"What is he called?" Kenko asked the stable master, watching her look the horse over in amusement.

"Buck,"

"What? No one would name a horse Buck. That is just asking for trouble," she sputtered, and the man laughed.

Orrian wandered over, checking the gelding's feet while murmuring in elvish, "He is a steady horse. He should make good time on the road and in the forests."

"What do elves name their horses?" Kenko asked glancing

"Much the same as anyone else, after the color, old heroes, or characteristics they have." Orrian said, shrugging, "My horse is called evening light, in elvish. You might wish to train it to come to a whistle if you hope to keep it for some time."

"Won't I keep him a long time?" she asked, frowning as both men chuckled.

"Perhaps ten years, perhaps less," the elf shrugged, "depends on the mount and where you travel. If you go across the sea, you will be forced to leave him behind, and it might be better to sell a horse than leave it to drift in a pasture for the rest of its years. You may also be granted a deer mount in Ernsari."

"Do you have one?"

"All rangers have a deer mount. It was decided to travel by horse when collecting an elfling. However, some of the humans raised will run from the deer if they are unaware of them."

"He is a sturdy mount but still young enough to teach you a few things or pick up bad habits if you let him," the stable master said, not commenting on elven mounts, "He will run from monsters, but most intelligent beasts do the same. It takes trust in the rider to keep a horse standing during a battle or monster attack. He has the training to respond to your hand and legs, so keep a light touch like you've been taught. I will have your tack and things ready in the morning; he will be ready when you all arrive."

"Thank you, sir."

"I've told you, I'm not a sir; you go live your life and do your best." he muttered gruffly, "You have an excellent master and a good mount; not much more you can ask for in a traveling life."

"Yes, sir," she agreed, grinning, stroking the horse's nose one last time; they would have plenty of time tomorrow to get acquainted.

They took the back way to the White Cat, avoiding the crowded main streets, and found Gatha presiding over a packed tavern. Dwarves, beast-kin, and a mix of elves and humans filled every table, and even two lizard-like men near the fire. They were joined by the other ranger, who dropped from a roof to follow them inside.

"Yarn for crafting?" Gatha blinked as she thought when asked, "That isn't a skill I know. You would probably be best asking one of the merchants who use it. I know the river folk often use knitted sweaters and such. It isn't popular at the moment, and with the summer heat, few will buy such things in the market, much less in the lowlands around here."

"Would anyone have some in stock for this winter?" Kenko asked, fingers spinning the colored flame she'd conjured absently.

"The weavers might," she said uncertainly, "oh, I know, check at Lawton's shop. He keeps the more unusual items in stock for those hunting for things."

"Where is Lawtons? I don't remember seeing it in the market," she asked, frowning as she fought to remember.

"I noted it in the byways," Orrian said, shrugging when the other elf raised an eyebrow, "the child is known to favor the more unusual shops, so I noted it when I passed. It is near the market and has a rather crowded storefront."

"You mean it's full of junk?" Gatha snorted. You wouldn't be wrong. Lawton is known for having a bit of everything. He will know where to find it if he doesn't have it hidden away somewhere."

"WELL, SHE WASN'T WRONG," Kenko said ruefully as they approached the shop that seemed to be bursting at the seams with random items.

Kenko wandered into the small store with Orrian behind her. Apparently, it was Gaelin's turn to watch outside. The rangers swapped back and forth on some schedule she couldn't work out. Gaelin seemed to prefer keeping her distance from the other humans and races. Only Orrian followed inside when she ran into a shopping district or a store for supplies.

The store was utterly without scheme, theme, or rhyme. Odds and ends were tumbled together everywhere, bolts of cloth next to rusted swords, hats by books, and random figurines. Kenko let her hands guide her, fiddling with everything as she hunted for tiny treasures. The proprietor watched in amusement as she gathered a small handful of items and books to return to the counter before approaching him.

"Excuse me, sir. I have a question."

"Ask away, my dear; Lawson's is open to all races and creeds," he said, gesturing widely at the overflowing shelves with a grin, "We have items for any and all; if you can't find it, I might have it tucked away in back."

"Do you have any yarn for knitting?"

"Knitting?" he asked, blinking, glancing between her and the items she'd brought forward. "That was the last thing I thought you would ask after picking out every magical item from my shelves."

"I did?" Kenko asked, blinking down at the small pile of trinkets she'd found.

"Well, you ignored the armor, but considering your size, none of it would fit you for several years to come." he huffed, waving her to the counter and pulling out a basket of skeins of yarn in a rainbow of colors from the back room, "Where in the world did an elf learn to knit?"

"The woman who watched me as a child knitted," she said, shrugging, ignoring the look that both men had shot her. "How are these items enchanted exactly?"

"The cup purifies water and most liquids it holds. I wouldn't recommend trying to drink spirits out of it," he said, snorting in amusement, setting the small banged-up metal cup to the side, "I won't explain the books; you can see for yourself when you read them. The ribbons and bells are enchanted to draw the eye, a cosmetic charm."

"Perhaps I should leave that then. I wanted something to tie my hair back, but I don't need more attention focused on me," she huffed, setting the white ribbon with silver tarnished bells to the side.

"Very well, the silver scissors are spelled ever sharp, and the sewing kit has a small charm that makes sure you never forget to return the needles," he said with a dry smile.

"Summoning magic is no small charm." Orrian huffed. "The kit will summon back the needles after a set amount of time, as long as they are not too far away. Generally, it is set to a day."

"These are dawn to dawn, so don't try to work on something over several days."

"Fair enough," Kenko agreed, "How much do I owe you?"

"With the enchantments, the lowest I can go is five silvers."

"Done," she agreed, ignoring Orrian's huff when she didn't bother to haggle; some needed the extra coin more than they needed her to bargain on a cost.

"Elves tend to be strange when dealing with human objects, but you are one of the more unusual people to grace my store. Is there anything else you need?" he asked, packing her items in a bag. "I also have a few plain ribbons you can look through."

"Can you recommend a cheap shop for small things to travel, like a tin of tea or sugar?"

"I have a few things here, but a guild shop would have more variety," he said, pulling down a few tins and laying a tangle of ribbons beside it.

"I don't need variety, just something to drink other than water if we can't find herbs where we camp."

"Most children your age would be looking for a good bow or candies to pack, not that you need a bow with him at your back," he grumbled, leading her to a back corner and waving her to a massive stack of tins and bundles when she ignored the handful he'd initially offered. Find what you like. I use most of it, so it is in good order and not molded. I'll throw in some dried fruit and medicinal cream as well."

"Thank you," Kenko nodded absently, fingers prying at one tin after another to smell the contents, to Orrian's amusement.

"I am sure your master has planned for your meals, Kenko." Orrian rumbled when she finally paid and left the shop with her sack of items.

"It doesn't add much weight, and I want to have my own supplies just in case."

"You like to be prepared for any eventuality, don't you?" he asked, frowning, "Do things often go badly for you?"

"Not since I arrived here, but they have before," Kenko said, leading the way to the merchant shop Lawson had recommended for her last few items: a few handkerchiefs and a pair of leather fingerless gloves.

———

Kenko *[Level 3]*

Race: Elf

Age: 8

Class: Artificer (Magical) [Level 1]

Skills:

Marathon, Archive (Artificer, beginner), Disengagement, Flight, Darkvision, Perception, Rune Carver, Inscription

Magical Skills:

Rune casting (Basic), Ward casting (Basic), Light (Basic), Shield (Basic), Thorn Whip (Basic), Environmental entanglement (Basic), Elemental Control (Basic)

Additional Skills:

Cooking (Basic), Crafting (Basic), Spell Craft (Basic), Housekeeping (Intermediate), Design (Intermediate), Organization (Advanced), Magic (Basic), Map Reading (Basic), Woodworking (Basic), Wood Carving (Basic), Drawing (Basic), Calculation (Intermediate), Gathering (Basic), Plant Identification (Intermediate, Racial Boost), Weaving (Basic), Basket Craft (Basic), Debate (Basic), Eloquence (Basic), Archery (Basic), Sling (Basic), Shield work (Basic), Dagger work (Basic)

Titles:

Blessed of Ume

Child of Elvish Clan, Unknown

Racial Passive Skills (Elven)

Longevity, Darkvision, Medication, Perception, Pathfinding, Stealth

Racial Skills (Elven)

Forest Sense, Spirit Sense, Taming

* Upgrades possible for Meditation, Stealth, Forest sense, Spirit sense, Taming, Rune Carver, Inscription, Shield,

Current Magic Level: 10 / 1000

CHAPTER
SIXTEEN

SEVERAL DAYS INTO TRAVELING, Kenko finally started asking the random questions about the world she'd been reborn in, which kept her up at night. Surely Anais would pass it off as youthful curiosity, right? She needed the information too much to keep silent entirely.

"What about the gods?" Kenko asked, chiding her horse a bit faster to keep up with the longer legs of Anais' mount, Blackthorn.

"What about them exactly?" The elf asked, raising an eyebrow; Gaelin had the habit of turning a question back on the asker that probably didn't endear her to many humans.

"Well, I know the beast-kin worship different gods and the dwarves worship a different creator god than other races. Are humans and elves the same? Do elves worship Ume?" she asked, turning to include Anais in the conversation.

"Elves worship the Great Tree and the light of life itself." Gaelin said, gesturing elegantly towards the distant green of the elven nation, "Each race's gods go back to our original lands before we became a mingled community."

"The races used to be separate? Completely isolated like the elves try to be?"

"The elves tell old stories saying we were once all one, but a great calamity struck the land and broke the world into pieces. Each race was confined to a unique piece, and we slowly diverged, developing our own abilities, religions, and cultures. However, these are only stories; we have no proof." Gaelin said, shrugging.

"Humans believe the gods created the world much like the dwarves. Ume is our creator god, while the others are subordinates who help give magic and abilities to believers." Anais said, glancing at the elf girl, "What do you believe, Kenko?"

"I believe in Ume, but I can see the magic and life within everyone with forest sense, so the elven beliefs make sense as well," she said with a shrug. She had a feeling the gods didn't care if they were worshiped or not; they would exist with or without the focused prayers and beliefs followers gave them.

"Wait until we reach the elvish capital, Ernsari. Then, you will be able to see the seedlings of the world tree and understand our culture more."

"A seedling?"

"It is a daunting sight," Gaelin said, smiling at the child's confusion. The original world tree was consumed to create this world and its magic. Only the seedlings remain to grant the world a second chance at rebirth should the darkness succeed in removing the balance of light and magic."

"Balance?" Kenko asked, "Orrian mentioned that before when we practiced forest sight."

"Balance is essential to elves." Orrian agreed, jogging out to join them, accepting his horse's reins and grinning when Anais cursed at his sudden appearance, making Kenko laugh.

"How do you hide from mage sense? I should have detected the magic in your weapons and clothes." Anais grumbled.

"That would be because no active magics are on our weapons or armor." Orrian laughed, grinning at Anais' annoyed glare, "Elves push magic into our weapons, not cast magic, and leave it as humans do."

"So you don't have any active spells on anything?" Kenko asked, "You don't use wards or enchantments?"

"Not and be an elven ranger." Gaelin said with a smile of her own, "We are trained to be invisible in the forest and to leave no trace behind. To do so, we use no enchanted gear unless necessary for the beast we hunt."

"Is there a reason beyond annoying mages?" Anais asked, chuckling while Kenko grinned; she'd noticed his approach using forest sense.

"A handful of monsters hunt by sensing magic in a fashion similar to mage sight. They look for the strongest source nearby to feed off of."

"I've never heard of something like that," Anais frowned, "are they common in the elven nation?"

"Only in places with large natural mana wells can they settle in and slowly drain the area before moving on. If they can't find a mana source, they will hunt anything in the area with magic."

"Are they hard to hunt?" Kenko asked, looking at the suddenly solemn elves. "They sound frightening."

"Only special weapons work on them, and they kill the most rangers outside of accidents of nature."

"What are they called?"

"It depends on their form; they are a perverted form of nature that has gone wrong. They can be stone drakes, ember-encrusted snakes, or deer crafted from rotting wood and flesh. The name we use in elvish does not translate easily."

"Perhaps we can move to a happier topic," Gaelin offered, "you will eventually need to learn elvish, Kenko. Would you like to have a few basic lessons?"

"Of course, I would love to learn." Kenko agreed, perking up, "Where would we start?"

"As with most languages, the children's songs teach the basic numbers and names of animals. If you like, I can teach you a few songs when we reach the camp." Gaelin grinned, "Do you know the song, Little Sparrow, Anais? It was popular for a while among the human settlements."

A clear ringing soprano, Gaelin, launched into the song in elvish while Anais did her best to translate in time. It wasn't the best way to learn grammar, but the song was pretty and passed the time while they traveled. Kenko listened avidly, humming along to the repeating harmony on the second verse, never noticing the considering look that Orrian gave her.

———

Orrian watched the two mages settle into camp as he got the fire going and a few coals glowing to one side to heat a pot of water for dinner. Kenko clapped along happily enough and struggled to pronounce the words for the rest of their evening, but she never joined them in song. Singing was common among elves to pass the day during tedious work or while waiting. Had she been told not to sing? Most elves grew up humming and singing constantly. Perhaps it had annoyed her human caretakers.

"Kenko, do you have any songs to share?" he asked when she returned from washing up while Anais started on dinner.

The young elf blinked down at him in wide-eyed surprise, those golden eyes making her all the more expressive, "You want me to sing?

"Elves typically share songs during our travels to pass the time. I am consistently searching for melodies I have not previously encountered," he agreed readily. It was accurate enough.

She frowned, sitting down to one side of the fire, "I don't know many."

"Anything is always better than nothing." Anais chimed in, adding herbs and vegetables to the simmering water.

"I don't know what to sing," Kenko said sigh, "can it be anything?"

"Anything at all," he agreed, wondering if it would be a song before her rebirth as an elf. Reincarnations were rare and to have one as an elf was even more, she would be both celebrated and hounded for any knowledge from her last world when she reached Ernsari.

She hunched lower as if trying to hide, even as her delicate voice rose to fill the glade. Low and throbbing, her alto reverberated in his chest with each verse of the song, which was about a daughter losing her mother.

I was standing by my window
On one cold and cloudy day
When I saw that hearse come rolling

For to carry my mother away
Will the circle be unbroken
By and by, Lord, by and by
There's a better home a-waiting
In the sky, Lord, in the sky
I said to that undertaker
Undertaker please drive slow
For this lady you are carrying
Lord, I hate to see her go
Will the circle be unbroken
By and by, Lord, by and by
There's a better home a-waiting
In the sky, Lord, in the sky
Oh, I followed close behind her
Tried to hold up and be brave
But I could not hide my sorrow
When they laid her in the grave
Will the circle be unbroken
By and by, Lord, by and by
There's a better home a-waiting
In the sky, Lord, in the sky
I went back home Lord, my home was lonesome
Missed my mother, she was gone
All of my brothers, sisters crying
What a home so sad and lone
Will the circle be unbroken
By and by, Lord, by and by
There's a better home a-waiting
In the sky, Lord, in the sky
Will the circle be unbroken
By and by, Lord, by and by
There's a better home a-waiting
In the sky, Lord, in the sky

.   .   .

After that one song, the music seemed to flow from her body like it couldn't stop. He didn't recognize the music, but it held them spellbound; he barely noticed Gaelin returning from her patrol to watch the child with shining eyes sing. Standing, he winced when the song broke off mid-word.

"Just heading out for patrol," he said, grinning, "Gaelin, teach her something in elvish. She has the voice for it, that is certain."

"Gladly," Gaelin murmured, still in shock from the song that had drawn her in from the woods.

"You didn't eat," Kenko protested, glancing at the still cooking stew.

"I have a pack of trail bars. You can save me a bowl for in the morning if you must, " he said, watching her with evident amusement. He caught Gaelin's arm and tugged her to follow him to check on the horses.

"Her voice," Gaelin whispered, glancing back toward the fire with awe-filled eyes.

"You felt it as well; it wasn't just my imagination then," he huffed. "I have no skill in healing songs, and neither do you. Who would they send along to teach such a gift?"

"There hasn't been a powerful singer since the last queen, and they may not let her travel if her gift is revealed. My blood is still singing, and I only caught the last song. It felt like it was drawing me back to camp."

"I have not cried from such a simple verse in decades. She will be a powerful orator when she comes of age." Orrian said, sighing even as his blood fuzzed with magic; it was both a gift and curse to be blessed with such a voice.

"And the magic? Does she even realize she is infusing her voice with forest magic?" Gaelin hissed, "The very trees are humming; the glade will be in full bloom by morning."

"We will have to limit her singing to one song a night. That should be enough to limit its effects on her surroundings."

"Not on the surrounding people. How do you feel after that long held in thrall?" Gaelin said, hugging her chest with her arms. Now that the song was over, it was like something warm had been stripped away.

"Not in thrall, in awe." Orrian huffed, "I'm full of energy and feel like I won't have to sleep for days, like after a visit to the sacred tree."

"She has such strength."

"Go, continue to watch over her. I will patrol; there is no telling what her song might have called our way."

"Surely it wouldn't have traveled that far," Gaelin said uncertainty.

"Better to not take chances. Watch over our young royal tonight. She is proving stronger than any of us could have imagined."

"ORRIAN, do the elves have stories about the reincarnated?" Kenko asked, fiddling with her carving. Anais was off hunting with Gaelin to supplement their store of food after some animals had stolen most of the dried meat from their bags while they stayed in a tiny town. Kenko wasn't sure she believed the story, considering the number of poor and hungry-looking refugees wandering through, but she wasn't going to protest sharing food with those who needed it more than they did at the moment.

"No, in general, the reborn are seen as a force of chaos, and there was the occasional story that they were to be avoided, but mostly, it was just that, a story. I have never met one before you, myself."

"Why are they viewed so badly? Is it because we aren't raised as elves?" Kenko guessed, needing to understand if she would be shunned in yet another place that should have been a home.

"It is more that you bring knowledge from another world that can easily upset the current stability of our time. A reborn might bring ideas and weapons that allow a weaker force to rule the area they previously would have never mastered. They change fates without thorough consideration of the consequences of their actions."

"So it goes back to balance?"

"Balance and the long-term consequences of their actions. Most sell their knowledge to the highest bidder for coin without considering how that knowledge will be used." Orrian said with a grimace.

"If they are from my world, then I can understand it; we survived only by acquiring coin and money. Without it, you would have no way of leading a valuable or productive life. Here, your skill is more valuable than money; it has changed my mentality."

"You live to acquire currency?" he asked, glancing at her in surprise.

"Yes, not all believe that is the best way to live; few do, but our society was impossible without it."

"Does no one live to work the land or protect it?"

"Some do but are often seen as powerless because of their views."

"And you?"

"I was sickly and weak, my treatments placed my family deeply in debt, and I wasn't able to live a genuine life no matter how I tried. I would not have been strong enough to work the land, so I worked wherever I could, trying to earn money to pay off my debts. It was not a happy life."

"And now, are you satisfied with your new circumstance?"

"Oh, yes!" Kenko beamed, "I'm not in pain. I can run and move how I want. I have all the time I need to learn and craft more than a human lifetime. Once I understand enough to level my skill, I won't have to work for money to support myself. I can craft and work to help those around me. It is wonderful."

"Good, as long as you consider the long-term consequences of your actions and preserve the balance of magic and the preservation of the land." Orrian nodded, "That is the chief value of all elves: balance and preserving the land and our magics."

"What of elven magic? Does it also use balance and natural energies?"

"That you would have to ask of someone in Ernsari. I can cast only a few spells, the smallest handful most elves can use. Light, Spark, Find Water, and Minor Healing."

"Is Spark similar to the small lights that human children cast?" she asked, remembering the town's children dancing under small sparklers of colored light.

"No, that is an illusion, I believe. Spark is used to start fires and light candles. It can be beneficial when the surrounding wood is too water-logged to be burned easily. With enough concentration, Spark can dry wet items or warm things without catching them on fire. It is a useful skill that all rangers use outside of areas where magic is forbidden."

"You can't do magic in some areas of the elven forest?"

"Magic can attract some monsters, and a few more remote areas can have powerful monsters that protect the vales and caves they inhabit."

"You mentioned that before. Is magic easy to sense?"

"Only for monsters and perhaps those with ward sight, like yourself." Orrian chuckled, "Are you worried about meeting other elves?"

"I dislike not knowing what is coming," she said grimly. "Will I be told I am the daughter of a lost prince or just a typical elf? A distant cousin to royalty or no one of consequence? So many things rest on the test that I can't plan for a future until I know the answer."

"Then take it day by day; as an elf, you have centuries of life to look forward to."

"But you still plan for the years to come, right? If I were a child of the lost prince, then the royal family would be my guardians. They will have some say on where I go and what I do, won't they?"

"There has never been a reincarnated elf among the royal clan. I do not know what they will do. You may be offered more freedom than most children by virtue of your past life's experiences."

"If they see me as a chaos bringer like the envoy, will I be sent away?"

"I doubt that would be the case, but you would still have a home with Anais even then, Kenko. You would not be abandoned. You would have a home among the elves even if I must take you in myself."

"And if they claim I am too young and must stay in Ernsari for training?" Kenko asked, "Would they make me break my contract with Anais?"

"That can only be done with the consent of your master. I doubt she would do so without your approval, no matter the opinion of your new guardians." Orrian huffed. "You worry over impossible possibilities, child. What will happen will happen. Save the fight for the actual battle."

"I like to be prepared," she huffed, "and if I know the worst situation I might find myself in, I can prepare for it."

"For now, prepare for several months in the elven nation; no decision comes together quickly regarding the elves."

"Will the royal clan support me?"

"That depends on how you are viewed. Many will view the fact that you are a reborn human as dangerous. I cannot say how most will treat you, but if you are found to be a member of the royal clan, reincarnated or not, you will be welcomed to our nation."

"And never allowed to leave? Gaelin seemed to think I'd have my brain dissected for information once everyone learns I'm reincarnated."

"I would hope not. Few royals have lived outside the elven nation, but some have worked as rangers or in other positions that took them outside of Ernsari in the past. Many of the royal family have occupations and work for our nation."

"Do any do so now?"

"You would have to ask someone in the royal family. I've never kept up with much gossip about the royal family."

"As long as babies aren't suddenly all being named Kenko," she muttered, waving away his questioning glance. "Ignore that. So, is the royal family treated like a celebrity? They are gossiped about, and people idolize them to an extent?"

"I believe that happens with most nations' royalty, " he said with a shrug. "I have never seen the draw myself; they are simply normal people going about their lives."

"Under massive scrutiny and expectation from those around them." Kenko added, giving him a pointed look, "Will it be a massive scandal if I do happen to be the dead child of the prince's brother? I don't want anyone thinking I would be trying for the throne."

"There will always be people who think the worst of you that can't be helped. You should focus on your studies and decide what path will help you achieve your goals."

"Easier said than done," she snapped before apologizing, "I know you mean well, but everyone I meet seems to want me to be their blunt instrument. Arrowview used me to get money from the elves; the elves will want me to create things from my last life for them, and the mages want me to hunt monsters with Anais probably or teach them any new spells I create. Everyone wants something, and I want to be useful. The gods sent me here to live a simple life. He said I didn't have to fight or kill even though the world was full of danger. I want that to be true."

"You are a crafter, an artificer," he whispered, "that doesn't mean you have to craft weapons for war. You can help the world in other ways."

"All anyone has talked about on this journey is monsters." Kenko pointed out with a sigh, "The knights said the war is tearing Arda apart, and with all the fighters at the border, the monsters are spreading unchecked. Either the war must end, or the monsters must be culled."

"That doesn't have to be a problem you solve, Kenko."

"Right now, I doubt I could even if I was held at gunpoint," she said with a watery smile, "I don't know how to fight a war; I never learned about war or battle in my last life. My world was mostly peaceful, and where I lived, there hadn't been a large war in decades, even longer since there was a battle where I lived."

"That is not your battle, Kenko. No one will force you to fight; it would be allowed if you truly wish to settle somewhere and make children's toys."

"The people I'm meeting are fighting, and I have no idea how to help them. I don't like feeling useless, Orrian," she said, wiping her eyes, "I don't want to lose the people I've just started to become friends with. Everyone I've met so far has dangerous jobs; they protect their land and the people around them, but I can't help. I am too small and weak to do anything to help."

"No," he huffed, pulling her against him. She gave into the tears, her armload of wood tumbling around them. "You are a child, Kenko. Let others take that burden while you learn and grow. You have years of knowledge and experience to gain before such an act would be expected of you."

"Expectations," she muttered with a sniff, digging out a handkerchief to blow her nose.

"If you dislike the expectations placed upon you in Ernsari, you only have to say the word, and I will take you away. If you wish to live a quiet life in a small town, I will make it happen, Kenko."

"You can't promise something like that."

"I was named your personal guard, Kenko. As a potential member of the elven royal family, it is my duty to protect you from all threats. If you demand it, Gaelin and I will take you and leave."

"You don't know if I'm royalty or not."

"You are, in my mind; Gaelin has said the same. I would offer you my oath here and now if you need it to settle your mind," he said, gently drying her face with his handkerchief.

"What oath?"

"Each child of the royal family has a personal guard who is bound to them for life to protect them and assist them however they need it," Orrian said, taking a knee and meeting her eyes. "Will you take my oath, Kenko?"

"No, not until after the testing," she insisted. If the testing shows that I'm part of the royal family, you can take the oath, but I don't want you bound to me for life. You have to have an escape clause or something."

"Very well," he said with a sad smile, "are you ready to return to the camp?"

"Will you tell me more about Ernsari?" she asked as they gathered their fallen wood.

"It is something that an elf must experience for themselves. The magic of our race permeates the forest, and its strength can be felt in the capital so near the sacred sapling."

"And you don't know the prince or royal family enough to tell me anything more," she said, sighing, "Will we be meeting other elves at the border?"

"Yes, we'll exchange horses at the guard post and head in. The going will be much faster on the elven trails."

"Are there any customs I need to be aware of?"

"None that any would expect you to know already," he grinned, "stop worrying, little sprite. What happens will happen, no matter how hard you twist your brain against it."

"I know that, Orrian, I can't help it. I need to plan for the worst potential outcome because the rest will be easy if I can survive that."

"Perhaps you can leave the planning and worst cases for the adults this time. You aren't alone on this journey, sprite."

"Why do you keep calling me Sprite?"

"Have you never seen one? They sing like birds in the mornings, and the dawn chorus differs in the elven forests."

"Are they like fairies? Tiny people with wings?"

"I would not call them people; they are more animal than not and will bite the hand that feeds them as easily as a feral dog if with less damage." he said, leading the way back into camp, "Gaelin, is it your turn to keep the fire tonight?"

"My turn to cook, sadly." The female elf said, wincing, "I did not inherit my mother's skill at the fire."

"I can help if you like," Kenko offered uncertainly. I have some spices we can add to even the stew if you need them."

"It is more that there was little enough to forage that will work in a stew; fiddleheads and mushrooms only do so much. We will be eating hardtack and dried meat tonight."

"Do elves like burdock roots? I know I saw a tree while we were gathering wood, and the roots are good with salt as long as you clean them," she offered, glancing at Orrian, who nodded.

"I'll go harvest some; it will add a bit of crunch to the meal if nothing else." he agreed, striding off in the direction they'd been working.

"I wish I could share some rabbit," Anais said, gesturing to her bowl of deboned meat ready to cook. "I did not take into account enough rations for traveling with three elves, I'm afraid."

"The foraging should be better as we leave the towns behind." Gaelin said, shrugging, "We are used to enduring with only what we can find; our primary concern is keeping the young one healthy, and there is more than enough stew for one."

"Still, I don't like leaving you both hungry," Kenko insisted, glancing over the mostly bare campsite. A thick carpet of pine needles covered the clearing, with only a few hardy evergreen bushes pushing up toward the light.

"We will have more than enough, don't worry. Eat your fill, and we will split the leftover stew between us and soften the hardtack. No one is going to go hungry, Kenko."

"Fine," she murmured, hating how off-balance she felt.

CHAPTER
EIGHTEEN

A TRIO of armor-clad soldiers rode towards them just as they discussed when to camp. A human and a beast-kin wore shining plate armor and carried lances, while a third watched with disdain in mage robes. Their white and blue surcoats, with the royal crest, marked them as knights of the realm.

"Hail traveler!" the bear beast-kin boomed, waving from his massive draft horse-like goat with massive black ram horns.

"Betha, the Poet, and Oak, the Illuminator, what do we owe the presence of such illustrious knights?" Adais asked with a smile, welcoming the approaching pair.

"Hail, Anais!" she said gesturing to the last member of the party, a slim man with dark red hair and a beard, "You probably have not met Sir Gregory Drake."

"I have not," Anais agreed, slightly bowing, "Well met, Sir Drake. This is my apprentice, Kenko."

"A pleasure to meet you," she said, bowing shallowly from her horse, uncertainly watching the other knights as they joined their party.

The broad-shouldered Bearkin and Betha were deep in discussion with Anais about the woods around the elven forest and its dangers while Sir Drake watched everyone with calculating eyes. Betha and

Oak chatted with Orrian easily, seeming not to have any issue with elves, but the mage was clearly not happy to be part of their mixed party.

Kenko kept to herself as they traveled, content to listen to the other knights and learn what she could. Betha and Oak were traveling knights like Anais, but Sir Drake seemed to stay mainly in the capital from the little he'd offered in conversation.

"Hail!" Gaelin called, riding up at a trot, "I've found a good campsite ahead if you are willing. It might be a bit tight as the party has grown, but there is a stream nearby and no sign of any beasts or monsters."

"Sounds good to me," Anais agreed, "is there space enough for sword practice?"

"There is a clearing not far away that can be used." Gaelin nodded, turning without another glance and leading the way back.

"You take the advice of elves rather quickly." Sir Drake said, glancing at the retreating ranger, "Are you willing to put your safety in their hands so readily?"

"They have more knowledge than I do of the land and the monsters that inhabit the elven forests. After all, we will be within their territory in a few days." Anais said amicably, "We will be their guests, and it is only right to allow them some say in the matter since we are escorting a lost elfling back to their lands."

"She does not appear lost to me," he sniffed, giving Kenko a long glance, "What exactly made you choose such a child for your apprentice? You are known in the capital for refusing many other and more accomplished candidates."

"Most of those candidates sought to add my name to their list of titles, the same as paying for a peerage. I have no interest in teaching those who have no interest in learning. Kenko is a quick learner, interested in several practical applications of magic, and has mage sight, a rare gift. I would be hard-pressed to find a more suitable candidate for an apprentice."

"Possibly," he said, changing the topic, "it has been some time since you were in River-deep. Will you be returning this year?"

"In the winter, yes, I still have several assignments to complete, and heading to the elven nation was not on my original itinerary," Anais said, smiling at Kenko that her comment wasn't meant as a slight.

"Has taking an apprentice put you behind?"

"Not enough to matter," Anais murmured, gesturing away the question, "What has been happening in the capital while I've been away? Have the renovations to the mage guild finished?"

Kenko ignored the rest of the conversation as they discussed different nobles and mages they knew and the gossip going around River-deep and the border. Settling herself on her saddle, she tried to pull forward her forest sense without losing her seat or closing her eyes. It was strangely like mage sight, but instead of seeing wards and lines of magic, she saw the echoes of energy and magic every plant and animal possessed.

The forest pulsed gently with green and gold mingled light, and each rider's light was a soft golden hue that pulsed in time with their heartbeat. The beast-kin had a second thread of reddish light, humans a soft blue, and the elves the same color as the forest.

She still couldn't hold the skill long, and magic seemed to spook her horse, even though it was the small magical flame tricks she used while practicing. Kenko assumed the similarity to real fire made the animal react. She was trying to find something safer around the horse that wouldn't get her tossed off or keep her attention away from her surroundings.

While she practiced, they reached the campsite. Separating, everyone started setting up camp, each dealing with tents and horses as needed. Sir Drake and the knights took one side of the clearing while Anais and Kenko took the other. The two elf rangers disappeared into the woods like always; Kenko didn't know when they bothered to sleep, if they did at all.

She still wasn't used to being treated like something precious or worth protecting. The elves saw her as worthy just by being an elf, but she could only hope these two saw her as more after spending weeks following her around. She hated that the elves saw her as worthy, while the humans mostly saw her as something to use to gain power.

Some elves were looking to use her, but they even seemed to accept her without the unease the humans seemed to wear around her constantly. Only the other races lacked that caution. Were humans really that race-centric, or was it caution?

———

The night felt warm, despite the arrival of fall, which had begun to change the color of the leaves. Kenko worked on her carving, carefully infusing magic into every twist and curve of the unusual shape she was creating; she relied on her elvish instincts to guide the wood in the most favorable directions for the magic. The attention of those around her was palpable, causing the soft melody she had been humming to fade away quickly.

"Have you been stationed at the capital, Sir Drake, or the border like so many others?" Anais asked while the others settled about the fire. She could feel the tension in the air, and it was still weeks of travel until they reached the elvish capital, Ernsari.

"Both, but I am mostly at River-deep," he said with a tight smile, "I have little to offer the offensive while the Empire insists on such juvenile tactics. I mainly deal with the merchants' guilds thanks to my powers of appraisal."

"That is a rare skill," Kenko murmured, glancing at Anais before forcing herself to continue, "do you also work on enchantments?"

"Very perceptive," the man sniffed, seeming annoyed that she'd intruded on the conversation, "I appraise most of the items coming and going from the mage college and those assigned to the royal crafter's hall."

"The army and knight orders often commission potions, artifacts, and enchantments for their gear before a long patrol from the crafter's hall." Anais nodded at Kenko, "We must visit and have your skills reassessed once we reach River-deep this winter. It could be useful for you to attend a few classes or shadow an enchanter for the day."

"Is she skilled in enchantments?" Drake asked, raising an eyebrow.

"Her class is magical artificer." Anais smiled when he blinked in shock, "She will need more grounding in enchantments this winter; for now, we are learning wards and more practical applications for traveling and combat."

"That would be prudent considering your general accomplishments, Blue Mage."

"Anais, please." she demurred, giving a gracious smile. Kenko hasn't leveled up to working with more than basic runes at the moment, but I'm sure you will be seeing her about your department in the years to come."

"Perhaps," he huffed, "much depends on the next year and how we repel the empire's forces. However, we should see some relief this winter once the mountain passes are snowed in."

"So you aren't with the faction that believes the war will resolve itself without our nation's interference?"

"Gods, no," Drake snorted, "I believe we will see a full invasion by some point next year; they will have to retreat for the winter, but without a firm border to resell their advances, Arda will be fighting a losing war soon. They have a much larger army and population that is fanatical in their faith, with that very faith prodding them closer and closer to all-out war."

"So that faction's influence isn't spreading? I was worried on my last visit given the number of speeches and flyers being given out on every corner."

"No, thankfully, the royal family and most nobility agree that a simple treaty will not end this. They believe they have the right to control how we live within our borders and how we interact with the other races that live among us. There will be no peace until their religion changes, or we have a mighty enough threat to force them to turn to someone else to threaten."

"Arda is not a military power; even if all the other races and surrounding nations joined us, we may still lose much of the coastline and northern border. We will have to see how the elves deal with the attacks; I've heard rumors that the entire northern wastes are unsafe for travel, and we can no longer keep them off the coastal areas. They have even started attacking our coastal cities up and down the country."

"I haven't heard of any attacks on the elven nation, but we will certainly find out either from the Baron or our elven hosts once we reach Ernsari."

"Sadly, that will have to be done without our band," Drake said with disgust, "the elves have refused us entry to their lands with your party."

"Political maneuvering," Anais sighed, "I always hope to leave such things behind when I leave River-deep, and it never seems to happen."

"If only it were possible," Drake agreed, chuckling. Every level of society has politics, even at a small personal level. We see the more complex aspects thanks to having to deal with local mayors, nobility, and guild masters on a nearly daily basis."

"That is exactly why I prefer to be a Mage of the Realm," Anais said firmly. "Let the guilds handle the local issues while I hunt those they can't handle."

"Is the Baron's land your only stop before the elven nation?" Betha asked, dropping onto a log and groaning, "I'm getting too old to be riding every day."

"Planning to retire?" Oak asked, curling up sadly, making him appear more like a teddy bear than a beast-kin, "You would leave me to some random scrapper from the lists?"

"No one stays on the road forever," Anais huffed, "I'm looking forward to a little downtime now that I have a reason for it. This last year was rough: ten packs of Tur, three Huld, a cave of Enap, and two griffins harassing a town where an idiot tried to steal an egg."

"At least you haven't been hunting water tigers. It took us three months to pin them down." Oak huffed. "We were ready to demand a replacement between that and the Devi."

"Everyone is stretched tight, but they should have sent a squad with you for the Devi." Anais huffed in surprise, "Those ogres are sometimes worse than hydra."

"You never answered the question, Anais." Betha prodded, "Are you planning more stops?"

"No, we will press on to the border as soon as we leave the Baron's land." Anais huffed, "There are simply too many unknowns once we reach the elven forest to tarry too long. What of you, Dante? Are you back to your students?"

"Not a moment too soon, I can assure you. No matter how well I craft my instructions, the apprentice appraisers never keep on schedule with their lessons." he huffed, turning to Kenko with a sharp look, "Well, apprentice Kenko, what can you tell us of the monsters we've discussed?"

"Huld are mountain ogres, often called frost giants for the white and blue furs they wear. Tur are monstrous bulls with red or black hides and are known to breathe smoke and flames when enraged." Kenko said carefully, listing each out, "Enap are gigantic spiders that live in caves and, given enough time, can grow larger than a man. Griffins are half eagle, half lion, and very territorial."

"Is that all? You would do well to work on enhancing your memory, Apprentice." Dante chided her with a scoffing tisk.

"Water tigers are semiaquatic and have tusks or large teeth protruding from their jaws. Devi are horned ogres with multiple heads that grow back if cut off before the heart is pierced." Kenko dutifully recited, fighting the urge to roll her eyes.

"Well said, Apprentice." Oak said smiling, "You are classed as a crafter, are you not? What have you made so far?"

"I've designed a number of things but do not know enough enchanting to complete them yet. Mostly, I am learning to ward insignificant items." she said, pulling out two of the small bird charms she'd finished, "These will keep you warm tonight if you wish to try them."

"Enchanted to soothe the wearer and keep the area close to their skin at a comfortable temperature." Oak hummed, handing the other to Betha, only for Dante to snatch the small tasseled charm and examine it, "Something like these would be welcome to most hunters or even the younger adventurers still learning to protect their camps."

"I like making useful items, but my carving still needs improve-ment." Kenko agreed, pulling out a small figurine and offering it to Betha, "This is charmed to glow softly when held; I thought it might be nice for a child."

"All of these are infused with nature magics," Dante snapped, snatching up the carved horse to examine it as well, "What have you done to the wood?"

"Just smoothing and carving,"

"The wood is infused with elemental magic and all but pulsing in my hand. What did you do? A simple light spell isn't all that was cast on this."

"The child is a natural elven mage," Gaelin said softly, "she will be taught to harness her gifts in the capital."

"Then she cast this unconsciously?" Dante sputtered, turning to Anais, "You are letting her cast spells without supervision?"

"She worked on that piece while we cooked dinner last night. I watched her enchant it and add the light runes." Anais huffed. "She is using elven techniques to smooth the wood by hand. I don't know enough to guide her, but she will receive training when we arrive. For now, I must ask you to return her work. Until someone with elvish abilities reviews it, I don't want it to leave her pack."

"They can't have them?" Kenko asked, annoyed, "I thought it was a human custom to give parting gifts?"

"No apprentice is allowed to gift enchanted items until they have been formally appraised."

———

Kenko *[Level 3]*

    Race: Elf

    Age: 8

    Class: Artificer (Magical) [Level 1]

    Skills:

Regeneration, Skin Deep, Marathon, Archive, Disengagement, Flight, Darkvision, Perception, Meditation

    Magical Skills:

Rune casting (Basic), Ward casting (Basic),

    Additional Skills:

Cooking (Basic), Crafting (Basic), Spell Craft (Basic), Housekeeping (Basic), Design (Intermediate), Organization (Advanced), Magic (Basic), Map Reading (Basic), Woodworking (Basic), Wood Carving (Basic), Drawing (Basic), Calculation (Intermediate), Gathering (Basic), Pathfinding (Intermediate), Plant Identification (Basic), Weaving (Basic), Basket Craft (Basic), Debate (Basic), Eloquence (Basic), Archery (Basic), Sling (Basic), Shield work (Basic), Dagger work (Basic), Riding (Basic), Camping (Basic)

    Titles:

Blessed of Ume

Child of Elvish Clan, Unknown

Known Spells:

    Elvish:

Light, Spark, Find Water, and Minor Healing

    Human:

Illusion, Ward Area,

"GAELIN, what can you tell me about the royal family?" Kenko asked carefully as they went about collecting firewood for the night. Having the knights watching her every move made her hesitant to ask many questions about where they might hear and report back to River-deep.

"I've only seen them during our festivals, Kenko." Gaelin said frowning, "Rangers rarely have a reason to deal with the ruling class. Generally, I am only in Ernsari at the end of the season while the rangers give their reports for the season and a small festival is held. Some rangers never return to Ernsari; they stay in the smaller villages and the wilds, only passing on reports through letters or representatives in the towns."

"Rangers work alone?"

"Only the most advanced among us can do so, but yes, some are more suited to a specific area, and so they are assigned a lifetime watch over the valley or mountain they have been assigned. The rangers on the circuit ride through those areas twice a year. It is simply too dangerous to send anyone to the remote outposts more often."

"But you don't do that; you work in pairs like the rest, right?" she pressed.

"Yes, I do not yet have a permanent partner, but I am rotated through those without or those in need of a larger party until I find someone I work well with. Orrian and I are well suited. I may ask him to consider a partnership if he is willing to take on another assignment with me."

"He prefers to work alone, doesn't he?"

"I was raised in the deep woods by my father. However, he is suited to long silences and spending time far from towns and cities. He was raised in a town not far from the border, but he too sought the quiet stretches of forest to patrol and learn from," she offered, shrugging, "At the same time, we are both drawn to the excitement of battle and protecting the nation from monsters and other threats."

"Do you have other family?"

"Yes, I have a sister and brother who work as craftsmen. My father was sad to see me taking the path of the ranger, but it suited me more than the life of a small village tanner or woodworker. What do you think will suit you?"

"I think I am more of a city elf," Kenko said with a small smile. I love traveling, but it is more about seeing so many new things and learning so much. Once I know enough, I want a quiet place to work and sell my items. Maybe a tiny shop in a mid-sized town or village, but nothing too significant."

"Wait until you see the elven cities. We do not pack close to each other like the humans do. There is more room to breathe and enjoy the space around you than you have known in Arrowview."

"Humans in my last life were the same. Everyone was packed close to each other in the city, and you couldn't go more than a few feet without seeing someone outside hurrying to work or off on errands. It was like a massive ant hill, everyone hurrying here and there."

"You may dislike the human capital, River-deep. While not as tightly packed as you describe, it holds several thousand within its walls and more outside. One of the envoys once described it as having more houses and refuse pits than trees."

"I guess I will find out when Anais returns this winter." Kenko mused, hefting her armload of wood as they started back, "Do the other races have their own kinds of mounts like the Elves? I know Oak uses a riding goat, but does all beast-kin use them?"

"Yes, most horses are flighty for beast-kin. Goats tend to be more willing to allow other races around them. Some of the northern elves also use goats in the high mountains, and those on the plains clans use a deer-like beast called a Pono. The dwarves use a rabbit-like beast; I've only seen one, but I can't tell you much. They keep to their own mountain homes like we do, and the mounts are rarely seen outside their kingdoms."

"What do they use outside then? I know there are several small clans of dwarves in Arrowview."

"Those are the younger members who have left to gain notoriety and fortune outside the clan. The rabbit mounts are supposed to be fast but are easily injured in monster attacks, so few leave their mountain homes."

"You have a deer mount. What is its name?"

"Tarron," Gaelin huffed with a small appreciative smile for her tenacity, "He stayed at the border so that you will meet him soon enough."

"Will I be given a mount when we leave the capital? I know all the attendants with the envoy came in carriages."

"It depends on the reason for traveling, the speed necessary, and who is riding." Gaelin chuckled, pointing to another deadfall from which they could collect branches. "An elven ranger always rides unless they are injured or ill. It is often the same with the guard and those tasked with protecting the civilians in the party."

"Would I be a civilian?" Kenko asked as she started trimming the limbs to a usable length with a small hand ax.

"It depends on the situation, where you are traveling, and if you want those around you to know your status among the elves. Rangers rarely hide our status when we want to be seen. Otherwise, we ride lightly, staying to the unseen routes where few would report word on to anyone of import."

"So the rangers do sometimes work as spies for the crown?"

"No, a select group is chosen for those duties; only the royal family and those of rank would know of them. I have never had such a task; mostly, we are glorified messengers, escorts, and protectors of the wilderness within the elven lands."

"I doubt I would be suited for any of those tasks. I want to craft and bring new things into being."

"There are many ways to do most things, but crafting new items and ideas takes dedication if you wish for anyone to know of your inventions."

"I wouldn't mind people knowing and using them if it made their lives easier or made them happy, but I doubt many would find my crafts useful."

"You have many talents and are still an infant to most elves. You have time to discover your usefulness, Kenko. No one is pressing you to decide about your life, is there?"

"No, but what if the royal family wishes me to study certain things and ignore my crafting?"

"Then you would be welcome to continue to live and travel with your current master. I doubt they will wish to force you into a profession or a certain path of study. You have centuries to discover what you wish to do, Kenko. There is no need to rush."

"I just feel like something is coming, and I must be ready for it," Kenko said, heaving a sigh and accepting the last few branches while Gaelin put away the ax and gathered his bundle of wood.

"Worrying over possibilities is a bad habit to cultivate; you have several hundred years to learn how this world works. Take your time, child."

"I don't think we have as much time as an elf would like." Kenko sighed again, following the older elf back towards camp.

CHAPTER
TWENTY

THEY RODE into Baron Armland's lands the next morning. It was a bare three days of hard riding to the beginning of the elven forest once they reached the next border, but at the pace they were setting, it would take at least a week, along with several more weeks through the forest, to reach the elvish capital, Ernsari.

Kenko suspected they were keeping to the slow pace to allow time to train her in the evenings, but she wouldn't complain. Since they started traveling, she had been learning constantly. Information on every plant or animal they passed and how it could be used, the history of the region or town, the nobility of the area, and random stories from both her master and her guard filled her days.

If there was enough light when they camped, they sparred each morning and evening. The two days it rained, they camped in a deserted barn at a rundown farmstead, waiting out the downpour. The adults taught her new magic and other skills she would need while traveling with Anais.

The knights and Sir Drake often kept to themselves during the training, watching Kenko practice, but once they were all confined to the camp, they joined in teaching her a few minor tricks with a dagger or fists. Sir Drake scoffed at the grappling and violence but taught her to weave actual fire into her lights and burn her targets with flames too intense and persistent to be non-magical. She dropped into her bedroll each evening, exhausted, but it was a satisfied, overextended feeling; she was stretching her abilities and strengthening her muscles.

Many things they pressed on her seemed ridiculous, but she diligently learned to tie knots, climb a tree, and scale down a rope thrown high into the canopy. She at least already knew the basics of fishing, to her guard's relief, as fish was one of the few meats elves ate when other options ran low. Her small carvings improved as well since she continued to practice each night once dinner was over if she wasn't too tired to hold a carving knife safely.

They would reach the Baron's manor that afternoon, and Anais would drill her on courtesies and manners all morning. The knights and elves watched on with amusement, but Sir Drake looked to be about ready to strangle the next person who asked him a senseless question.

"Will the Baron be harsh if I do miss a courtesy he is due?" Kenko asked, fighting to remember the correct forks and bows she'd be expected to use.

"He is one of the more forgiving nobles, so I doubt it will be an issue, but it will mean even more lessons on deportment when you arrive in the capital this winter," Anais said, turning back to Betha and drawing the other knights into a conversation about their recent travels near the elven kingdom.

"What will the elves need? Are their courtesies different?" Kenko asked Orrian, letting her horse slow down to give the others some space to chat; Gaelin was riding slightly behind them since she couldn't scout ahead so close to the manor without possibly angering the baron's guard.

"Stick to the human courtesies for now. None of the elvish nobility will expect you to have learned the greetings and language so quickly."

"Will the envoy have returned by now?"

"Yes, if he traveled swiftly and took the direct route. We are going much slower and not pressing the horses. He will deliver his report to the King; however, my report and your master's will have proceeded him by several days, if not more."

"They won't think bad of me for upsetting the envoy?" she asked, shifting in the saddle to try to ease her aching legs; they were pushing further than they had before to reach the Baron's manor before full dark.

"I expect he will be chastised for his part in upsetting you and your master more than any offense he took from your behavior," Orrian said with a frown. The man had been well aware of his blunders when they left Arrowview.

"Will any other elves take offense that I've upset the elvish envoy?"

"He is not the envoy for all elves, Kenko. He was merely selected to accompany the lost young elflings to the elven nation and deal with any debts they may have incurred outside the forest. Even if you were not a royal clan member, his attitude would have been unjust. He will be removed from his duties and set a more suitable task in the capital."

"Then his clan won't be punished?"

"No, the clan healer and guard performed as they should. We have reported as much to the king in our reports." Gaelin added with a kind smile, urging her horse to meet them, "His clan will not face reprisal from the king; at most, those he placed previously may be reviewed to ensure he was not taking advantage of their situations."

"So they will be waiting for us to arrive," she added with an uncertain frown; she wasn't sure how she felt about visiting the elven forest for the first time. She was an elf, but in her mind, she still saw herself the same as a human as in her first life.

"Come take a look, Kenko. You should be able to see the walls of the Baron's estate over the next rise," Anais called, waving the girl forward as they crested a slight rise.

"Wow," Kenko murmured, standing in her stirrups to try to see clearer.

The manor was on a long plain, with grass and small clusters of trees scattered throughout. However, what drew the eye was the sharp glare of the sun off the glass structures throughout the compound. The manor was farther back from the walls, partially hidden by a screen of cedar-like trees that lined the drive leading toward the main entrance.

. . .

"Welcome to Armland Manor. It is nice to see you again, Madame Mage." A servant called out, waving for them to ride to one side, where several stable hands emerged to take their horses to the stable.

"Nice to see you again, Umo. How has the Baron been recently?"

"The Baron is in high spirits. A new monster arrived a fortnight ago and is settling into its new home."

"He must be ecstatic. Please inform him of our arrival and ask if he is available to dine tonight."

"Of course, my lady." The butler said with a bow, "And the others of your party would be?"

Anais rattled off everyone's titles and names, waving the two rangers forward. "These are rangers from the elven nation assigned to protect my apprentice. Please alert your guard to their presence around the compound."

"I shall do so. If you want to freshen up, you and your apprentice will be housed in your normal wing. I will see to finding rooms for the rest of your party," Umo said, giving a low bow.

"Thank you, Umo, you are as competent as ever." Anais grinned.

"You are most welcome, Madame; Alice will show you the way," he said, gesturing a maid forward to guide them inside.

The manor was opulent but minimalist, and it was elegant in its design to Kenko's more modern sensibilities. Clean lines, a few sculptures, and landscapes adorned the walls, but the baron's wealth mainly was displayed through the high-quality materials of every object in sight. Nothing was extreme like a solid gold knickknack or massive painting of himself; instead, fine velvets and exotic woods were used in the furnishing, and a soft scent of sandalwood drifted through the vast halls.

Kenko followed behind Anais and the maid silently. She'd never been around people with a lot of money, much less anyone with a title. It appeared to be a common theme while traveling with her master. If her testing in the elven capital, Ernsari, showed she had the royal bloodline, then she might never be able to travel easily without a guard or spend time with the upper classes.

She hoped to avoid dealing with politics or currying favor from the other nobility. There was no way she was going to deal with the rich snobs who saw everyone around them as someone to use or abuse to improve their station. Her skill was rare, so hopefully, she would be able to decide on her projects in the future. Only time will tell.

"What has you so quiet?" Anais asked once the maid had been sent away after a promise of a drawn bath and light refreshments for both of them.

"I don't like not understanding things." Kenko huffed, "Where does the Baron sit in everything? I don't understand politics, but he is clearly very wealthy. You've said he treats his tenants fairly, and the farms we passed seemed well cared for."

"What is the main question you have?" Anais pressed when Kenko trailed off.

"What power does he have over matters outside his lands?" Kenko asked, hating that she sounded so hesitant and childish, "Does he hold power in River-deep as well?"

"He is well-liked by many, and while he does not hold any personal connection to the royal family, Baron Armland does hold considerable power over the local councils, regional trade, and economic policies of the area."

"Does he use that to influence the royal family and their decisions?"

"It would depend on the items being discussed; of course, he would try to influence decisions affecting his lands and powers. No noble wishes to see their powers lessened."

"What are his stances on the war and the mixing of the races?"

"As far as I am aware, he is tolerant, given that his lands border the Elven nation. His people do brisk trade with the elves, and much of what is sent to the capital for trade from the region comes through his hands. He would be against restricting such trade or placing restrictions on the elven nation as that would affect his region's prosperity."

"But they don't tolerate the elven rangers to travel his lands? Why were the rangers so careful to stay in sight while we approached the manor?" Kenko asked pensively. It bothered her that so many appeared to tolerate her new race, much less the beast-kin, dwarves, and so many others outside of humanity.

"I believe that is more of a point of courtesy. It is rude to send what could be viewed as spies to another nation and to cross borders illegally without due cause."

"So they are ignoring that they could easily travel through those lands without any notification."

"Yes, it is politics at its finest." Anais agreed with a smile.

"Right," Kenko sighed, "So politics is ignoring reality and pretending it isn't possible to circumvent every protection on a neighboring country to travel through it anonymously at the smallest whim. Only the fact that elves seem to hate leaving their home forest and dealing with humans generally keeps them from infiltrating any place or nation they wished."

"What would be their reason to do so?" Anais asked, settling back into her chair.

"The fact that there are nations and religions that propose the eradication of all races not human?" Kenko said slightly sarcastically, "I would have a permanent watch on the border of their country and the other nations' governments and religious leaders."

"I don't believe the elves function that way as a people or within their government." Anais said, glancing at the younger woman with a frown, "They patrol their borders but have little power outside their nation and lands when it comes down to it."

"Then the elves assume no one would be able to attack their nation?" she asked, becoming concerned. Were the elves that complacent?

"They are extremely long-term planners; unless an attack came without warning and they had only a few scant months to prepare, they could hold their borders indefinitely simply from the innate magics within the forest itself."

"And what of their allies outside of their borders? Would the humans of this territory be granted assistance, or have elven troops fought alongside the humans before?"

"I don't believe the elven nation has ever been attacked in such a manner," Anais said, looking over her apprentice with a slight frown as the maids came in with several small trays and moved to the bathing room to set up the tubs. "Let's unpack and get ready for dinner. We can discuss this later."

"Yes, Master," Kenko said, pressing her frustration down; there was nothing she could do about the situation until she found someone in the elven courts to discuss the matter.

Kenko stayed silent as they worked, moving to unpack her bags in the smaller room she had been given. She gathered a change of clothes and allowed the waiting maids to undress, wash, and massage her with oils while her mind continued to churn. The women cooed over her blue tresses, happily braiding them into an elaborate style they claimed was all the rage in the capital. She only drew the line at the perfumes and makeup they offered beyond a bit of lip stain and color for her cheeks.

The elven nation had not been to war in anyone's recent memory, barring the elves themselves if they had ever suffered from a civil war. She had to assume they had at least one point in the distant past, considering there were splintered groups of elves outside of the central forest nation. She had no idea if they were willing to protect their allies should war come to Arda, but she was willing to bet that most of their forces would stay safe in the elven nation's forests.

Arda was fighting to protect those mixed blood and non-humans within its borders while the elven nation watched on, offering zero support that Kenko could see. Maybe they would get lucky, and the Empire would stick to skirmishes and random attacks on supply caravans.

Either way, she planned to speak with the elves about how they planned to support their neighbors during this crisis because clearly, they saw the issue as resolving itself before they ever needed to set foot outside of their forests, given the lack of patrols or guards along the route towards their nation. It wasn't until they were both eating a light meal that Anais brought up the subject again.

"Kenko, I must ask that you keep your opinions on the state of the Arda kingdom and the Elvish nation to yourself while traveling with others. The Knights are duty-bound to report all mentions of possible security breaches to the proper authorities of the kingdom."

"I understand, and I have no intention of discussing those matters with them; however, I will ask the royal family what they intend to do to protect their allies if the current conflict becomes an all-out war," Kenko said firmly, ignoring Anais's wince in that statement.

"Either way, please wait until after your testing to bring up such things. I don't want your chances for training and education withdrawn because of a curious mind."

"I'll be careful, Anais." Kenko agreed, reassuring the troubled woman that she wouldn't burn her bridges before arriving at the river.

Bathed and changed, they ate a small snack before Anais led her to the library to pass the time until dinner was ready. There was no sight of the others in their party, but Kenko did her best not to worry over them; the elves and knights could take care of themselves.

The baron kept an extensive collection of illustrated works on the monsters of this world, which Anais helped her browse for an hour before they each moved on to something they wanted to read until dinner. Shortly after their arrival, a servant appeared to serve them tea, but they were mostly left alone until another came to call them for dinner.

Kenko assumed you needed numerous servants for such a large estate, but it was strange to suddenly have a maid or butler pop out from behind a tapestry with tea and biscuits on a ready tray. She had dozens of questions about the servants, including whether they were forced to wait behind the tapestries for their master to call them or if they were assigned other duties while everyone else was busy.

The way most of the others treated the servants as invisible rankled Kenko, making her murmur thanks for every action they performed for her. They didn't react to the praise, but she couldn't stop the soft words whenever they helped her. Anais at least seemed to approve of the quiet support of the staff.

They were led to the dining room, one of several. The butler informed them that this was the smaller family room, given that they were the only guests in residence.

"The baron favors our visit by not insisting on a more formal setting." Anais murmured in Kenko's ear, "Do your best and keep an eye on what is discussed during dinner."

"Yes, Master," Kenko murmured internally, wincing at the title she was forced to use; even Anais had insisted it not be used unless they were in a formal setting.

The table could have easily seated thirty or more for what the baron considered a small family dining room. They were shown down one side closer to the head of the table. She noted Orrian standing to one side on guard and assumed Gaelin was outside on patrol.

"Welcome, Anais Gens, the blue mage! It has been too long since you graced me with your presence." The baron boomed in delight, waving them forward without rising from his chair.

"It is an honor, as always, to arrive at your estate, Baron Armland." Anais said, dropping into a formal curtsy, "May I present my apprentice, Kenko. We are on our way to the Elven nation to discover the name of her clan. Kenko, may I present Baron Charles Armland."

"This is the lost elfling? There has been nothing but chatter about it and even the merchants along the border." The Baron said, gesturing for them to be seated, "I did not realize you had taken an apprentice, much less an elfling. This will be the highlight of the season."

"I am sure it will be the talk of River-deep until we can return for the winter sessions." Anais agreed mildly as the first course was brought out.

There was minor shuffling, but Kenko was happy to see her meat-free meals still fairly closely resembled those served to the rest of the table. Not that she would have minded otherwise. Food was food, in the end. Enduring the small, careful bites, ridged posture, and banal conversation was much more challenging.

The rest of the group arrived then; the Baron was delighted to have so many guests at his table. The conversation quickly skewed to what monsters the knights and mages had encountered recently. Kenko nibbled and listened, but most of their discussion had been mentioned once or twice during their travels.

She tried to decide how the seating reflected the person's rank, but she didn't understand enough about the Mages to see why they were placed above the knights at the table. Mage Dante, Knight Betha, and Knight Oak sat across from them on the baron's left-hand side while Anais and she sat on his right. Was Oak further away because of his beast-kin race or because he was technically lower in rank than Betha? It was hard to understand what she mostly deemed stupid social rules of ranks and position among the many races and the nobility.

"I am looking forward to showing Kenko your collection." As the main meal was finally plated and placed before them, Anais said, "I have had her studying the various types of monsters and their traits, but seeing them for yourself is always startling."

"Exactly why I keep them," Baron Armland nodded. I could not go adventuring like many of my ancestors; however, I continue our legacy of providing monsters for research and study. In the winter, I will be moving several new specimens to the academy during the winter sessions. Our youth must understand the dangers we face and the necessity of the adventurers and their guilds."

"There is an exhibit in River-deep as well?" Kenko asked carefully, unsure if she was allowed to ask questions.

"Yes, in the adventurer's academy there," Anais agreed, sipping at her wine, "the mages and knights also use the monsters on display to help train and those that die to further our knowledge of their anatomy. The baron donates his specimens to the guilds to allow their parts to be used for further research on their use and in creating new potions or artifacts."

"In the morning, I will take you on a tour; there are several new species since the last visit, Mage Gens."

"Please, just Anais," the mage huffed, "You know I can no longer claim that name."

"Forgive me; it is hard to separate the young mage I met in my youth from the Blue Mage, Mage of the Realm and custodian of the royal flame." The baron laughed, "I must insist you call me Charles during your stay. We have known each other far too long to bother with such formalities."

"As you wish, Charles. However, I must insist that my apprentice continue using your title. She needs to learn the appropriate use of such formalities and courtesies during our travels."

"Of course," he agreed, waving the matter away as the conversation moved on to other people who had visited recently and news of those they knew in common.

The dinner ran late into the evening, and eventually, Kenko could not hide her yawns. Anais waved her off to bed with indulgent chuckles as the rest of their group moved to the salon for after-dinner drinks. She was excited to see actual monsters the next morning, but the long ride and stress of the day finally caught up with her, and not long after her maids tucked her in, she was asleep.

———

Mounted cases showed stuffed specimens of monsters as they worked their way through the estate to the walled-off garden that housed the zoo. The bestiaries Kenko studied in Arrowview had lacked the scale to prepare her for exactly how large a troll really was. She stumbled forward next to Anais as they were guided past the massive taxidermy, its snarling lips showing off sharp, pointed teeth.

A butler pushed the Baron's wheelchair along at a sedate pace, allowing them time to examine the cases and specimens that lined the hall. Anais had said nothing about the baron's disability, and Kenko had no intention of commenting. She'd spent her adult life as one of the mobile and functional chronic illness sufferers. She had no intention of making the man uncomfortable by staring or implying he was limited because of his body. Until now, she hadn't seen disabilities caused by sickness or genetics, only those that were caused by injury in this world.

"You will notice I have no human-like monsters in my care. While there are some like lesser goblins that spawn from pure magic, there are other races bearing similar features that do not. No speaking race will ever grace my home as a specimen or live its life in a cage if I have my way. Separating our many races and kinds into human and not human is an attempt to treat all others as lesser, and I will not have it done in my presence."

"That is kind of you, Baron Armland." Kenko murmured as they finally reached the outer path to the garden and its inhabitants, "Many of the people I've met feel the same, but some agree with the Empire's views that humanity is the greatest of the races and all others are beneath them."

"I hope you were not treated poorly on your travels?" The baron asked, frowning in concern.

"There were protests in Arrowview but no actual violence, thankfully," Kenko murmured, trying to think of how to change the subject.

"Most of the unrest seems to be coming from the refugees fleeing the war; they have been indoctrinated from their contact with the Empire and cling to those beliefs even in the face of the poverty and violence that awaits them." Oak rumbled as the others joined them, "Have your troops been rotated through the border yet? I wasn't sure if your lands would be exempt, given you hold the border between the mixed-race lands and the elves."

"No, our detachment leaves in another month. They are garrisoned on my southwestern border now and will sail to the closest port before heading on foot. It should shorten the journey by several weeks if the weather holds."

"Here is one specimen you might be interested in, Kenko. Those specific to the elven forests and their mountain counterparts tend towards camouflage and mana-infused abilities. Many more magical species dwell in the forest nation's hidden valleys and remote areas, such as this minor example of a forest ape. They don't show their true strength until threatened and, once killed, revert to their resting state, which you see here."

The molted green and brown ape, long-limbed and clawed, looked nothing more than a large sloth, slow and weak to react to any attack. "They are one of the more commonly known hazards of the forests but thankfully are shy and generally stay away from settlements or human paths."

Outside, carefully laid paths guided them between large enclosures. Each cage or pit was enchanted heavily to keep the animals and monsters inside and humans out. Still, some amount of care was required in placing the plants and structures of each exhibit to show something close to the creature's natural habitat. A horned bear, a noxious deer, and a rhino unicorn, which was as unusual as it sounded, lined one path. At the same time, a fine mesh cage kept the deadly flesh-eating butterflies inside but did nothing to hide the rabbit corpse they were feasting on, making her shudder.

The hornet hyena, a hybrid of insect and canine, was a nightmare-inducing beast. Thankfully, this was a single specimen. They primarily hunted the high plains in small packs, and it was rare to hear of any attack.

Fulgurite are a different matter. The tiger-like beast paced the front of its enclosure, clearly agitated, a cat-like ape with dark orange and black stripes with massive saber-like fangs hissed at them as they passed.

"Unfortunately, I've not had much luck with Fulgurite. The species does not take to captivity well, " the baron mused absently before leading them to the next pit, strangely covered in sheets of metal and showed a thin layer of earth below.

"Where in the world did you find an earth snake?" Anais asked, sounding impressed, "Even the elves refuse to hunt them unless they occupy a mana source."

"I was owed a small debt recently and was offered several earth-type monsters as payment. It probably has cost me beyond the debt to house the snake, but I also received a rock troll that is off being mounted and several vine and herb species your ward may be interested in."

"Elvish forest animals?" Anais asked, glancing at Kenko, who stayed quiet, watching as the strange crystal-like worm tunneled back and forth through the loose soil, a steady grinding of stone and crystal jaws accompanying the never-ending movement.

She understood that keeping these animals meant educating the masses and those who may never see a living monster. However, she could feel the exhaustion and anger burning from the ape, the frustration of the stone worm, and its hunger for actual stone. These animals were not mistreated, but they were not happy or even mildly content. At the first slip of the caretakers, they would attack and escape if they could.

"You may have heard of thorn hounds and vine monkeys. However, a recent new species was discovered in a remote valley," The baron said with a wry smile as his guard showed them to a larger greenhouse-like structure, "They are one of the few monsters to be completely docile as long as they aren't threatened. We can enter without fear."

"They feed on sunlight, rainwater, and the occasional fruit," he said, waving them further into the glass enclosure. A large tree filled most of the space with moss, and finely manicured grass was soft underfoot. A few random bunches of flowers sat near the far wall and around the tree.

A rustle in the branches drew the eye, but Kenko was already stalking the flowers near the base of the tree; with a steady, unflappable gait, a small grey and green capybara sauntered out of the blooms before settling down to nibble a stray leaf with the species usual Zen-like serenity. Bursting from the branches with a crash, something landed on her head and chattered into her ear with frantic cheeps. A grey squirrel hung in her face, patting at her temples in frantic delight; only the near desperate yearning from the beasts stopped her instinctive flinch from having something in her hair.

"Oh my, that is unusual. I don't believe I've ever seen a humming-bird thorn species or, is that a sparrow?" Anais asked in amusement as Kenko held out a hand for the tiny bird that seemed more blossom than an animal to land on while the flying squirrel continued investigating her braided hair.

"They seem quite taken to you." The baron said kindly, like she was a five-year-old playing in the dirt, making her wince as she pulled the squirrel from her hair to examine it.

"They are rather desperate," she muttered, her attention on the animals while the humans looked on in shock. Acting on instinct, she pulled magic from her hands and let the small beasts sip the mana from her hands like dew.

"Are they injured?" The baron asked in surprise, stepping forward only for the squirrel to chatter at him aggressively and even the capybara to trundle over and sit in her lap to block her from moving or being moved.

"They don't have enough magic to survive, your land isn't mana-rich, and they are slowly starving," Kenko said, absently gathering the squirrel to her shoulder and offering the capybara a palm of mana to drink delicately from.

"Would you mind continuing to tend them while you stay? I will have to discuss a possible remedy with the rangers." The baron asked, frowning as he watched the animals. As they watched, a handful of new blooms opened along the capybara's back, tiny purple stars amongst his moss and stone.

"I don't mind tending them, but I'm not sure your land has enough mana for them to survive here. Keeping them in your collections would mean a slow, painful death."

"That would not do. I will have to consider options for their welfare." The baron sighed, "I appreciate your insight into this issue. They rarely come out for more than a moment, so I did not realize how poorly they were faring."

"If you are comfortable traveling with them, can we view a few more enclosures before lunch?"

"The other monsters won't aggravate the thorn beasts?"

"No, at most, their instinct is to flee during an attack, and the entire area is enclosed with warding spells and protections to keep all monsters and beasts as docile as possible."

"It would still be an unnecessary stress for the beasts. Perhaps we can continue after lunch? I wouldn't mind staying here until then." she offered, glancing at Anais, who stepped forward to claim the group's attention.

"Perhaps we can continue the tour and collect my apprentice on the way out?" With a slight bow to the baron, the mage said, "I know you are busy with other affairs of state and duties to your lands, Baron."

"I always have time for my guests; however, you are correct. If that suits you both, we will collect your apprentice on our return."

"Thank you, Duke Armland," Kenko murmured, stoking the capybara with light fingers; she'd expected the armful of thorn beast to be heavy, but he was light as driftwood.

The soft swirl of magic in each thorn beast was a comforting hum against her skin. Thorn beasts were known for protecting lay line crossings and pools of residual magic in old-growth forests. The elven forest was known for them, even if they were often culled for being territorial and sometimes attacking even the rangers who tended to their forests.

Gaelin slipped into view and gave her a small smile, "Orrian is guarding the door. Are they well?"

"Yes, just weak from too little magic. They won't last long here. Do you think the baron will be able to find a new home for them?"

"Perhaps we can offer to bring them to Ernsari? There are several pools of ambient magic nearby that they might like. As long as they aren't combative, the thorn beasts of the elven woods are allowed to do as they wish."

"The baron received them as a gift. He might not want to part with them."

"Only time will tell," Gaelin shrugged, settling into the shade and relaxing, "don't feed them too much magic; they could become dependent on you."

"Are thorn beasts really that dangerous?" Kenko asked, settling the capybara in her lap and pulling the flying squirrel from her braid again.

"These three are too weak to do much, but they embody nature, magic, and all. That is not something to ignore lightly. Nature is as savage as it is kind. A thorn beast will defend its grove to the death."

"A full-grown capybara can attack a jaguar, so I know they are fierce, but how does a hummingbird fight off those threatening their grove?"

"Even the smallest can be fierce." Gaelin chuckled, making Kenko roll her eyes.

"I'm not that small."

"For an elf child, you are small for your age, but many of our kind hit their growth later than most humans."

"What if I'm a mountain elf instead of a forest elf?" Kenko asked, stroking the beast in her hands. The hummingbird started with a barely heard peeping snore, basking in the magic she naturally gave off.

"We don't yet know your full parentage. You may be part mountain elf, but your coloration is pure forest elf. I have never been to the mountain elf clans, so I cannot comment on their looks beyond what I have seen at the great gatherings."

"What exactly is a great gathering?"

"Once a century, all the elven clan leaders are gathered. It alternates between the forest, mountain, and sea elves of the north. You may yet see members of the other clans, but if you stay in Ernsari long enough, the next gathering will be held there."

"I just want a normal life, Gaelin. I want to be a normal elf and learn as much as possible about this world. I didn't come here to become all-powerful or be the elves' next ruler. I want to live the life I never could in my last life."

"We aren't allowed to choose our own destinies, Kenko. You may yet have a normal life, but I doubt a child as special as you will be satisfied with such an existence."

"As all the elves keep pointing out, I have nothing but time to try. I might as well live one normal human life before attempting anything more complicated."

CHAPTER
TWENTY-ONE

TREES TOWERED OVER THEM, old hardwoods and evergreens with trunks big enough that her entire party couldn't span them with their arms. Two days ago, on leaving Baron Armland's estate, the trees started, growing from small pine and oak and slowly expanding; the forest never ended or changed to mark the beginning of the Elven Nation. The forest near the Baron's land was well cultivated and more of a park than a wild space. The elven forest was wild in a way the forests around Arrowview were not.

Wide-spaced massive oaks and other trees reached towards the sky, leaving only a filtered green light to reach below. Kenko tried not to be relieved as the knights waved goodbye and turned back towards Arrowview and the capital beyond. Her forest sense grew each day they came closer to the elven forests. She wasn't sure what was different, but the trees and air seemed to hum with energy.

The feeling of being watched and constantly caressed by magic made her alternately twitchy and so comforted that she rode in a daze. The elven magic shivered along her skin, filling her lungs with every breath, and having the vine animals around at least seemed to ground her. Baron Armland's final decision was to send the animals back with her to the elven forest, where the rangers could decide what must be done with the beasts.

Kenko was struggling with not naming the vine beasts. The hummingbird and flying squirrel refused to be parted from her while the capybara took her to Gaelin, and she was riding happily on the back of her saddle. Orrian didn't seem bothered by none of the animals taking to him; he'd murmured something about cats and continued with his task about the camp the first night they rode away from Armland estate. The knights were uncomfortable around the magical monsters and kept to themselves on the last days of the ride to the elven forests.

Only a guard house marked the end of the mixed races' nations and the start of the elven lands as the road narrowed, continuing past into the distance as the path rose and fell. The elven guard watched as they approached a small pen housing elven deer mounts waiting on their masters.

"Welcome; what business do you have in the Elven Nation?" A molted green and grey-clad elf called out in challenge, stepping forward to block their progress.

"Well met, Ruthan! We are on our way to Ernsari to test this young one for her birth clan," Orrian announced as the others dismounted. Kenko glanced around curiously at the approaching guard, and her forest sense made them seem to glow as they stepped out of the gloom.

Kenko blinked, surprised to see two elves wearing light plate metal armor waiting by the gatehouse; she had only seen it once before with the envoy's party. The elven rangers tended more towards light leather armor with woven and layered leather treated with some compound to make it light, flexible, and hard enough to stop an arrow or sword.

"Who have you brought? I wasn't aware you were out on escort duty." One guard asked suspiciously; only her week of contact with the rangers let her catch the tiny frown he sent towards Anais.

"This is the Blue Mage and her apprentice, Kenko. The child has been lost to the elven nations and will be tested for her parentage."

"Well met, Kenko, child of the wood." Ruthan said briefly before turning to her master, "Would you be willing to leave your charge at the border?"

"I will not, as you should well know. I would not leave any child alone without anyone to stand at her side in an uncomfortable situation. I will be staying until she requests I leave or I am required to return to the capital." Anais said firmly, looking exasperated at the question.

"Your pardon, I must ask," Ruthan said, "some humans do not wish to walk the forest paths no matter their duties."

"I have visited your lands before as an ambassador for the King of Arden. While few humans are comfortable for long among the winding paths, I will not let such a thing deter me."

"As you like," Ruthan agreed, turning back to the other rangers, "Will you be collecting your mounts?"

"Yes, we will also use a spare mount for the child if available. She has never ridden a true elvish mount and should learn to care for one."

"Will they mind the vine beasts?" Kenko asked, pulling the squirrel from her hair, sighing as the beast tried to cling to her braid; the hummingbird twittered at him in agitation, poking its head up from where it was sleeping against her neck, making the ranger break his calm mask to blink, in surprise.

"The child is god-touched," Orrian murmured. Even as the rest of the group dismounted, Kenko doubted Anais could hear the soft murmur.

"Extraordinary," the other ranger murmured, watching Kenko as she stripped the pony of its tack and led it behind the horses the guards used.

A tiny stable, a lean-to, and a round pen of deer watched them with expectant fidgets, hooves scraping the ground. Two forced themselves forward to meet Orrian and Gaelin at the rail, soft chuffs greeting them even as they nosed for reassurance and treats to the woman's laughter.

"Such greedy things," Gaelin said, chuckling before turning to Kenko once she'd placed her pony in a waiting stall; Anais would pick it back up on the way out if Kenko couldn't return with her.

"Come meet my Snowdrop," Gaelin said smiling, guiding the child forward to her pale-colored mount, who eyed the vine beasts uncertainly but allowed the elf child to approach.

The antlered mount snuffed at her offered hand before carefully poking the flying squirrel and giving a snort before returning to her master. They were more like reindeer in shape, large and muscled with heavy, sharp antlers. The ones in the pen mainly were shades of tan, but a smaller grey and white piebald deer nosed through the hay to one side.

"Are they all waiting on their riders?"

"No, we keep one or two at every station, rotating to receive training until they find their match."

"How do you know you've found your mount?"

"You will find out once we reach Ernsari. After your heritage has been confirmed, we will perform several small rituals in the following days, one of which is calling your mount."

"They come to you?"

"Sometimes a young elf will find their mount during an emergency or a time of great stress without the ritual, but most receive their mount during the days following the ritual after their naming day."

"Naming day?"

"That will be explained once you've been accepted into a family."

"Right," Kenko agreed, sighing, petting the squirrel as it patted her cheek in concern.

"Don't worry; even if you aren't who we suspect, you will find your place among us." Gaelin said confidently, "Let us tack up, and we can head out; there is a chance of heavy fog tonight, and we might be delayed in the morning."

"How can you tell?" Anais asked, leaning on the rail to watch as Kenko was shown how the specialized tack was settled onto the waiting Snowdrop.

"On the weather?" Gaelin asked absently, hands automatically checking fastenings and fit. "It is a gift from my clan. We all have some weather sense. It is a useful talent for a ranger, and many of my clan members have that calling."

"So Kenko may need specialized training for the innate talents of her clan?"

"Depending on how strong her gift is, it is possible." Gaelin nodded, finishing up and giving her deer a pat, "Considering her talents with magic, it is suspected her inborn clan gifts will be strong, but she will be tested for those as part of the clan naming ritual."

"Is everything a test?" Kenko asked petulantly; she was tired of being forced to show precisely how worthy she was of another's attention at every turn.

"It will only be this once since you were not born among us. After this, you will be considered a full elf and start learning your true heritage and magic." Orrian said, coming up with his mount, which was already tacked and ready. "Ruthan has offered for you to take Mist. He is still training and without a master."

"Mist," Kenko asked, glancing at the dark-colored deer. Orrian chuckled and led her towards a pale-blonde deer near the edge of the group. The deer was a bit more skittish than the ranger's mounts when presented with the vine beasts, but it seemed willing to tolerate them as long as Kenko was carrying them.

She was instructed on how to pack the lighter saddlebags with her small pile of belongings. On a whim, she left a carving with each station ranger, offering Ruthan a pale purple fish she'd carved from a dried root he took with far too much ceremony as if she was gifting him something precious.

Her instincts and magic still tugged her back and forth, and the gesture felt right. He needed the talisman; if nothing else, it lightened her pack for the new mount. Trell, the other ranger, was much quieter and accepted the offered carving without comment.

Tucking her tools carefully away, Kenko did her best to ignore the soft argument behind her as they exchanged maps and notes on the road to Erisari. She was only days away from meeting possible family and finding a new home among the elves and couldn't focus on anything else.

"She does not know her worth," Ruthan argued, watching as Kenko was tossed into the saddle by Gaelin and walked through the small area, getting used to the motion of the deer.

"It is my duty to keep her safe, Ruthan," Orrian said firmly, "I will not allow her to be used for her strength before she is ready to weld it."

"Good, she will need a champion among the royal family."

"You see it as well."

"Few would miss it that have known the prince and his brother." he sighed, "She is strong but offers herself without the knowledge to protect her fire. Protect her well, Orrian."

"Do you see something?"

"Only shadows, some monumental challenge is coming, and we will need her strength to guide us."

"I will keep watch."

———

Towering trees and the soft colors of magic pulsing at their cores lead the way down the slowly widening road. Kenko expected to see other travelers, but the road was deserted except for the random bird or animal. The hush of the forest should have felt unnatural, but instead, the magic drew her eyes to small hidden features and shapes deep in the trees, watching their progress.

At night, they were housed in small hidden ranger stations, most little more than lean-tos with a small paddock for their mounts and a sealed box of supplies. The last night before they reached Ernsari, she was fed up with the eyes on her and stomped into the tiny cabin, collapsing into a corner and cuddling the squirrel while the others unpacked.

"Getting nervous?" Anais asked in concern, offering her a cup of tea once it was ready.

"Yes, but mostly, I'm tired of all the watchers." she said, leaning around Anais to ask Gaelin, "Why are we being followed?"

"I'm not surprised you noticed," Gaelin said with a chuckle, "the new rangers are often tasked with keeping watch over the road. Few travelers use this path, so they try to be diligent in their duty and follow a bit too closely."

"So this road is only for humans?"

"Only those not fully accepted by the clans take this path. Since you are being escorted and passed the guard without incident, they will keep a loose watch until we reach the city."

"So the elves keep their smaller towns and homes hidden in the forest where outsiders can't reach them?"

"We are a private people," Orrian agreed from where he was tending the fire, "dwarves and other non-humans are often the same.

Arden uniquely allows all races to mix and mingle in their towns and cities."

"You don't discriminate against the other races, however, right? You don't allow them to live amongst you?"

"I can not speak for the entire race as I mostly deal with other ranges. We see more of the other races than those rarely leave the forest homes."

"Does the royal family travel?"

"Some do, many act as ambassadors for the various nations and our own."

"You will have several weeks if not longer, to get to know your clan." Anais reminded her to smile as she took a seat by the fire. "You don't have to make any decisions now."

"I just don't want to be locked in place. I'm finally learning about this world, and I don't want to be forced to study only one area or have the royal clan refuse to let me continue to be your apprentice. I've learned so much in just the last few weeks."

"You are my apprentice. That isn't a bond they can sever easily. I will make it happen if you want to stay or come with me. It will be several weeks before any decision needs to be made; at the latest, we will need to be on the road before the first snow."

"Is that when you are expected back at the capital?"

"Yes, the mage's council holds yearly meetings to review positions and reports. I'm required to attend and to report any changes to the King."

"Do you stay in the capital all winter?'

"I have a small home, but many council members keep rooms at the mage's academy or in the government quarter."

"You could stay in the elven embassy as a ward of the elven nation if you wished."

"No, I would rather stay with you if I had to," Kenko said, sighing. I hate not knowing how anything will turn out. Will I be tested the first day we arrive?"

"I doubt it, and it may take a day or two to arrange the ritual," Anais said, glancing at the rangers.

"She isn't wrong, and the royal family will wish to meet you even if you are simply a lost elf returning to the forest." Orrian nodded in agreement, "Especially considering the reports we have sent of your mistreatment from the ambassador, they will wish to mend any issues you may have suffered at his hands."

"He was rude, not torturing me." Kenko said, huffing in annoyance, "They don't need to mend anything as long as they don't act the same way."

"I hoped there would be a message waiting at the border; however, we were left with no instructions. Tomorrow, I will take you to the palace and present you and your master to the royal steward. They will arrange rooms for you and arrange for a meeting with the royal family and the ritual. Gaelin and I will continue to be your guard until you are confirmed to a clan, and we hand your care over to a new guardian."

"So you won't leave me at the palace?" Kenko asked, hating the tears welling in her eyes; she had grown to know the quiet rangers in the months they trained and traveled together. She would miss them once they were forced to part; they were her first friends in many years.

"One of us will be at your side at all times. Gaelin will watch you within the palace while I watch from a distance; she is much more skilled in the diplomatic arts and royal courtesies."

"Only because you have never bothered to learn," Gaelin scoffed in mock annoyance, making Kenko chuckle wetly as the two elves picked at each other.

The stew was served with bread and slices of sharp cheese warmed on the hearth. Kenko ate hungrily, trying to forget about the next day. Chatting about random things, they finished quickly before laying out the bedrolls for the night.

"What about the vine beasts? Will I be allowed to keep them?" she asked, stroking a finger down the delicate leaves and petals that mimicked feathers on the hummingbird she was absently calling Flit deep within her mind.

"Normally, I would not. However, I hesitate to tell you a possible falsehood." Gaelin said carefully, setting the washed bowls in a stack for the morning, "It will be the King's decision in the end. I know other lost children have kept their pets; however, yours are more unusual than most."

"We simply will have to hope for the best, Kenko." Anais offered, "Don't worry over something that hasn't happened yet."

"Not sure I know how to not." Kenko huffed, dropping onto her bedroll and rolling onto her back, holding the small flying squirrel between her hands and letting him jump from one palm to another and twine between her fingers.

She'd spent too long planning and preparing for every possible emergency her body and health might throw her in her past life. She wasn't sure she knew how to stop trying to anticipate the issues she might encounter. Here, no one saw her as less because of illness or disability, but they also expected more of her now, it seemed. Were healthy people not allowed to have emotional days or take random days to rest?

Everyone needs rest sometimes, but it felt like she had been running nonstop since arriving in this world. Was she still allowed to stop? How would the elves expect her to live? Would they pressure her to continue her headlong charge into life? Only time will tell.

Kenko *[Level 3]*

Race: Elf

Age: 9

Class: Artificer (Magical) [Level 1]

Skills:

Regeneration, Skin Deep, Marathon, Archive, Disengagement, Flight, Darkvision, Perception, Meditation

Magical Skills:

Rune casting (Basic), Ward casting (Basic),

Elven Clan magics

Additional Skills:

Cooking (Basic), Crafting (Basic), Spell Craft (Basic), Housekeeping (Basic), Design (Intermediate), Organization (Advanced), Magic (Basic), Map Reading (Basic), Woodworking (Basic), Wood Carving (Basic), Drawing (Basic), Calculation (Intermediate), Gathering (Basic), Pathfinding (Intermediate), Plant Identification (Basic), Weaving (Basic), Basket Craft (Basic), Debate (Basic), Eloquence (Basic), Archery (Basic), Sling (Basic), Shield work (Basic), Dagger work (Basic), Riding (Basic), Camping (Basic)

Titles:

Blessed of Ume

Child of Elvish Clan, ?

Bonded Animals: Thorn hummingbird, Thorn squirrel

CHAPTER
TWENTY-TWO

THE ALREADY MASSIVE trees were slowly spiraling larger and larger. It was all a bit too manicured, like a park where a gardener was just behind the hedges, waiting to spring forward and rake up every fallen leaf. Kenko hoped other sections of the woods were left more to nature; she could almost feel the spells forcing the trees to grow as the elves willed, making her skin itch.

If this is what the elves showed the world that came to visit, what cage of propriety and ritual would the royal family be locked into? She was afraid to question the rangers too closely in case her questions were reported back when they arrived. It was better to seem a bit naïve than to show her hand too quickly and be chained before she entirely viewed the restrictions.

The sounds of a bustling city slowly filtered through the trees as they finally approached a wide wood and stone gate blocking the road. She eyed the lines of spellwork that flowed within the stone, tried to pay attention to the guards as they were shown a letter, and waved through on their way. A soft groan of oiled hinges on heavy wood heralded the gate opening, giving them their first sight of Ernsari.

A soft green light filtered through the leaves, filling the city. Wooden walkways and sloping ramps led into the canopy far above. However, they passed these by making their slow way through crowded markets and youth running errands, much like in Arrowview. The only difference was that everything was done with stately grace and soft voices. No one shouted or rushed unless it was necessary for their purpose.

Even the children seemed to move with purpose and focused determination. Two using wind magic to keep a kite-like toy in the air had the same blank air that the rangers often presented when in the company of humans. Was it because of Anais, or was she still considered an outsider to everyone they met since she didn't have a clan name?

She decided that the surrounding interactions were missing some subtext, as even the guards on the avenue to the palace didn't react to them at all. The massive tree was surrounded by carefully crafted gardens, streams, and fountains cunningly cut to appear natural. They dismounted and handed off their mounts and luggage to waiting grooms in the open courtyard amongst the tree's roots.

There wasn't anything else she could call it. It was a tree so large it could have housed an entire city within its trunk. The bark and leaves glowed with magic and a soft pulsing light of energy and life. Smooth yet not slick floors of polished wood, lush carpets, and draperies greeted them as they stepped through the first set of massive metal and crystal doors worked into intricate flowers and leaves with hidden animals to tease the eye.

Elves dressed simply in weapon harnesses or sashes to denote their position or employment. She assumed the colors denoted different clans, or perhaps the intricate braids many wore served that purpose; she had so much to learn. There was just too much unknown right now to start asking questions.

What if they insisted she stay with them? What if the royal family insisted she stay because she was reincarnated? What if they took away the thorn beasts? What if she was forced to relinquish her apprenticeship? What if they didn't want her to craft as an artificer?

Just how isolationist were the elves? Would they force her to stay in the forest until she was older? Would they allow her to travel at all?

How would she continue to learn? Would she have elven tutors?

Travel to the capital with Anais or stay in the capital? Would she have to move wherever her clan insisted she lived?

She could only hope for the best and wait for the ritual to be performed. Anais, Gaelin, and Kenko were shown into a small suite of rooms to rest until they were called. She hated waiting; most of her life previously had been waiting for appointments, job interviews, calls back or refusals, and staying in bed for sleep to claim her. It seemed that this life would be much the same.

She let the elves draw baths for each of them and whisk their nice clothes away to be pressed without comment. Her magic felt too unstable today with her nerves to trust it to do the task herself. The thorn squirrel seemed determined not to be parted from her, wrapping himself around her throat like a leafy choker while Flit nested at the end of her braid as a living tie, wings fluttering occasionally.

"Go get cleaned up, child." Gaelin guided her to the steaming tub. "I'll be outside keeping watch and arranging for a meal to be brought, if possible."

"If possible?"

"The royal family may wish you to join them for dinner tonight."

"Is it that late already?" she asked, starting to unbraid her hair, careful not to unseat the animals from their perches.

"We skipped lunch since the city was closer and time can run unusually on the forest paths. We took a bit longer than normal to arrive."

"Does that happen often?"

"It is too varied to say; the forest has a mind of its own at times and will lead an elf where they need to be instead of where they are traveling."

"Then the forest didn't wish us to arrive early?"

"Perhaps we will have to see how events play out. It could have been that the magic was needed elsewhere in the forest, which led to our path changing. We generally only find an explanation after the magics return to balance."

"Did you report the imbalance?"

"The guards at the first gate were already aware. Several rangers traveling with us were sent on before we arrived instead of keeping pace as they intended. Two even tried to retrace their steps only to exit the forest close to the gate."

"And that is normal?" Kenko asked, glancing around the bath.

"It is known to happen," Gaelin shrugged, "don't forget to wash your hair. Try the green soaps. They should suit you."

"Alright," Kenko nodded, forcing down a sigh as the door was shut behind her, and she eyed the steaming stone tub sunk into the floor, "Maybe I don't understand how the elves measure time; what is a few months to someone who lives hundreds of years."

Once she was undressed, Kenko gently settled the two thorn beasts into a towel before slipping into the water with a hum of appreciation. It was just this side of too hot, but all the better for it. The green soaps were soft and foamed in her hand, wafting a pleasant herbal scent as she washed her hair, finger-combing out her braid and tangles as she went. The beasts fussed but waited until she climbed out to clamor to be picked up again.

A maid was settling up a light meal of fruit and tea on the table when she stepped out in a towel, Gaelin watching with hard eyes from a far corner. Kenko ignored them, gathering her waiting clothes and retreating to change.

"Would you like me to fix your hair?" The young elf servant asked, holding up a wooden comb.

"Do you mind thorn beasts? These two are rather attached to me and might get in the way." Kenko asked, showing the hummingbird cupped in one palm while the squirrel peeked from behind her hair.

"It should be fine if you don't mind holding them out of the way?" the maid said gently, smiling with repressed delight at the tiny creatures.

"That will work, thank you." Kenko agreed, settling into the waiting chair and untangling the protesting squirrel from her wet hair.

"Have you had them long?" the maid asked, combing her long hair carefully. Then, using magic, she dried each section by softly pulling out the excess water and adding the small globes to a waiting basin.

"Only a week, but they have become dear to me," Kenko murmured, carefully petting each with gentle fingers.

"How would you like your hair? Most ladies at court are wearing their hair up at the moment."

"Would a crown braid be improper? It is how I normally wear my hair up." Kenko asked, fighting not to fidget as her hair was sectioned for braiding.

"What color ribbons?"

"Gaelin?" Kenko asked, unsure of how to answer without saying too much.

"Keep them to white for now; it would be rude to wear a color tonight while you are still an unnamed child before the royal family."

"Few follow that tradition anymore, but they will look wonderful with your hair color." The maid agreed and started to arrange the girl's hair quickly. A knock on the door had Gaelin hurrying to answer, returning a few moments later with a folded note.

"A note for you, Kenko," she said, offering her the letter as the maid put the finishing touches on her hair.

Waiting to open it until the maid finished, Gaelin guided her out, and she fingered the expensive paper with concern. Anais came in as she forced herself to pry back the wax seal and unfold the thick parchment.

"We received a message?" Anais asked, sitting to one side, resplendent in her blue mage robes and gem-covered belt.

"The prince is requesting a private meeting after dinner."

"Will the king and queen attend?" Gaelin asked with a carefully blank tone, making Kenko glance at her sharply.

"It doesn't say, would it be a problem if they did?"

"It would be seen as acknowledging your suspected parentage if they did. They may not wish to show you favor before your clan is confirmed."

"It isn't acknowledging me publicly."

"The staff would still know, and rumors spread like wildfire, as they say. Most of the nation would know within the week."

"What if I agreed to abdicate any position my birth may afford me?"

"You would lose what little power you have among the elven nobility, and even so, some would still seek to use you to curry favor." Anais said frowning, "You are not in an easy position as a possible bastard of the royal line; however, I doubt you will be cast aside. Elves treat all relatives respectfully, especially children, since they have so few births per generation."

"Don't stress yourself over possibilities, child," Gaelin said, moving to make the girl a plate of sliced fruit. Eat something and rest for a while. We still have a while until we are called for dinner."

"I don't know how not to worry," Kenko said grimacing, picking up a small square to try, "what if they don't want me?"

"The prince wishes to speak with you; that does not sound like rejection to me," Anais pointed out, pouring each cup of tea and taking up her cup. "No matter the outcome, you will always have a place with me should you want it, Kenko."

"Thank you, Anais," Kenko said, wishing she had time to retreat and rest her eyes; it felt like they had been on the road for months instead of a few short weeks.

Curling up small in her chair, she shared a nibble of fruit with the thorn beasts and did her best not to think beyond what she hoped to study in the coming weeks. She needed to see how the local shops made their wares and arrange with Anais for more set lessons while they were stationary. Perhaps every morning would be for magic while she worked on elven knowledge and crafting in the afternoons?

Her hands itched to pull out her carving knife, but the last thing she needed was to arrive disheveled and covered in wood shavings at tonight's dinner. Twirling her fork, she speared another sliver of fruit, trying to decide what the flavor was closest to, not apple and not plum, but it wasn't a berry either.

"Have you decided on names for the beasts?" Gaelin teased, smiling; her capybara happily slept in the stable with her mount.

"I think I need to wait until after the King decides what will be done with them," Kenko said, carefully setting the fruit aside and cuddling the beasts closer.

"But you do have names picked out," Gaelin teased, trying to cheer her up.

"What are you calling the other one?"

"Rin, it means a still pond in the winter." Gaelin said, "I'm hoping he does okay traveling. If not, I may try to have him stay with my father. He could use some company now that we have all left the house."

"Do you have brothers or siblings?"

"All the above," Gaelin snorted, "I was the eldest of three, two girls and one boy. We were all wild growing up, and all went into the rangers; my brother may have been one of our shadows coming in."

"You don't know where they are posted?"

"We write, but it is hard to know where to send messages when constantly moving. My father tries to convince the head ranger to allow us all to be on leave simultaneously, but it rarely happens. Last year, I saw them twice before I had to ship out for the winter."

"Is your father close to the capital?"

"He is a woodworker in a nearby town, not too far but not in the capital itself."

"You should visit him if there is time while we are here."

"Perhaps I will send him a letter; he may want to come to the capital for a meal instead."

"Have you considered what you would like to study while we are in the capital?" Anais asked. They discussed magic and different craft workshops she might like to attend until they were called to dinner.

———

Several hours later, the call for dinner finally came. Kenko was grateful as the conversation went dry, but she struggled in the last hour. The others were concerned for her while she tried to maintain a carefree attitude, but forward movement at least gave her a destination to strive towards, even if it was stressful.

The room was deserted except for a few guards, and the table was much smaller than she'd expected. This was a private dinner, not the formal one she'd prepared for. She was ready to be ignored until after dinner, not analyzed for the entire time.

"Presenting King Taegen, Queen Nimue, and Prince Ivaran of the Royal Clan Valera."

All the elves in the royal family were as beautiful as most elves; they were tall, thin, and athletic even as they aged. The King and Queen could be in their hundreds; however, they would continue to look middle-aged until they reached at least three hundred. Taegen was red-headed, amber-eyed, with freckles across his nose, which wasn't common in elves, perhaps some human blood resurfacing. Nimue was a classic elven beauty of blue eyes and silver blonde hair that would have made movie stars weep, while her son, Ivaran, was of a darker blond, seeming to lean towards his father's coloration.

Kenko would have said that she looked nothing like them, but the prince had the same golden eyes that her father was supposed to have. The same golden eyes that she woke up with at the forest outside of Arrowview.

"Thank you for coming. I am sure you must have questions. Let us have the meal served, and you may ask whatever you require, " the king said, taking a seat at the head of the table with the queen on his right and the prince on his left.

"Please have a seat," the steward said, pulling out a chair for Kenko next to the prince; there was no chance they were hoping to refuse the relationship altogether.

"Thank you," Kenko murmured, nodding slowly, taking a seat as Anais was seated across from her by the queen while Gaelin took up a post next to the door.

The food was served, and she had no idea what many of the dishes were, but fruit, salad, stews, and small slices of fresh bread alongside sauces seemed to be the main staple. She waved away the offer of wine and kept to the water as everyone started eating, wondering who would break the silence first.

"I believe apologies are in order for how you have been treated by our ambassador, child. We received a number of reports of his horrible treatment of you from several members of his clan and others among the guards. He will be removed from his position and investigated for any other children he may have mistreated during his years of service."

"No apologies are necessary," Kenko said carefully, "His actions didn't harm me; however, I am grateful for the investigation into his past conduct in case it harmed others."

"You are very forgiving," the queen noted coolly.

"Perhaps, however, in the end, his actions had little effect on my life, and I am willing to leave it in the past," Kenko said, shrugging.

"Do you have any other questions you wish to ask of us?" the king asked. " No matter your future placement in the clans, you will be a subject of ours, and we wish to see you have an excellent start to your education and life here in the elven nation."

"Many of my questions will have to wait until the testing of my heritage," Kenko said hesitantly, picking at the salad in front of her, "what tests would generally be required to test a new elf's abilities?"

"A magical gift testing can be done if the elf wishes; however, it is not required. Some wish to pursue certain occupations, and those with skills in those areas are often apprenticed to allow the child to gain knowledge of that occupation over a year before deciding on some- thing more long-term. Our race is rather long-lived, and we often take on several subjects to the point of mastery during our lifetimes."

"I am already apprenticed to the Blue Mage. Will this cause issues with my elven education?"

"It should not be a barrier. We will ask that you continue your education, even if you return to the human nation's capital, in time to continue your mage studies. You may wish to study elven magics once you have been released from your apprenticeship. We have no set age for an elf to take an apprenticeship."

"That is good to know," Kenko said, nodding to Anais; she wanted to stay with the mage for now, and that would make things much easier if there were no proper time limit or schedule she was forced to keep.

"The only caveat I can perceive is if you are chosen for the royal clan. We require training in any magical gifts that come with the clan magics to show control before you can leave the forest; however, most gain control in less than a month. You may also wish to stay for a time to learn our history, culture, and courtesies." The queen offered gently as if knowing this wasn't what Kenko wished to hear.

"I can understand wanting magical gifts tested before traveling outside the nation." Anais agreed, "If she is required to stay for a few weeks, this would not cause any issues. I would like to continue to mentor Kenko in her magical education; however, an elven teacher while we are within the elven nation would be appreciated for her gifts. This winter, we are planning to travel to the capital where she would receive continued training in runes, elemental magics, weapons, and other more mundane subjects as we find the need."

"It is three months until the snow makes the roads impassable. If you both are willing to allow us, we can arrange tutors for her needs and quarters for your stay."

"That would be appreciated," Anais agreed, glancing at Kenko, who nodded.

"What do you wish to pursue in your career, Kenko?" Prince Ivaran said with a low tenor, watching her with slightly pained eyes.

"I wish to learn to craft," Kenko said slowly, watching the royal family for their reactions. However, they all wore a careful mask of polite interest. I am learning how to defend myself. However, I dislike fighting and violence. I wish to travel and learn all I can about magic and other nations' inventions."

"You aspire to become a scholar?" Ivaran asked, eyes dark with emotion.

"No, I simply want to understand the best techniques for each project. I want to invent and craft useful items."

"You wish to be of use," the prince said, a knowing, sad smile flitting across his face as if remembering another conversation.

"Exactly, Prince Ivaran," Kenko murmured uncertainly. Had she upset the man?

"Lien was much the same; he was determined to bring progress seen in the other nations back to the elven nation." The queen murmured, sharing a look with her family.

"He crafted many enchanted items, they are in the gallery if you would like to view some of his personal collection." The king added.

"I would enjoy that," Kenko agreed, returning to her meal as the conversation moved on to more straightforward topics. They discussed what Kenko was learning, Anais' lesson plans, and what she believed the child needed to focus on, along with possible subjects and skills she should acquire as was expected of elves to know.

"She will need to learn elvish as well," the queen pointed out to Anais over dessert before Gaelin offered a soft interjection.

"My queen, if I may, the child already speaks high elven; we hoped to use it to speak privately; however, when tested, Kenko spoke it fluently."

"I did?" Kenko asked, blinking in shock, "When was this?"

"The first day after you met the ambassador," Gaelin said, bowing, "we kept to human common afterward since it was more polite to include your instructor when she was present."

"I didn't even realize I was speaking a different language." Kenko said, glancing between the two elves in confusion, "Is that a skill you can gain?"

"A language-based skill?" Anais murmured. "We checked your magical talents in Arrowview but not your full skill list. You may have a hidden skill you haven't discovered yet since you are still young. Sometimes, the gods hide a talent until it becomes useful or is shown not to be useful to the person."

"We have a method listing all skills, even those not normally listed on a person's status. I will speak to the priestess to arrange for the full ceremony." The queen said firmly.

"Thank you, I was considering asking for the same in the capital," Anais said nodding, "at times the human religious temples get annoyed at the mage's council refusing to release a student's skill list and they would certainly be interested in any skill check done on an elvish apprentice mage."

"Are the mage's guild and the healers still having issues in the capital? For a time, it was all anyone could talk about." The prince asked, sipping at his wine.

"Not the last time I was in the city. They continue to monopolize the priesthoods and healing talents, but some students make it to the mage academy and the other guilds."

"So the violence has ceased; that is wonderful news."

"Yes, mostly we have war protests at the moment, but I cannot blame them with the growing violence at the border and the number of refugees fleeing from other countries."

"Yes, those rejecting any that are not human." The king murmured, "It is most distressing to see such beliefs flourishing."

"It is indeed."

KENKO STEPPED into the private meeting room, frowning. None of the royal family had followed her after they had left the dining room. Anais headed up to see to some correspondence while Gaelin prowled the small study, identifying potential dangers. Kenko wasn't sure what to expect from a meeting with the Prince. He could be her uncle, but there was little discussion until after the testing in the coming days.

The steward opened the door, bowed the Queen in with an expansive gesture, and followed behind a maid to set up a small tea set and cups for two. It was clear no one else was going to join them. Gaelin stiffened at the deception, but Kenko settled into a chair without comment. The queen wanted her off balance so she would be more honest in her answers.

Everyone waited as the tea was poured, and the maid and the steward left. Gaelin took a guard position along one wall and performed her trick of becoming one with the woodwork. She was easily ignored by those who could not see magic. Kenko watched and waited. The queen would speak when she was ready.

"No questions?" the woman finally asked, taking up her cup while Kenko ignored it. She had no intention of drinking from a cup that could have been tampered with when the person who arranged this meeting lied to do so for utterly no purpose beyond gaining a perceived advantage.

"You seem disappointed. Should I have acted more childlike?" Kenko asked lightly, wishing she'd dared to bring the thorn beasts to dinner, "I generally dislike being lied to, and a lie simply to deceive or gain an advantage is much the same as any other lie; all they do is bring distrust."

"Sometimes deception is necessary." The queen said gravely, sipping at her tea.

"While true, I doubt today was one of those times." Kenko said bluntly, sighing, "Is it because I am a reincarnated child?"

"Would you consider yourself a child? You have already lived a full life."

"Hardly, I died rather young for a human." Kenko said, swallowing another sigh, "I am not here to take anything from you or your people. If you don't trust me, send me away, and I will get by completely alone."

"No elf child would be abandoned so callously." The queen said flatly, "You will receive the care and training you require no matter your heritage."

"You just said I wasn't a child."

"This world will view you as one." The queen said, sighing and setting her cup aside.

"Perception is rarely the full reality of anything."

"At least you aren't one of those prophesied children," she said, looking over Kenko with tired eyes, "the last elf reincarnation was forced to slay demon-possessed dragons to end the war at the beginning of the last century."

"Is there any way to make sure of that?" Kenko asked, "I'd rather not have that kind of life hanging over me, pressuring me to change."

"You can ask for a divination at the temple, but some consider that to be drawing the god's attention. It could cause a prophecy to be foretold that might have been withheld if you hadn't asked."

"A self-fulfilling prophecy, ask, and you shall receive," she murmured.

"Exactly," the queen sighed, "do not take us as uncaring; we must simply weigh the nation's well-being above that of ourselves and our family's welfare. It is not an easy distinction to keep in balance."

"So you would consider the prince a romantic in his hope that his brother is alive?" Kenko asked carefully, hating that even mentioning the dead prince seemed to age the woman further.

"He wastes resources that could go to his people on a faint hope that we have no proof of," the queen sighed. "He is now insisting you are the proof of his survival. However, the gods had a hand in your creation and reincarnation. You woke to consciousness as a grown child, did you not?"

"Yes, the god Ume said I would be eight years old when I woke. I have no memory of this world before then. I can't say if I was created from nothing or if the god used another body to create mine. I wish I could help but wasn't told anything else."

"I do not blame you, only the circumstances. Tomorrow, the temple has agreed to hold the testing for your blood clan to see if you are compatible with the magic of our clan. If you are willing, I would also like to test your skills and gifts; it will help with your placement should you not be a fit for our magics."

"I have no problem with that," Kenko said, nodding. They might as well get all the testing over with so she could move on. One of the rangers mentioned a ritual to call my bonded mount; would that also be done?"

"No, that is generally done on the child's fifth birthday, so the two grow up together. I will speak with our hunt master about a private rite. It could be done in the next few days if he is willing."

"Thank you. I know I am causing you many problems, and I hope the path is smoother for us both." Kenko said, giving a small seated bow.

"You are a very polite child," the queen noted with a slight frown, "was your family very strict in your last life?"

"I was very ill and seen as something of a burden for much of my life. Even once I moved out on my own, I was expected to repay the money they had lost from my upkeep; it meant I was rather poor and struggling to survive. I honestly doubt they miss me." Kenko offered a shrug, knowing that explaining her former culture would be pointless; she was here to learn a new way to live.

"Do you miss them?" The queen asked after a brief pause.

"At times, they were still my parents, no matter how I was often treated. They gave me a lovely childhood at first, but once I became sick, that was quickly discarded."

"Do you regret your last life?"

"No, I lived it the best I could and still accomplished much for someone so disabled. At least here, I can run and craft as much as I wish and learn all I can manage each day. I am content with that much."

"You truly do not wish to rule?" The woman pressed.

"I have no knowledge of your nation and your laws. I would make a bad ruler of any nation." Kenko scoffed.

"And yet, by acknowledging your faults, you are better than many others who have held the title of king or queen."

"Perhaps in my old age, I would do my best, but not for many years and adventures to come."

"Then you would not turn down the position of heir?"

"Would you be comfortable with your heir traveling with a human mage and learning to craft things with her hands?" Kenko pressed, needing to be sure.

"We elves live a long time. You would bring a fresh perspective to our halls if nothing else. As you said, it would be years before you were asked to serve in such a capacity."

"Are there no others? I thought there were cousins and other members of the clan?"

"I expect you will be marked with a gift seen almost exclusively among our royal line tomorrow; once that is revealed, very few will argue with the posting."

"It can't be that simple."

"You have the royal eyes, much like your father and his brother. He lacks the gift, but his brother carried it in his blood. It was why he was marked as the heir once their testing took place. However, we withheld the results to protect them both from attack. If I am right, you will need training to use your gifts, and there are few, even among the forest elves, with such abilities. You would be sent to the mountain elves to train with their prince, who has a similar ability."

"You are that confident?"

"My lost son burned with an inner magical flame; I can see the same strength in you. You will be a powerful crafter and mage in the years to come. As long as you are committed to assisting our people, I have no qualms about claiming you after tomorrow's ritual."

"Even if I'm a reincarnated elf? I wasn't born the normal way your sons were."

"You still had parents and a childhood before you became what you are. Do you have regrets from your first life?"

"Of course," Kenko said blankly, unsure what the woman was asking.

"Good; ensure that you do better within this new life. If you made no progress in your second life, it would be a waste of a long life and a lifetime to learn."

Kenko agreed, giving a determined nod; there wasn't much point in this second life if she didn't manage to craft a better life than her last.

"I will arrange a meeting with the prince after you complete the ritual."

"Of course, there is no reason to get his hopes up or to become attached when I might not even be related to the royal clan."

"I'm glad you are more logical than your possible uncle," the queen sighed, standing and gathering her skirts. "I will arrange a meeting with the family after the testing. Perhaps a late lunch will suffice; we can discuss matters further once all our trees are grown."

"An elvish idiom?"

"We are a race connected to nature at our heart," the queen said, a rare smile making her glow as she waved for the door to open. Once you are confirmed as our heir, you will be taken to see the Tree. You will understand then."

Kenko watched the queen leave, retaking her seat. Tomorrow, she would be tested for the royal inheritance, the royal clan's magics, and her complete skills and abilities, and she would find out if a prophecy were attached to her rebirth. It was going to be a busy enough day without adding meeting a new family on top of everything.

"Are you alright, Kenko?" Gaelin asked, returning to her side and kneeling next to the chair.

"Is there a quiet garden or balcony I can sit at for a while?"

"Give me a moment to speak to one of the guards. I'm sure we can find somewhere quiet."

"Thank you, Gaelin," Kenko stood and paced while the guard went back out for a moment.

Ten minutes later, she was pacing a small garden and fountain built stories above the ground from massive woven branches. The paved stones in the courtyard were even, and everything was far too perfect. She longed for the regular forests she'd been traveling through for the last month. Kenko had a slight sense that she should be worried about the height from the ground, but whatever elven instincts were driving her left her surefooted and ignored the long drop off the edge hidden behind a screen of ornamental trees.

"Would it help to talk?" Gaelin asked tentatively after she'd been pacing for nearly an hour without a pause.

"I'm not even sure where to start." Kenko huffed, dropping to sit on the grass to one side, "I need to let Anais know about my reincarnation eventually, but I want to wait until after the testing. What if my magic is too out of control, and I must stay with the elves longer? What if I am a member of the royal clan and the other possible heirs are against my appointment? What if my magic isn't the same as the clan, and I need to find different teachers?"

"You don't need to worry about teachers for your magic. The royal family will see you placed with a clan and teachers if you aren't a member. Even if you don't have the clan magics, you could still be the daughter of the lost prince and be a member of the clan. All of that will be sorted after your testing. Try not to worry about it now."

"What will the royal family expect of me? The queen seemed to think there would be little I would need to do beyond learning the basic courtesies, but I still know so little about this world and its people."

"You have a lifetime to learn, Kenko. You are thinking like a human. You have centuries to catch up on the things you might have missed in not growing up as an elf."

"Would you want to stay?"

"Here in the palace?"

"I don't feel comfortable here. The forest is nothing like staying here. The town was nothing like this. Even staying with the baron wasn't like this. I don't know how to deal with servants or people treating me differently because of my birth. I wasn't anyone in my last life."

"I would say cling to that; the more down to earth you are to those around you, the easier you will have with those below your station. You only need to bow to the King and Queen or royalty from other kingdoms. You can be polite and still be yourself."

"You think I am the daughter of Prince Lien," she murmured, watching him tiredly; it would make sense in some twisted way that the gods forced her into a birthright she would never have claimed willingly but simply withholding the information even to know enough to ask.

"During the journey, I felt your magic. Those of us who served the prince as a child still remember how he charmed animals or called for rain with a song. It isn't something that can be taught; only those of the royal bloodline can sing the trees to awakening, sing the wind calm, or call a hurricane. You are a member of the royal clan, no matter what your lineage is shown to be."

"And if I decide to leave?"

"Then we will walk together through the world for a time. I would not mind traveling afar again if it meant keeping the royal bloodline of Prince Lien safe until such time as you have an heir or wish to take up your mantle."

"And if I never become queen?"

"Then I will have served at the feet of one who might have been, and that is enough."

———

Kenko went through the ritual bath, changing into white silken robes, fighting to keep her nerves calm, and could only hope the thorn beasts weren't destroying her rooms while she was gone. They seemed to pick up on her mood and act accordingly if she was scared or nervous. They had someone destroy a door with magic at the baron's manor to get to her when she had a nightmare.

The acolyte guided her to the altar, where the priestess waited once she was dressed in the thin white robe and veil. The hallway was carved from some dark crystal-streaked stone, making her feel like she was walking to her own sacrifice as she padded barefoot down the empty, echoing halls into the temple. Buried underneath the great tree, the temple walls glittered with rich embroideries and gems; however, the floor was left unadorned except for the wandering roots that dug through the walls, ceiling, and floor, wandering where they would.

Prince Ivaran and Anais waited nearby, representing those who supported her claim to the royal bloodline, while royal guards lined the walls. The lack of guards she knew was grating after having a personal guard for the last two months of travel. The king and queen waited at the back of the room, and they wouldn't acknowledge her until her bloodlines were confirmed. The ceremony itself was simple: holding a crystal orb while praying to the gods, the orb extracted magic, and a small amount of blood was then offered to test her heritage.

"Accept this wandering lost child as a child of your light. Accept this wandering child as one of our own." The priest chanted, devolving into the more formal tongue of elvish that she was still learning and droning on in what she assumed were prayers for several minutes.

"Accept this orb and present your magic to the tree," the priest said with the annoyed voice of someone repeating himself as he pressed a crystal orb into her hands. Kenko pressed magic into the orb in a steady flow until it pulsed with an inner light.

The priest accepted the glowing orb, pressing it into a slot on the altar, the entire thing carved from a root of the great tree and polished to a lacquered shine. A wooden card underneath glowed, blazing her stats, skills, and titles into it with a flash. This was a formality reconfirming her current titles, status, and class. She would have instead done this outside while wearing more than a glorified silk bathrobe.

Next was the test to confirm that her clan magics and birthright aligned with the royal clan. The prince, her potential new father, stepped forward as a priest offered a bowl and several drops of blood. The small wound quickly healed with magic while the priest emptied several potions into the bowl and waved Kenko forward to add her blood.

Pouring the bowl's contents across a small sapling's root, the priest set the bowl aside and cast a long enchantment over the tiny tree. The small trunk seemed to pulse with life, leaves glowing as the small stem shot up several inches and new leaves began to unfurl. The priest gashed the primary root, making her bite back a gasp at the pain the action seemed to cause in her chest, catching a thin stream of glowing red liquid in a wooden cup.

"Now the test begins, kneel supplicant and pray to the gods." The man intoned, handing Kenko the cup. "Drink and dream of the tree so you might be guided on your journey."

Kenko drained the cup of sweet sap and handed it back, settling onto her heels on the cold floor as the rest of the room silently filed out. She would be locked in, expected to meditate on the powers that be until morning. The prince clutching her status plate made it evident that it already showed her elven clan name, but she would follow the rules. The only issue was who she was supposed to pray to.

Ume had brought her to this world so he would receive her first prayer. After all, he was the god of reincarnation, and she owed him for this second chance at life. The sap clung cloying to her throat like cough medicine, exhaustion tugging at her even as she fought to recite the handful of prayers she knew.

Waking in a fog-filled room, she glanced around before the massive tree in the distance drew her forward like a beacon. She could feel the magic pulling at her, demanding her attention as she walked. At the base of the massive oak tree sat a dozen beings having tea from crystal cups while the fog shifted and filtered around them. Voices rang and moved with the mist, only becoming apparent as she neared the table.

"*We shouldn't meddle with such things; the races do much better when left alone.*" One woman said softly, golden hair trailing along the back of her chair, voice echoing like bells in a distant church.

"*Something must be done to shift the tides of fanaticism before the balance is lost.*" A man murmured, cloaked in dark blue robes that shifted and swayed about his body. Kenko drifted closer, trying to see who was speaking, but each figure wore a mask or shifted constantly so she couldn't see.

"*The balance must be upheld.*" Another agreed, features hidden behind a heavy metal mask, dark shadow-like robes shifting and stirring in the light breeze.

"*We do not mettle in the affairs of mortals. We are in agreement that the balance is tipping, but surely the conflicts will end before it endangers magic itself?*"

"*And if it does not? The winds speak of death and abandonment of the traditions we have guided and blessed. Even those of the classes are being abandoned, and only the strong are left to survive. An entire generation with no magic to offer to the land.*"

"*We are already meddling by bringing the new souls to our lands. How is offering more guidance wrong?*" An armor-clad being asked, shifting in his chair, voice like grating steel.

"*New souls bring creation and innovation to the world. Are you saying we should abandon those that have worshiped us since time immoral?*"

"*We will not abandon those who have faith in us.*" The first being stated, making the others murmur in agreement.

"*Even those who do not pray or believe in us are still under our domain and deserve our protection, as does the world.*"

"*How can we protect the world when the races refuse to live together, and entire kingdoms call for the death of other races? There is no balance in this.*"

"*There must be balance, or they will destroy themselves.*" The one with the metal mask said, voice pressing at Kenko like a buffet of wind.

"*Some still cling to tradition and continue to pray.*"

"*Clinging to the point of imbalance, they learn nothing new.*" The masked being rumbled, making the armored man slam his fist down.

"Then let the new bring forth the balance, those we have gifted new lives and abilities. Let them pay for their gifts." The warrior snapped flames dancing along his cape.

"They come from a world of burden and pain; to burden them further with the problems of a new world is unbalanced, " the masked being said, simply making Kenko stop as he seemed to meet her eyes.

"Someone must,"

"Let them choose." The masked being said, watching her with haunted eyes; somehow, she knew the man was crying as he spoke, *"Let the prophecy be spoken and let them choose to maintain the balance of the world or leave it be."*

"What prophecy?" Kenko demanded, trying to step forward only to fall to her knees as the deities before her departed, only the metal-masked god continuing to watch her with sad eyes.

"You are not yet strong enough. Grow and find the other who walked across worlds to find a new life. You must choose to rebalance the world or to stand and watch as it falls."

"Who is the other? Someone reincarnated?"

"The reborn brother and sister shall stand on the edge of time and weave fate onto a new path. The path is yours to choose."

"Who is the brother?!" Kenko shouted as the table receded into the mists, "What am I supposed to do? Where do I find him?"

Kenko sat up with a gasp, scrambling to her feet on the cold stone floor. The tree's roots glowed with magic, filling the room with harsh pressure and light. She was drowning in magic. The tiny sapling filled the air with the scent of its blooms as it steadily grew, roots covering the altar and branches spiraling towards the ceiling. All she could see or feel was the magic, more and more filling her with every breath.

CHAPTER
TWENTY-FOUR

KENKO WANDERED THE PARTY, trying to keep the smile from falling from her lips. The room swirled with mingling elves and elven nobility, whom she was expected to meet and ingratiate herself before her formal introduction as part of the royal family. So far, it wasn't going well.

She ignored the glare from one of the priests as she passed. Destroying a sacred altar was frowned upon, even though it showed her power and nicely confirmed her bloodlines. The royal family was all linked directly to the great tree per their magic, in some convoluted fashion she didn't fully understand.

The prophecy from her vision just made things worse. She hadn't spoken about it with anyone yet, and even knowing the gods were real and inclined to meddle in this world hadn't suddenly prepared her to become an object of their interest. She wasn't anything special.

Only the final line gave her any relief. She might have been chosen; however, she wouldn't be forced to act. She and the other reincarnated boy could select if they helped turn the war and restore magic to the world that had been gifted to them.

It just felt too big and overwhelming even to contemplate. How did anyone stop a war when it was just her and a boy she knew nothing about? How was she even supposed to find him?

Once officially announced as the next in line to the throne, she would be gifted her own royal guard. For now, members of the guard swapped out with Gaelin and Orrian. Once her new guard started working, she would miss her two protectors. In the months they'd lived and traveled together, she'd come to count the two elven rangers as friends.

She would begin lessons on living as an elf at the start of the next ten days. All the small lessons an elf child would learn would be condensed and given to her rapidly for the next several years until she was deemed competent in each area. Learning elven history, elven noble bloodlines and who was who, how to ride an elven deer mount and calling her own. She would learn the expected etiquette for those in line for the throne and lessons in elven and human magic.

Anais would stay through the fall, and then Kenko would be alone in the elven forest for the rest of the year until she was seen of age or too proficient to need a master. It would be several years before she could travel outside the nation to other lands. Her only respite would be the yearly visits from her master until she was about to join her at the college.

She could only hope the mage's college in the human capital moved faster than the elves. Very little seemed to be rushed when it came to elves, and after a lifetime of information at her fingertips, being constantly put off was starting to get annoying.

"You must be the new bastard that arrived hoping to steal an inheritance." An older elf with pure white hair sneered behind her, interrupting her musings.

"My name is Kenko," she said, turning and facing the elf behind her with a sigh; for a race meant to be long-lived and wise, the population seemed determined to get on her nerves. "Was there something you needed?"

"Just attempting to understand the perpetual need of half-bloods to try and ingratiate themselves to the monarchy in hopes of proving a distant relative. One pops up every few decades. It is truly tiring. I don't know how the king and queen are still so willing to deal with such usurpers."

"Funny, but no one has bothered to ask me about what I want in this entire fiasco," Kenko murmured tiredly, trying to ignore the tugging of the bonds between her and the thorn beasts. They had become extra protective since the night of the ritual, and she suspected the influx of magic influenced them in more ways than she knew of so far.

"Coming to take what you can get from a royal inheritance?" The elf sneered, making Kenko glance over the thin elf with a sigh. He was as pretty as any other elf she'd seen, but the interior did not match.

"I am sorry, but have we been introduced?" Kenko asked, starting to get annoyed.

"Why would I want to introduce myself to someone here hoping to steal from those in power? You are nothing to those of us raised on elven lands."

"And yet you are telling a child to give up and go home." Kenko muttered, "I don't want anything from the elves. I wanted to be an artificer and work as an adventurer in the guild. I don't want to fight or deal in politics. I want to craft and be left to live my life as a useful member of society. I apologize if such a small aspiration is beneath you."

"Watch your tongue, heathen!"

"You are the one who approached me, sir," Kenko said with a heavy sigh, turning and heading towards the garden doors. Behind her, the man sputtered, complaining to anyone who passed about how rude the half-blooded child was.

"Where are you two hiding now?" Kenko asked, wandering the garden, doing her best to ignore the guards that moved as she sat by a magically sculpted tree, the trunk marked with rune-like swirls.

"I still need to name you two," she sighed as the hummingbird whirled out of a low hedge with the squirrel not a moment behind. At least the guards were getting used to the constant motion of the animals and Kenko's care for them each day requiring her to take them outside at several points, not that she minded that; she was getting tired of the constant study the tutors she'd been assigned required.

Cupping the hummingbird in one hand, she looked over the preening thorn beast with a smile, "What about Dori for you?"

The squirrel was too busy with a nut to care as she stroked the fragile leaf-like feathers of the beast. "You would be Risu on my old world," she told the squirrel, who chittered at her in response, sprinting up her leg and settling on her shoulder to continue the perusal of his nut.

For all that she was supposed to be learning about her family, she felt very disconnected from the elves. This wasn't her world, life, or heritage, really. She was some impostor forced upon them with no chance of much good coming of it if she followed the path of the other reincarnations before hers.

Was it worth learning about her heritage when it wasn't hers? Even the royal family had kept their distance since the night of testing, leaving her unsure of her genuine welcome. She needed something to do, she decided, pulling up her status screen. She was still only a level one artificer, and that was something she could work on.

Settling the hummingbird into her hair as it liked, she let herself drop into the light meditation Anais had drilled into her in their lessons on magic. She needed a framework, a simple spell that did something easy but noticeable. Light was standard, and she'd already charmed small rocks to glow when needed, so something different was required.

With a slight grin tugging her lips, she leaned down and picked up a smooth pebble from the path. She let the magic pool in her palm and guided the looping lines of the elvish rune onto the stone, humming to herself as the magic shifted and stirred around her. The natural flows of magic in elven lands lent themselves to this kind of magic. Being so near the great tree amplified most spell work, leading to the firm belief that the elven forest protected those within it and naturally augmented spells the forest and magic itself approved of.

Singing softly, she crooned to the stone, nuzzling her sleepy thorn beasts as they nestled against her, curled in the collar of her tunic. As she pressed the simple song into the stone, she didn't notice the trees around her pulsing with magic and unfurling early blooms.

"Princess Kenko," a guard murmured, breaking her concentration; with a shiver, the stone cracked, sound escaping in a sharp burst of magic.

Kenko eyed the broken stone, fighting back tears. Nothing was going right today. "What do you need, guard?" she asked with a sigh, pocketing the shards of stone.

"Your personal guard has been assembled in your quarters. The Prince wishes to speak with you there."

"Thank you," Kenko murmured, standing and biting off another sigh; her rooms were changed after the tests, and she now had a suite in the royal wing of the palace.

Four guards waited for her in her sitting room while her uncle, Prince Ivaran, set his tea aside and stood as she entered. She gave Orrian and Gaelin a small smile as she passed them; at least they were still here to watch her back until her new guard was comfortable and on the latest schedule.

"Thank you for coming, niece. I hope the gathering was going well?" Prince Ivaran said, settling back into his chair and waving her towards the one beside him.

"Yes, I wondered when I didn't see you." Kenko agreed with a sigh; the prince was allowed to get out of most of the parties as he arranged events on the backend for her debut into elven society.

"Once you are formally announced and have your debut, things should start looking up for you. Parties and events will be open to you, and you can attend the academy here or apply for apprenticeships once your first year of training is complete."

"And my apprenticeship with Anais?"

"She has agreed to hold the apprenticeship until you can join her at the human magical college." The prince sighed; they had already had several arguments over the suspension of her apprenticeship with the mage. Elven children didn't take up an apprenticeship until they were in their twenties, if not older, and fifteen was the lowest the Prince was willing to compromise.

She turned nine only a few weeks ago, and it would be six years before she could travel outside the Elven nation. Elves weren't considered adult until they were in their fifties or older, most not leaving the home until they completed their first mastery.

"Was there another reason you wished to speak with me?"

"Yes," the prince said, gesturing the waiting guard forward. Your current guard has petitioned to remain at your side as part of your guard. Are you willing to continue their service?"

"I thought you both wanted to return to your quiet ranger patrols in the forest?" Kenko asked, hoping they weren't pressured to accept the position.

"We have time to return to the forest, and the forest will be waiting should we take longer than planned," Orrian said with a slight grin while Gaelin nodded firmly.

"We wish to guard your path for as long as you allow it," Gaelin said, nodding to the other two guards. We worked with Ruith and Amra during our apprenticeships, and they will serve you well. They have previously worked outside the kingdom and are accustomed to working with the other races as necessary."

The two elves, both women, were older than her regular guards and might match the prince in age if she was honest. Both looked to be in their late thirties to early forties if they were human, but given how slowly elves aged, they probably were at least two hundred years old, if not more.

"We are honored to serve in your guard, my lady," Ruith said with a short bow that Amra mirrored.

"Have you served the royal family before?" Kenko asked

"I served under Lady Sael until she passed this last winter here in the palace," Amra said, her pale golden hair braided intricately to keep it out of the way while blue eyes gave her an almost absent look that made others underestimate her.

"I have served under several of the royal lines; however, recently, I have worked as a general guard in the palace," Ruith murmured, falling into the still, silent stance all the palace guards took; her light brown hair was highlighted with a pale green reflected in her leaf green eyes.

"Thank you for joining my guard. I will depend on you as I adjust to the palace and elven society."

"Lady Sael requested reports each morning on the state of the palace and the rumors flowing about the court. Would you wish the same?" Amra asked, glancing at the other guards.

"Yes, it would be good to know more about the state of the palace and the other nobles." Kenko agreed with a sigh, "I have minimal experience dealing with those in the courts. Before now, I was simply an orphan who worked to make my way through life. I will work to learn all I can in the coming years and need all the guidance you can provide."

Ruith seemed about to say something before subsiding making Kenko suppress a small surge of annoyance, "You may both speak as needed while we are in my rooms. I have no wish to curb your tongues when the question or advice might be needed."

"The palace is rife with rumors of a bastard child who has proven their blood relation to the prince. Is this true?"

"I am Prince Ivaran's niece," Kenko said with a sigh. My father was Prince Lien; however, I didn't know him or my mother."

"There is a small ceremonial binding that is performed for your guard. That will be done in the morning, my lady." Orrian nodded, catching her eye. Until the guard was bound, she would have to keep her true origins to herself.

"What skills can you bring to the guard? The prince and queen wish me to stay in the capital for more training and education. I will also be presented to society soon."

"You will have little time to yourself if you are taking the standard lessons of a noble child; most study several instruments, dance, archery, magic, dictation, go on hunts with the other nobles their age, and attend many dances and events in the evenings throughout the year." Ruith said, looking concerned, "Have you arranged for tutors and your maids yet?"

"The queen has offered to arrange my tutors, and I wished to hire my guard before looking for more staff." Kenko said with a slight wince, "You will have rooms in my suite assigned to you and whatever additional items you require for your duties provided."

"You speak well for your age," Amra murmured, "The rumors circulating about the lost princess are broad; however, most appear to assume you are older than ten."

"Then they will have to live with disappointment after the formal introduction to the courts." Kenko sighed, "Now that we have met, you have the evening to consider your positions and see if you require changes. In the morning, we will hold the bonding ceremony and assign duties as necessary to fill out the rotations with the other royal guards."

As the guards filed out, she tried not to slump in exhaustion. She hated feeling so out of her depth. Kenko had no idea how to deal with royalty and nobility. Look at tonight's disaster; she'd insulted an elder elf and left the party to sit with her pets. I was still a socially awkward introvert, even in a new world.

She could only hope the lessons sorted out her social issues. Hiring new staff and finding guards to watch her back was unreal. How would she be expected to act now that she was technically rich and royalty?

In her last life, she'd been riding the edge of poverty her entire life. Medical bills and fighting to work while ill, constantly being behind on payments thanks to low wages and unemployment after too many absences. She didn't know how not to be working on something. Now that she was healthy, she wanted to plow ahead at top speed while everyone around her told her to take her time.

Three hundred years of life at the minimum for an elf was mind-boggling. There were hundreds of things she could learn and study in just that amount of time, and if she was lucky, she might live even longer. Kenko wanted to do everything, but everyone around her seemed determined to delay her.

Ducking into her bedroom, she changed out of her party frock into something more comfortable. Gaelin had worked out with the royal guards to allow Kenko onto the training grounds to practice her weapons. Maybe she could talk a guard into going on a long run tomorrow. She returned to the outer rooms and settled by the windows to read while the thorn beasts played outside.

Their bond continued to grow, and the low pulse of the beasts' amusement and energy was infectious, making her smile as they darted about. Orrian settled to the other side of the door so the light wouldn't hurt his view of the door to the palace. Pulling her latest project into her lap, she adjusted the fall of yarn and started knitting steadily, pausing only to turn to the next page of her book.

"What exactly have you reading so avidly?" Orrian asked when, several hours later, the thorn beasts were asleep at her side on pillows, and she was several feet into the hooded wrap she was making.

"Did you know this world has prophecies?" Kenko asked carefully, "I met the god Ume when I was reincarnated, but I didn't realize they were still so active in this world."

"The gods have not abandoned their children. Is your world so isolated from its creators?"

"If they are, we don't know," she said with a shrug, "I never saw their influence, and we don't have magic or monsters like this world. Maybe they still act in the background, but the belief in our gods is very low for many. I prayed as a child, but it seemed useless when there was nothing it could do to improve my life with how sick I was."

"The gods are much more involved here," Orrian said slowly, watching her quietly, making her feel like an infant. The elves worship magic itself, so we are outliers of most races. Those who devote themselves to a god's path are guaranteed blessings and extraordinary gifts should they prove themselves; however, many die in the pursuit of such power, and most avoid quests given by the gods. They often lead to more pain and struggle than most are willing to cope with."

"Such quests are rare, however, reserved for heroes and those the gods see great things in their futures."

"Elves are given prophecies, however?"

"Yes, however, prophecies are often not understood until after they happen. In elves, we record prophecies but do not believe in trying to change or force an outcome. What will happen will happen with or without our efforts."

"So you just let it happen? What if it isn't a good thing?" she pressed, leaning forward and catching the other man's hand.

"Prophecies are rarely welcome things." Orrian said, watching her with a sharp gaze but not taking his hand back, "Fighting the gods or the flow of time and magic as we believe guides our actions is the path of madness for an elf. To step outside nature's natural flow is to reject our very being. You have received a prophecy."

"Yes, and I don't know what to do."

"Does it say anything definite?"

"The reborn brother and sister shall stand on the edge of time and weave fate onto a new path. The path is yours to choose."

"Then you must choose if you wish to find this missing brother and accept your path or find a new one."

"I don't even know who it is or how to find out."

"Then don't learn what you need and continue the path you wish to take until the gods place you on the path you require."

"Just let the magic guide me," Kenko huffed. I'm still learning to feel the magic, and here in Ernsari, the magic surrounding me is so strong that it feels like I'm drowning."

"Continue your lessons and learn what you need to take your place among your clan. You will find your way to the path needed to move you forward in time. You must trust both yourself and the magic within you."

"Should I tell anyone of the prophecy?"

"Does it impact them?"

"Not now, but it sounded like a quest to save the magic and the world." Kenko said uncomfortably, "Eventually, everyone is going to be in danger if the balance of magic isn't restored."

"That is a noble quest for an elf," Orrian said, squeezing her hand before letting go as he stood and resumed his post. We strive for balance in all things, especially magic."

"Balance in all things," Kenko muttered with a sigh, gathering her knitting and the thorn beasts into her arms. "Would I be allowed to travel the forest to learn about the rangers and their skills and learn how to be a noble?"

"Perhaps that is something to discuss with the prince and your grandparents. I would have thought you wished to stay in the city."

"I want to do both; I think I'll have enough dealing with people from the parties and such I'm expected to attend. I also want some time to myself, time outside with the thorn beasts learning to ride an elven mount, time learning about the elven forest."

"You would do well to take up an instrument as well."

"And finding a day a week to work on my designs for inventions."

"I do not see it being too much of a strain. However, truly learning to serve the forest will take more than a day or two at a time. Most beginning scouts and rangers spend weeks in the forests learning to survive. We will discuss it when you meet with the royal family next," he said, giving her an amused look before glancing at her bedroom door with a raised eyebrow.

"Right, sleeping is required." Kenko said with a mock, sad sigh, "I know you keep telling me to slow down, but how am I supposed to when there is so much to do?"

"Step by step, child, step by step. Have a good night, Princess Kenko."

———

The hall below them was full to bursting with elves; dazzling bursts of color swirled and swayed as they mingled below. Kenko had never been so glad not to have to speak before a crowd; there was no telling how the elves would take her recovery and return to the forest. The royal family sat on their thrones to one side, watching their people with a detached air of disinterest.

Prince Ivaran stood next to her on the right of the thrones, "Don't be so worried; they may denounce you in private, but no one will say such to your face."

"They had no issue spouting nonsense last night at the party," Kenko murmured, knowing he would hear over the sound of the crowd; elves were much sharper of hearing than she'd ever thought previously.

"They did not know you then,"

"So insulting random children is common?"

"There are outliers in every race and creed," the prince said, giving her a tired smile. The man seemed exhausted, as if losing his twin had aged him a century.

"I would be considered an outlier." Kenko pointed out with a matching sigh, she'd spent most of the morning arguing over changing her name to something more elvish. So far, the compromise was to take an elvish use name to use in polite company while her actual name was used for friends and close acquaintances. It felt like a betrayal after earning her chosen name on her rebirth.

"You are no longer an outcast. You have family and a large clan waiting to embrace you here." Ivaran said, watching her with a small smile, "You will find your balance in time."

"Is balance that important to elves?" she quipped, trying to keep her tone light and make it a jest, not a complaint.

"It is what we all strive to achieve in our lives."

"Let me stop you there, son," the queen said with a sly smile, "He will talk you to deafness on balance if you allow it."

"Later, perhaps," Ivaran said with a nod to his mother. The royal couple stood, and a horn sounded, bringing the room to an unnatural silence.

"Presenting the royal clan, Valera. King of the elven nation, King Taegen, Queen Nimue, and Price Ivaran." the announcer brayed before he stepped forward.

"Tonight, we have a most auspicious announcement. An elf long thought lost to us has been found, and their child welcomed back into our embrace." The King thundered, sweeping his arms out as if to embrace the crowd, "Her bloodlines and gifts have been confirmed, and her claim is indisputable. Tonight, we welcome the daughter of Prince Lien, Princess Leilatha Kenko."

Prince Ivaran took her hand and led her to the platform's edge. Her hair fell down her back, carefully brushed straight while silken robes trailed down her arms, and a gown covered in vine-like lace hid the tiny slippers she'd been forced into. She'd already stubbed her toes three times.

"Let us welcome our new princess!" The king shouted as the royal couple stepped down and kissed her on her forehead from each of them

A slow clapping started, and the noise gradually rose until it filled the hall, echoing and completely overwhelming. It was a rolling roar of sound, somehow natural and jarring, like a discordant echo of waves against a breakwater. Kenko faced the crowd frozen, watching the shifting mass below them as the elves celebrated their new princess.

Continued in Book 2: *I don't want to go to war!*

———

Kenko *[Level 4]*
    Race: *Elven*
    Age: *9*
    Class: *Artificer (Magical) [Level 1]*
    Skills: *Regeneration, Skin Deep, Marathon, Archive, Disengagement, Flight, Darkvision, Perception, Meditation*
    Magical Skills: *Rune casting (Basic), Ward casting (Basic), Elven Clan magics*
    Racial skills (Elven): *Surefooted, One with the Forest*
    Additional Skills: *Cooking (Basic), Crafting (Basic), Spell Craft (Basic), Housekeeping (Basic), Design (Intermediate), Organization (Advanced), Magic (Basic), Map Reading (Basic), Woodworking (Basic), Wood Carving (Basic), Drawing (Basic), Calculation (Intermediate), Gathering (Basic), Pathfinding (Intermediate), Plant Identification (Basic), Weaving (Basic), Basket Craft (Basic), Debate (Basic), Eloquence (Basic), Archery (Basic), Sling (Basic), Shield work (Basic), Dagger work (Basic), Riding (Intermediate), Camping (Basic)*

Titles: *Blessed of Ume; Princess of Elvish Clan Valera*
    Bonded Animals: *Thorn hummingbird, Thorn squirrel*

ABOUT THE AUTHOR

Amelia G. Sides is the author of fantasy, science fiction, and alternative history novels. Her books are filled with complex heroes, political intrigue, and finding home amongst the chaos that is life. Amelia lives in the southern US and enjoys long walks with her dog, Reuben, and late nights at her computer, plotting out her next book.

A gamer at heart, Amelia will be self-publishing the first in a new series, "I Don't Want to Fight!": A GameLit Novel, which will become available in the summer of 2025.

Please feel free to check out her social media sites at the link below and give her a follow.

https://linktr.ee/asides3

ALSO BY AMELIA SIDES

The Stone Mage Series

The Mage's Daughter (Book 1)

Shattered Stone (Book 2)

Fusiliers Series

An Unkindness of Magic (Book 1)

Writing as Grace Reid

Coming in 2026 from Gold Dust Publishing,

Hound and Dagger Books 1-3

A Sci-Fi Romance series